THE
WRONG SIDE
OF THE
GRASS

THE WRONG SIDE OF THE GRASS

STEPHEN SOLOMITA

MYSTERIOUSPRESS.COM

OPEN ROAD
INTEGRATED MEDIA
NEW YORK

ISBN: 978-1-5040-7868-9

Published in 2023 by MysteriousPress.com/Open Road Integrated Media, Inc.
180 Maiden Lane
New York, NY 10038
www.openroadmedia.com

THE
WRONG SIDE
OF THE
GRASS

ONE

So, what do you think?" Mike Tedesco asks. "Should we contact Noah, put in a request for the ark's blueprints?"

The question's valid because it's raining so hard that cars parked on the opposite curb might be apparitions climbing out of a misty hell. There's no wind, a small blessing, and the rain falls in straight lines that shimmy back and forth, opening and closing, the dance of a billion veils. Just fifty feet away, the facades of the bow-front townhouses are at times invisible, as if they'd been ripped from time and space. Tedesco might be looking past the edge of a flat earth at an empty universe beyond.

That's not the weird part, though. The weird part is that Tedesco's talking to a dog, and not his own dog, but a large pit bull, a stray male that's decided to huddle next to Mike in a shallow doorway that offers minimal protection from the downpour. Dark scars, long-healed, crisscross the dog's head and shoulders, testament to his time in the pits, and to what must have been victories.

"You got used up," Tedesco says, his voice barely audible over the pounding rain. "Used up and dumped out."

The dog whines softly and wags its stubby tail. Fighting dogs are usually gentle around human beings, and this one proves no exception. His whole life has been about training and fighting. Now he's worthless, not good enough to breed, not good enough to feed.

A lightning bolt obliterates the gloom, followed in less than a second by thunder sharp and close enough to make them both cringe, man and dog. For just a second, time freezes, every drop of rain suspended in a lingering afterimage that reveals a face in a window across the street. Then the dog begins to shake, and Tedesco reaches out to trace a long scar running from ear to ear. Calmed by this small show of affection, the dog arches his head, mouth opening, tongue lolling.

For Tedesco's purposes, the rain is a blessing. He knows this, and he's additionally pleased with the eighty-degree temperature— if it were ten degrees colder, he'd be shivering. But he's soaked through and through, from a full head of curly hair tucked beneath a Yankees ball cap to the soles of his large feet. His clothes offer no protection, nor do his four-hundred-dollar Armani sneakers that are being ruined by a sheet of water that flows down the steep hillside, washing sidewalk and roadway alike.

Another flash of lightning, another crash of thunder. Tedesco removes the blue Yankees cap and shakes off the puddle accumulating in a fold at the top. He's not a baseball fan, not at all. The cap is designed to conceal his features from a security camera mounted on the facade of St. Luke's Church. The camera's almost a block away and unlikely to produce a recognizable likeness, especially with the rain, but Tedesco's spent time in prison and has no wish to return. Better safe than sorry.

"The good with the bad," he tells the dog. "Today, we eat the bear."

Tedesco's always been an optimist. In his heart of hearts, he knows there's nothing he can't accomplish, as he's certain that his past failures have resulted from bad luck or betrayal. Both elements played their part in the five years he spent upstate, but that was long ago when he was young and foolish. He's a lot smarter now, or so he believes.

The dog sniffs at the pocket of Tedesco's jacket. Despite the rain and the plastic wrapper, he's discovered an unopened bag of pretzel sticks Tedesco bought last night. Tedesco shakes the pretzels into his hand and offers them to the dog. The animal's not gaunt—that will come later—but he takes this small soggy offering without hesitation. Again, he whines and wags his tail.

Maybe he's hoping I'll take him with me, give him a home, Tedesco thinks. That's not going to happen, of course. Tedesco's agenda is set and it doesn't include the company of a seventy-pound bulldog. Nor can he imagine bending over to scoop the poop. That's for suckers. That's for the assholes who crowd into subway cars every morning and every afternoon, sharing one another's stink. And for what? A paycheck that doesn't pay the bills? The privilege of doing the same thing tomorrow?

One thing sure, Vladimir Putin doesn't scoop poop. Neither does Bill Gates or Jay-Z or Beyoncé or even Crash Patterson, a notorious dope and coke dealer who lives only a few blocks away.

Tedesco's crouched in a gentrifying West Harlem neighborhood called Hamilton Heights. To his right, at the bottom of a steep hill, Harlem is a flat expanse stretching all the way to the East River. To his left, the hill continues up to Amsterdam Avenue, the crest of a rocky palisade that runs along the Hudson River from West 72nd Street to the northern tip of the island. This early in the morning—it's not yet six o'clock—only a few cars pass, wipers flashing madly as they fight the downpour and the incline.

The cell phone in Tedesco's pocket, a burner to be sure, gives off three quick beeps. Tedesco's groin tightens in response. The package is on the move. He stares into the rain, toward West 154th Street on the other side of the island, less than a mile away. A truck loaded with a thousand cartons of cigarettes has just pulled out of Legrand Transportation's small warehouse. At the end of the block, on Frederick Douglass Boulevard, it will turn south. On West 141st Street, three blocks from Tedesco's position, it will turn west to come straight at him. The trip will take between four and six minutes, depending on the lights. Tedesco knows this because he timed the run so many times that he's lost count.

Tedesco takes the burner from his pocket and taps in a number. It'd be a big joke if the phone shorted out in the rain. Talk about shitty luck. Talk about factors you can't control. But the call goes through, ringing once before a man's voice mutters, "Yeah."

"The horse is out of the barn," Tedesco says. "Are you ready?"

"Piece of cake."

Hijacking trucks hauling cigarettes or liquor is never a piece of cake. In fact, it's nearly impossible. That's because the trucks are equipped with tracking GPS units. These units don't provide drivers with a little map and a disembodied voice to guide them to their destinations. Instead, they allow the vehicle to be tracked from a remote location, usually the warehouse. There's an added feature, too, for trucks that haul especially valuable cargo. The units can be programmed to alert the base, and track the vehicle, if a truck varies by as little as fifty yards from a specified route.

Most owners, including Tedesco's boss, Skippy Legrand, deem this precaution enough. Yeah, you can steal one of his trucks, but the cops—not to mention a private security firm on call 24/7—will find you before you unload it. There's just no place to hide.

The solution to this problem, for a crook like Tedesco, is on the other end of the phone, a punk named Asher Levine. Asher works for a company in Queens that installs and maintains tracking GPS units. He claims he can disable the unit in the Legrand truck in less than three minutes.

"Just be on time, Asher. Forgiveness is not part of my nature."

"I'm ready, Mike. Jeez."

Tedesco ignores the whiny, irritated tone. He's focused on the gray mist that conceals the lower part of the hill as he takes a sodden face mask from his jacket and hooks it over his ears. A minute passes, then another and another as a giant SUV rolls past, an Escalade with its sound system wide open, the bass loud enough to echo from building to building. One note, regular as a metronome.

The dog moves closer to his new friend just as the Legrand truck finally makes an appearance. Painted a color somewhere between maroon and purple, the vehicle is instantly recognizable as it lumbers up the hill. Tedesco's pretty sure the driver—a newly arrived Mexican named José Sepulveda—doesn't want to stop on the wet slope. But he won't be given a choice. José's twenty feet from the corner when Asher guides an ancient Lincoln Town Car into the intersection and stops directly in front of the truck.

Tedesco's on the move before the truck comes to a halt. Byebye, doggie. He flies across the road, leaps onto the running board, and smashes the side window with the butt of a .40 caliber Smith & Wesson.

"Set the brake, motherfucker. Set the brake or I'll splatter your brains all over the cab. Set the fucking brake."

José's eyes are two Ping-Pong balls with black dots at the center. The dots are fixed on the barrel of the gun as he yanks at the parking brake, pulling so hard he bends the metal rod. Tedesco rips the door open, jumps to the roadway, then jerks José out of the cab and slams him onto the pavement.

"Don't look up. You look up, you won't go home to your little *mamacita*. You'll go straight to fucking hell."

His point made, Tedesco steps back and looks around. Asher has the truck's hood up, which is good. Also good, the cross street, Convent Avenue, is deserted. But there's a minivan coming up the hill, and Tedesco prepares to wave it around the disabled truck. That proves unnecessary when the driver executes a U-turn in record time and heads back toward St. Nicholas Avenue.

Tedesco grabs José by the back of his jacket and pulls him onto the sidewalk. A second later, as he watches over his prisoner, Asher taps him on the shoulder.

"You got it done?" Tedesco says.

"No, see, the booster's mounted in front of the unit. I can't get to it, not without pulling the booster."

"What the fuck are you talkin' about? What's a booster?"

"The hydrovac."

"The what?"

"It's part of the brake system, the part that supplies the power. It's blocking the GPS unit."

"So take it off. What's the problem?"

"Tools. I don't have the right tools." Asher stares at Tedesco for a moment, his eyes as wide as José's. "Mike," he finally says, "I can't do it."

"Are you kidding me? What happened to piece of cake?"

"Mike, please, I can't pull half-inch bolts with my fingers."

A shudder runs through Tedesco's body, from the base of his spine right into his skull. The gods have struck again, the bad luck gods. They've shoved it right up his ass, shoved it up to the elbow, and without grease. Not only will the job have to be abandoned, the asshole actually said his name. Twice.

Bad luck for Tedesco, bad luck for José and bad luck for little Asher. Tedesco deals with Asher first, putting a bullet in his chest. Then he turns the gun on José.

"Por favor, por favor, por favor."

The problem, for José, is that he and Tedesco both work for Skippy Legrand. They know each other, and José's sure to identify his coworker if the cops tighten the screws, which they surely will. After all, somebody had to reveal the truck's route to the hijackers. Why not the driver?

"Please, Mike," José says, this time in heavily accented English. "I won' say nothin'. I swear. Don' kill me."

Tedesco's brain lights up as an idea takes form. He kneels down beside José and puts the gun against his ear. "You got relatives, maybe live in another state?"

"*Mi hermano*, in Los Angeles."

"You go visit your brother, José. I mean right the fuck now. Don't go back to the warehouse, because if you do, Skippy's gonna put a bullet in your head. Skippy's not like me. He's not a nice guy."

One more thing to do. Tedesco returns to Asher, who's moaning softly and shoots him in the head. Calmer now, he walks over to the Lincoln, opens the door, then pauses long enough to check on José as the little man hightails it down the hill. The dog seizes this moment, this opportunity, almost knocking Tedesco to the ground as it leaps into the car.

Tedesco shakes his head as he slides behind the wheel. *I'm dead,* he tells himself. *I'm fucking dead.*

TWO

Tedesco's brain runs from thought to thought, the procession as relentless as the raindrops falling on the Lincoln's greasy windshield. He should have made Asher prove he could disable the GPS unit, should have killed José, should have introduced Asher to Skippy instead of using the creep to gain a better cut of the pie. A thousand cartons of cigarettes at sixty bucks a carton, with ten grand for Tedesco's end? Skippy had jumped at the deal, what with the cargo insured and Skippy in hock to a vicious and very impatient loan shark. Not that Skippy had liked the cut Tedesco demanded. He hadn't, but Tedesco had Asher and without Asher . . .

"You're vouchin' for this kid, Mike, and he better put on a ten grand performance."

If failure wasn't an option, a body left in the road makes failure a thousand times worse. That's because Tedesco and Skippy are co-conspirators when it comes to the penal code. If the cops focus on Tedesco, which they definitely will, and Tedesco rolls on Skippy, which he probably will, Skippy's gonna be looking at twenty-five to life. Skippy won't like that, and neither will Paulie Bancroft, who has the brain of a mosquito, along with a mosquito's appetite for blood. Bancroft is Skippy's man for the underside of Legrand

Transportation's business, hauling contraband for a number of local thugs. He's big and powerful and his little black eyes are as dead as a doll's. Nobody wants to fuck with Paulie. You put him in the truck, riding shotgun, you don't worry about a double-cross.

Mike Tedesco's computed Skippy's bottom line many times. Between the legit business and the contraband, mostly hijacked merchandise, the man probably made a couple of hundred grand last year. That would be enough to live nicely if Skippy Legrand wasn't the kind of degenerate gambler every bookie dreams about, a compulsive bettor with enough income to pay the vigorish at the end of the week. Basketball, football, baseball, hockey, soccer, boxing, and the horses. The only time Skippy doesn't have a bet down is when his bookies cut him off.

Tedesco pulls himself together. He's still alive, after all, which is more than he can say for Asher. But facts are facts. He's left a body on the street and is now driving a stolen car in the vicinity of the crime, a car sure to be on the NYPD's hot list. What's more, he's soaking wet.

Tedesco rides over the crest of the ridge at Amsterdam Avenue, then down the hill toward Riverside Drive and the Hudson River. He's feeling like he wants to pilot the car right into the water, just get it over with. Unfortunately, Riverbank Park, Riverside Park, and the West Side Highway block the path to that particular solution.

Next to him, the dog sits erect, staring out through the streaked windshield. Looking for what, exactly?

"Hey, asshole."

The dog turns his head, and Tedesco sees that half of his lower lip is missing on the right side, revealing the animal's back teeth. Tedesco shakes his head. The dog must have been a winner at one time or his handler would have dumped him before he accumulated all those scars. Still, despite everything, the animal's soft brown eyes seem hopeful.

Tedesco's running north on Riverside Drive. He's headed toward the George Washington Bridge and New Jersey, indulging his first instinct, which is to run as fast and far as he can. But now he pulls to the curb next to a fire hydrant.

All right, I killed a man, he tells himself. A mistake, obviously. But leaving José alive was a stroke of genius. Once the police connect Asher's occupation to the truck's open hood, they'll start looking for an inside man. Someone who knew the truck's route. That could be Skippy or any of several employees, or it could be the driver, who conveniently fled the scene.

Will José give Tedesco up? Does it matter? Maybe the cops aren't his biggest problem. Maybe his biggest problem is named Skippy Legrand.

After another moment, Tedesco's thoughts finally settle. He reaches into the back seat for a plastic bag containing half a doughnut, which he feeds to the dog. The Lincoln, he decides, must be dumped immediately because he can't chance some overeager cop spotting it. Ordinarily, that wouldn't amount to much. He'd simply park the car and take the 1 Train, only a block away. But Tedesco's soaked to the bone, and there's no way to get into the subway station without passing numerous security cameras and people are sure to remember him.

Tedesco laughs as he imagines walking onto a crowded subway platform accompanied by a scarred pit bull with one side of his face missing. No question, he'd find a seat on the first train into the station, maybe even get the whole car to himself.

There's a solution to this dilemma, though not one to Tedesco's liking. Not at all. But maybe he should have considered the consequences before he sent little Asher off to the Promised Land. Or before he decided to believe the prick when Asher insisted that he could defeat any GPS device out there.

Now it's too late.

Tedesco puts the Lincoln in gear and pulls away from the hydrant. Five minutes later, he finds another parking space on Riverside Drive, this one legal, at least until noon tomorrow when the street sweeper comes by. The Lincoln will probably be ticketed at that point, but not by anyone likely to check the hot list. In fact, it might sit there for a couple of weeks, accumulating tickets and then be towed over to a police compound before it's identified as a stolen car. How likely is the Lincoln to be connected to the hijacking after that much time? Little to none.

The dog follows Tedesco out the door and onto the sidewalk. The rain has almost disappeared and the sky, looking back over the Hudson River, is rapidly clearing. Tedesco hesitates, wondering if the animal will run away if he kicks it really hard, or if the dog will take his foot off. The muscles behind the mutt's jaws, the muscles that control the bite, are the size and shape of tennis balls.

An image jumps into Tedesco's consciousness, the face of a man who turns up regularly at a Long Island City bar called Tasso's. Tedesco can't recall the man's real name, only his nickname, Pug. A retired boxer, Pug's brow, thickened by keloid scars, has always reminded Tedesco of a long wriggling worm.

"Pug," he says. "That's your name, got it?"

The dog looks up at him, its head turning to the side. Tedesco interprets the expression to mean, *I don't give a damn what you call me as long you feed me and put a roof over my head. You can beat me, too, if it gets you off.*

One block over, on West 153rd Street, Tedesco approaches the redbrick apartment building called home by a woman named Daniela Castillo. Tedesco and Daniela were a hot item until he walked out on her almost a year before. To his surprise, and maybe his disappointment, she hadn't followed him, hadn't even called. That would have been demeaning for a priestess and if there was anything Daniela feared on this planet it was humiliation. Talk about a control freak. Daniela had remained a couple of steps ahead of him throughout their relationship. And maybe she was still ahead of him. After all, the key to her apartment still dangled from his key ring.

Tedesco finds the lock on the door leading to the building's lobby to be broken, as it was when he left. Ditto for the elevator. Undaunted, he takes to the stairs, the dog trailing behind.

On the second-floor landing, they run into a man walking a small female boxer on a blue leash. Pug reacts instantly, but not in the way Tedesco expects. The dog presses himself against the wall as the man scoots past, an ex-con trying to avoid trouble.

Tedesco leads Pug to a door at the end of the hall, then stoops to rub the dog's head. "Now here's the thing, Pug. You wanna make friends with Daniela right away. Otherwise, you'll end up on her altar. In pieces."

A moment later, Tedesco unlocks the door and throws it open to find Daniela's altar right where he last saw it, between two windows that look out over Trinity Cemetery. There's a poster on the wall behind the altar, a standing female cradling a child in one arm. The woman wears golden robes that flow to the ground, while the child's head is crested by a halo. To either side, darkened skies flash lightning and pour down rain. Beneath her feet, a small boat, its sail in shreds, founders in a heaving sea.

There are three helpless men in the boat. Two cling to the gunnels, while a third lifts folded hands in prayer. Tedesco had assumed the robed figure to be the Virgin Mary when he first saw it, and that was true as far as it went. But when asked, Daniela had identified the woman as *Lu Caridad del Cobre*, Our Lady of Charity, one of many Christian manifestations of an orisha in the Santería religion named Oshun.

Daniela's standing before the altar lighting a candle when Tedesco walks into her home. She whispers something as she lays the candle before a statue of the saint, then finally addresses him without turning.

"Bienvenida a casa, Miguelito," she says. "Welcome home."

THREE

Although Detective Dante Cepeda's tour doesn't begin until eight o'clock, he pulls up to the crime scene at seven twenty. Ordinarily, jobs that require the attention of a detective between midnight and eight are handled by Nightwatch, a skeleton crew of detectives who process crimes scenes and interview witnesses, then pass the paperwork to the day tour. But the Nightwatch crew was otherwise occupied when Mike Tedesco put two bullets into Asher Levine. Only a mile to the north, a collision between a city bus and a private sanitation truck had resulted in three fatalities, along with multiple, life-threatening injuries to riders and pedestrians.

"The vic's still lyin' in the street," Lieutenant Kelly Barnwell had explained to Dante Cepeda, the only detective under her command who lived in the city. "So do me a personal favor and get over there before the media shows up."

Cepeda hadn't argued with his boss, although he knew the scene had already been recorded a hundred times on a hundred different cell phones. Selfies, probably, with the victim in the background. Hey, look at me, I saw a dead man.

Dante pauses for a moment after stepping out of his car, ignoring the gawkers on Convent Avenue. The storm of an hour ago is now gone, replaced with a hazy sunshine that bleeds through a milky layer of high cloud. The humidity, on the other hand, has settled in for the long haul and the July heat is already building. The forecast is for temperatures to reach the low nineties by midafternoon.

If you can't handle weather, Dante tells himself, as he has on many occasions, *don't become a cop*. New York's never been about the climate. Still, should he be forced to work outdoors this afternoon, both he and his suit will be sodden by the time his tour ends.

Directly ahead of him, a purple truck, maybe twenty feet long, blocks the right lane. The hood has been raised and the driver's door is open, with the window obviously broken out. The truck's rear doors are also open, revealing scattered boxes marked with the names of various cigarette brands. Several boxes lie in the road behind the truck, evidence of a hasty retreat when the first responding officers came on the scene.

The victim lies on the far curb, his head on the road, his feet on the sidewalk. A blanket covers his body, a blanket that could only have been placed there by the uniformed cops charged with protecting the scene. The Crime Scene Unit will surely be pissed, assuming they show up, but dealing with trace evidence is their problem, not Dante's. At age thirty-eight, he's been a cop for twelve years and a precinct detective for seven. While he's not exactly burned out, he's not gung-ho. either. The years have blessed him (in his estimation) with a deeply felt humility. Talk about a cog in a wheel. Dante Cepeda's professional wheel has been turning since Cain bludgeoned Abel.

"Hey, Dante, aren't you up a little early?" The voice belongs to Sergeant Patti O'Hearn. Patti has overall responsibility for securing the crime scene prior to the arrival of the Crime Scene Unit.

"When duty calls, Patti, this trooper responds. What do we have here?"

"A hijacking, probably, followed by an execution. The vic was carrying a cell phone, a burner, but no identification. Right now, we're canvassing for witnesses in the rooming houses on either side."

Dante takes a step back. He's attracted to Patti O'Hearn, and has been since she passed the sergeant's exam and found herself assigned to the Three-One. Something about the red-orange hair, the freckles, and the knowing smile demand further exploration. But Dante has a problem, one that's haunted him throughout his life. After his junkie mother took off, he passed into the hands of New York's foster care system. The good news was that he survived the prison atmosphere of the group homes, a miracle really. Playing it safe all the way, he graduated high school without acquiring a criminal record, then joined the military, then the cops.

Now, a couple of decades later, while most of the kids who shared his fate are dead or in prison, Dante Cepeda, the scared Dominican three-year-old taken from his mother's bedside to a group home in South Jamaica, has risen high enough to claim middle-class status. This is a matter of some pride to him. Dante owns a small condo and a decent car and doesn't sweat the bills at the end of the month. Still, there are times when he feels like a tourist in a foreign land. The customs, the body language, the little signals that his peers instantly recognize are to him at least ambiguous, if not actually opaque. Case in point, Patti's knowing smile. Is it an invitation? Or is she mocking him?

"How about the looting?" he asks.

"Dante, they were swarming the truck like ants when we came up the block. In the pouring rain, OK? Men, women, and children.

I thought we were in for a fight, but when I flipped on the light bar and the siren, they scattered."

Patti doesn't bother with the obvious punch line. The condition of the man lying on the curb demanded immediate attention. By the time she established the obvious, that her possibly wounded victim was an actually dead victim, the looters had disappeared.

Patti's regular driver, Patrolman Vasily Vashnikov, crosses the street to join Cepeda and his boss. "We got a witness, Detective." He points to a townhouse across the way. "First floor, front. Says she was looking out the window."

"Let's bring her into the precinct, get her statement on paper."

"I could do that, OK, but she's an old lady and pretty crippled up . . . I mean, she uses a walker to get around, so we'd probably need an ambulance."

Dante stares at Vashnikov for a moment too long. The man is young, fit, and reasonably attractive. Are he and Patti getting it on from time to time? Is that what her smile's about? Screwing in the back seat can result in dismissal from the force, especially when the participants are of different ranks. Meanwhile, it's only happened a million times over the years.

"What's her name?"

"Myra Cuffee."

"What's her attitude?"

Vashnikov frowns. "She wants to help. She's cooperating."

"OK, put someone in front of her door. I don't want anyone going in or out until I speak to her. I'll be up as soon as I can." Dante finally turns to Patti. "What about the trucking company, the owner. Has he been notified?"

"That would be Theodore Legrand. He's on his way over."

Followed by Sergeant O'Hearn, Dante walks over to the body and pulls the blanket away. "You said you checked him for ID?"

"Nothing."

"Not even a driver's license?"

"Nothin', Dante."

"What about the cell phone?"

"It's still in his pocket."

"But you removed it, right? You said it was a burner."

Dante notes Patti's blush. Even if she wore gloves, there's the possibility that her DNA will show up on the phone. The Crime Scene Unit will now be doubly unhappy, assuming she admits to her misdeed. Dante kneels by the corpse and slides the blanket down. He examines the victim's hands first, drawn to the greasy black smudges on the fingertips, palms, and knuckles. That he had those hands inside the engine compartment is a near certainty.

Satisfied with the observation, at least for the moment, Dante turns to the man's injuries. The right side of his skull is missing a chunk the size of a baseball, and Dante knows he could not have lived for even a second after sustaining this injury. At the same time, his blood-soaked T-shirt clings to his narrow chest like a second skin. The blood must have flowed from this wound for a significant amount of time before the final shot was fired. Was the shooter angry? Dante files the possibility away.

"He can't be the driver, right?" Patti says. "He doesn't have a license."

Dante doesn't answer this question because the truck's owner is on the way and there's nothing to be gained by speculating. He rises to his feet, then waits a second for his right knee to stop throbbing. Finally, he takes out his cell phone and makes a call to a detective stationed at the medical examiner's offices downtown.

"I have a body coming down to you, a vic," he tells Detective Gavin Homart. "Unidentified. If you can get his prints and run them asap, I'll owe you a cup of coffee."

"Will do."

Dante shoves the phone into his pocket. "I'm going upstairs, speak to the witness," he tells Patti O'Hearn. "I want you to come with me. That'll make it harder for her to change her story down the line."

Patti frowns, leaving Dante to wonder if she's annoyed because he didn't respond to her question, or because he's ordering her around. Technically, she outranks him. But then she cocks her head and smiles.

"Lead the way, Detective."

FOUR

The four-story townhouse where Myra Cuffee lives—and which, as it turns out, she owns—has seen better days. Perhaps twenty feet wide and fifty feet deep, much of its original splendor is still evident in Myra's first-floor apartment. A latticework of dark wood separates the front parlor and the dining room, while the fireplace surround is of white marble. Though painted over many times, the crown moldings are still intact and a stained-glass window above the door reveals a faded fleur-de-lis. The three upper floors, on the other hand, have been carved into small apartments, or even rooms, as the number of bells on the intercom makes clear.

Cepeda's passed the last six years toiling in the Three-One, and he's familiar with the basic arrangement. A hundred years ago, in the early decades of the last century, this and the neighboring row houses were owned by upper middle-class professionals, virtually all of them white. An influx of southern Black families escaping the Jim Crow south, followed by the onset of the Great Depression, sent most of those families packing. The new owners, many of them unable to maintain the property or meet the tax burden, converted the single-family townhouses to high-occupancy rooming houses. But New York is a city in eternal flux, the only constant being the certainty of change. The proof is right in front of Cepeda as he climbs the short stoop and knocks on the door of Myra Cuffee's townhouse. The entire neighborhood is rapidly gentrifying. Townhouses that sold for a hundred thousand dollars fifteen years ago are now selling for two million, even in this condition. Restored, their asking prices can exceed five million.

When she finally answers the door, Myra's leaning on one of those wheeled walkers that include a seat and bicycle-style brakes on the handlebars. She is indeed old and frail, just as Vasily described her. Her back is bent and a plastic tube feeds oxygen from a portable concentrator to her nostrils. Still thick, her gray hair is parted in the center and pulled into a bun tight enough to make Cepeda wince.

"Hello, Ms. Cuffee. I'm Detective Cepeda. I understand that you witnessed the . . . the incident."

"Yes, I did. Please come in."

It takes Myra Cuffee a minute to turn around, then lead them into the parlor. She sighs as she drops onto a camelback couch set behind a mammoth glass coffee table. There's a complex arrangement of silk flowers on the table, roses, peonies, and gladiolas tied into a nest of English ivy.

"First thing," Cepeda says, "thank you for speaking to us."

"It's my Christian duty."

Dante nods to himself. A church lady for sure, the woman is all about preserving her dignity. That's no problem for the detective. As long as she cooperates, he's perfectly willing to show respect.

"I have coffee brewing in the kitchen. Would you like a cup?"

"I surely would, ma'am. I left the house without breakfast this morning."

Myra starts to rise, but Patti beats her to the punch. "I'll get it," she says.

"I thank you kindly." Myra turns to Cepeda. "Please sit down."

Cepeda drops into a heavily padded easy chair, a massive piece upholstered in a floral pattern that resembles the arrangement on the coffee table. "You have a beautiful apartment."

"I've tried to keep it up, but the taxes these days are a disgrace."

"You own the building?"

"For twenty-seven years."

Myra's taxes are rising for a good reason. The townhouse is worth ten times as much as she paid for it, and property taxes are based on assessed valuation. Cepeda doesn't mention this uncomfortable fact as he waits in silence until Patti returns with three cups of coffee on a tray. The cups are patterned with violets and rest on gold-rimmed saucers.

Myra sips at her cup, then sets it down and says, "Well, you probably want to hear my story."

"Whenever you're ready, ma'am."

"You know, this neighborhood, it's supposed to be improving. Gentrification, white people moving in, restaurants opening up. But I don't know. What I saw is white people shooting white people, so maybe the neighborhood's only changing color. You said your last name is . . ."

Cepeda's been here before, what with his tightly curled hair, pale olive skin, and morning-blue eyes. He also knows that tribal identities are important in a city as multi-ethnic as New York, especially when it comes to cops. "Dante Cepeda, Ms. Cuffee. I'm Dominican."

Myra nods once and folds her hands in her lap. As she begins to speak, her chin rises. "You see that rocker over there by the window?

That's right where I was sittin'. I often sit in that window, just watchin' folk come up the hill. Lord knows, I don't get out much these days." She stops abruptly, eyes blinking. Then she smiles. "I need to stop right here. Ain't nothin' on the face of this planet more pitiful than a whiny old woman. If I don't like bein' eighty-nine, I should have had the good sense to die at eighty-eight."

Myra goes on for several minutes despite her pledge. Patient by nature, Cepeda's not unsympathetic. The elderly poor often become trapped in their apartments, especially in buildings without elevators. The alternative, a homeless shelter, is worse than the disease. Myra, of course, is not poor, just lonely.

"I tell you, Detective, it was rainin' hard enough to drown the fish in the ocean. I could barely see the houses across the street. Now I did have that cataract surgery, which helped, but I can't say my eyes are what they used to be. In fact, if it wasn't for a bolt of lightning, I don't believe I would have seen a blessed thing before that truck come up the hill. Seemed like the bolt come down right on top of us and the whole street just lit up. That's when I saw the man. He was sittin' in a doorway and the rain was pourin' down on him, a white man."

"He was white?" Patti O'Hearn interrupts. "Not Hispanic?"

"Yes, I believe he was because the other one, the man he shot, was definitely white. But you see, that's not the part that was most peculiar, because there was a bulldog sittin' right next to that man. Now why a man would bring a dog to a robbery is beyond me."

Myra pauses for effect, leading Cepeda to flash an encouraging smile. "What were they doing?"

"Well, as I did say, if it wasn't for the lightning, I wouldn't have noticed the man or the dog. But once I knew they were there, backed into that doorway? Well, I could make them out pretty well. At first, they did nothing, just sat there in all that rain. Then the man took something out of his pocket and put it to his ear, most likely a cell phone, although I couldn't see clear enough to be sure. He slipped it back into his pocket after a few seconds and then put on a black mask, the kind that pulls down over your head. Nothing else happened for about a minute, until that truck arrived, the very one that's out there now. It was almost to the top when a car pulled into the intersection and blocked it off."

Out of breath, Myra stops long enough to adjust the settings on her oxygen concentrator. She takes several exploratory breaths before returning to Cepeda.

"Well, that man in the doorway, he ran toward the truck and pulled out a gun. Now I can't say what happened next because it took place on the other side of the truck, but a couple of seconds later, the driver of that truck was over by the curb on the far side and the man with the gun was standin' over him. Then a second white man, the one who drove the car, opened the hood on the truck. I don't know what he was up to, but he wasn't at it long before he walked over to join his friend. They talked for a minute, then the first man, the one holding the gun, just up and shot the second man."

"There was no struggle?" Cepeda asks.

"The shooting came out of the blue. One minute they're talking, the next . . ." Myra pauses again, the memory now sharp and obviously painful. She draws a breath and continues. "The man who did the shooting, the first man, he went and spoke to the driver. A minute later, the driver was flyin' down that hill like the devil was on his tail. Then the first man shot the second man again, shot him where he was lyin' in the road. It was just point and shoot, one time before he walked over to the car and drove away."

Cepeda glances at Patti O'Hearn who nods. She, too, finds Myra's story essentially unembellished. "What about the dog?" he asks. "Did the shooter take the dog with him?"

"Yessir, the dog jumped right into the front seat and off they went."

"And the looting?"

"That was folks from the neighborhood, much as it shames me to admit it. They busted open the back door with a crowbar and the boxes came flyin' out. Didn't pay the man who got shot no mind at all. Then you police arrived and everybody ran."

Cepeda spread his hands apart and shrugged. Smokes go for twelve dollars a pack in stores and a dollar per cigarette on the street. For the looters, it must have been like happening on an unguarded bank vault.

"I don't suppose you got the license plate of the car?"

Cepeda's joking, but Myra surprises him. "No, I didn't, Detective, but I believe the car was a Lincoln, an old one. Back in the day, it seemed like every gypsy cab was a black Lincoln with enough room in the back to stretch out. I must've ridden in one of those Lincolns a hundred times."

"That's excellent, ma'am. Very helpful. But do you think you could identify the shooter if you should see him again?" Though he'd saved the big question for the end of the interview, Cepeda knows the answer. Still, it's a question that has to be asked.

"I most surely cannot, Detective."

FIVE

Theodore "Skippy" Legrand is a big man. He stands six-four and weighs almost three hundred pounds. Much of that weight is muscle, or so he'd like to believe, but the rest, the extra sixty pounds, is killing him as he walks up the steep hill from St. Nicholas Avenue to where his truck sits near Convent Avenue. He has no choice in the matter, because the cops have closed off the block. Walk or crawl, as the owner of a hijacked truck loaded with cigarettes, he has to get there. The cops are expecting him. Meanwhile, it's ninety fucking degrees and he's sweating from his scalp to his toes, which is not good news for a psoriasis outbreak that covers his testicles and the inside of his left thigh.

"They stole everything," Paulie Bancroft, Skippy's companion, says.

"Do me a favor, Paulie, and shut the fuck up. I mean it. I don't want you to say one word to the cops. Not one."

Paulie is Skippy's oldest friend, which is why Skippy hired him, even though he has the IQ of a frog. No, make that a cockroach. Which is not to say that he's proved himself useless. The asshole definitely has his uses, but he's also a gym rat who could run up the hill backward. Maybe that's why he's wearing that idiot grin, the one Skippy hates.

But Paulie's got it right for once. The truck's almost empty, the cargo a near-total loss. That wouldn't be a big deal, ordinarily. The cargo's insured, and he can always add enough cartons to cover the deductible. No, the problem is that he's been through this before, and he knows the insurance company won't cut him a check for a few months. These are months Skippy doesn't have because he owes fifty large to a Russian loan shark named Arkady Alebev. If he doesn't at least pay the vig, he's gonna get his ass seriously kicked.

Five thousand dollars a week? Yeah, right.

About halfway up, Skippy decides to take a rest. The Crime Scene Unit has finally showed up and white-suited techs are swarming over the truck. There's also a meat wagon from the ME's office and a man leaning over what's obviously a body. Skippy's hoping against hope that the body belongs to an employee named Mike Tedesco.

All right, he tells himself as he shoves off, *you've been in the shit before and you always found a way out. Stay cool, offer nothing.*

Skippy eyes the cop on the other side of the tape, a detective in a sweat-soaked white shirt and dress trousers that cling to his legs. Some kind of blue-eyed spic would be his best guess. The cop's smiling as he offers his hand.

"Mr. Legrand?"

"Yeah, that's me."

"Thank you for coming. I'm Detective Cepeda."

"Glad to meet ya."

An awkward silence follows. The cop's trying to get Skippy talking, but Skippy's unwilling to take the lead. Answer the man's questions, then go back to the warehouse and figure out how best to kill the asshole who put him in this position. If he's not already dead.

"I assume you want to know what happened here," the cop finally says.

"I already know what happened." Skippy shifts his position until he's standing above the cop on the hill. The cop's six feet tall at most and Skippy now towers over him. "What happened is I'm out a thousand cartons of cigarettes."

"Was that the load?"

"Approximately."

"I understand that you weren't in the warehouse when the truck left." Cepeda waits until Skippy nods. "Is that normal? Sending a truck out at six o'clock in the morning?"

Skippy knew this question was coming, knew it before he started his car on the way in. He answers without hesitation. "The Arab stores and the bodegas . . ."

"Arab stores?"

"The delis. They sell lottery tickets and smokes, carry some groceries, make sandwiches, like that."

"Right, right. There's one on every corner."

"And they're mostly owned by Arabs. But it's the same with the bodegas and they're Spanish-owned. These little stores, they don't order smokes in advance because how many cartons they're gonna buy depends on how much cash is in the till when you get there. With them, it's strictly cash on delivery."

"And they open that early?"

"The bodegas open early to catch the breakfast crowd and the Arab stores run twenty-four/seven."

"This is actually fascinating," Cepeda says. "Tell me how often you make this run, if you don't mind my asking."

"I don't mind. I send a truck out twice a week, always the same driver, José Sepulveda. José knows the route and the customers, and he keeps on going until the truck's empty. That's usually around nine o'clock at night."

"Fifteen hours?"

"José's got a wife and four kids. He needs the money." Skippy hesitates. Only a few minute ago, he decided to volunteer nothing, but now there's a question that has to be asked. The cop will be expecting it. "The body over there? Is that José?"

"Actually, I'm hoping you can tell me. Would you mind taking a look?"

Skippy minds very much because he can't stand the sight of blood, a failing he's overcome more than once, but that left him nauseated for days afterward.

"Whatever you need, Detective, I'm here."

SIX

Skippy Legrand's in his office. He's standing in front of a window air conditioner, his pants and underpants around his ankles, rubbing a handful of Topicort cream onto his crotch. He's turned the air conditioner's vents down, directing the stream at his chest and belly, as if that could take the stink out of his shirt. Right now, he's having a hard time being in the room with himself.

Nevertheless, he tells himself that he's an optimist, like all gamblers, and his luck will eventually turn around because it always has. He just needs to think.

But the man under the sheet, the man with half his head blown away and what was left of his brain leaking out? Skippy's guts are still churning. At least it wasn't José, the only innocent party on the scene. Skippy had instructed Tedesco to leave José in one piece, even though he knew full well that Tedesco, in a pinch, would dispatch the little wetback without thinking twice. Tedesco was just that kind of a guy.

So, the dead man, if he wasn't José or Tedesco, must be the kid Tedesco brought in to disable the GPS unit. Which he probably didn't do, which is probably why Tedesco killed him. Fortunately, the cop, Cepeda, didn't know who the kid was. Or maybe he did know and just wanted to eyeball Skippy's reaction. Maybe . . .

"Fuck this," Skippy says out loud. "Fuck this."

His pants still around his ankles, Skippy shuffles into the bathroom and washes his hands. The bottom line, the one on the lowest rung of the lowest ladder in hell, is that Mike Tedesco can put him in prison for the next twenty-five years. Meanwhile, Tedesco faces exactly the same fate if he's caught, which he probably will be. The hijacking has inside job written all over it.

Skippy pulls his pants up and cinches his belt. First order of business, dry clothes. He walks through the outer office, past Martha Proctor, who keeps his books and takes phone orders, and onto the warehouse floor. As he walks, he dials Tedesco's number. The call goes directly to voice mail, which comes as no surprise. For a moment, he considers trying the burner Tedesco supplied. But no, he needs to get rid of the burner, maybe on the way home.

Tedesco out of the way, Skippy calls his insurance broker, only to be told that the claims process can't begin until he, Skippy, obtains a report issued by the NYPD.

"Hey, Skip, what could I say? We need proof that a crime occurred, right? Or else anybody could claim anything."

This news isn't entirely bad. Given a little time, Skippy can fabricate enough invoices to pad his claim by a good 40 percent. Meanwhile, he's occupied by more immediate concerns. He approaches his shop foreman and determines that the day is unfolding routinely. With a single exception, of course.

"I'm heading out to my house," Skippy says. "I gotta get a shower and a change of clothes. You need me, call."

Next, he runs down Paulie Bancroft at the other end of the warehouse. Bancroft's stretched out on a pallet behind a stack of boxed Parliaments. Skippy has to be careful here because Paulie played no part in the hijacking.

"Get up, Paulie. You got work to do."

"This about Mike?" Paulie says as he rises to his feet.

"Everybody else showed up for work this morning and the scumbag's not answering his phone. What does that tell you?"

Paulie thinks it over for a minute, then says, "I never liked that guy. He's all like his shit don't stink."

Skippy lays a hand on Paulie's shoulder. "I want you to find him, understand?"

"Yeah, no problem."

"Actually, it is a problem because he's not gonna be sittin' with his feet up on the coffee table, maybe watchin' *Sopranos* reruns, when you ring his bell." Skippy notes his cousin's perplexed expression and shifts gears. "Look, Mike's been stayin' with a woman named . . . named Sanda. Yeah, that's her name. He's stayin' with Sanda somewhere in Brooklyn. Martha has the address."

"Right, Sanda. I got it."

"Good. Now here's the thing. Mike's gonna get in touch with Sanda. He's got no choice because she'll call the cops and report him missing if he doesn't. So what I want you to do is go to her place and talk to her. And I want you to start out talkin' nice and polite, Paulie. Give her a chance, OK? To cooperate? But if she doesn't open up, if she gets all stubborn, you got my permission to hurt her. Not kill, little buddy. Hurt."

Paulie smiles. Not his usual dumb-fuck smile, but a smile that says thank you, Lord. Then a pair of obvious questions, late as usual, pop into his mind.

"What if the bitch don't open the door? What if she calls the cops?"

"Come with me."

Skippy heads for his office with Paulie trailing behind. Inside, with the door closed, he opens the bottom drawer of his desk and removes a gold badge. The word DETECTIVE is stamped across the top of the badge.

"Here, try this."

Paulie takes the badge, but doesn't put it in his pocket. "Is this real?" he asks.

In fact, the badge, which Skippy purchased online, is a replica of the badge issued to detectives on the San Antonio police department. Nevertheless, he nods his head and says, "Absolutely. You just show it and she'll open the door. Guaranteed."

Skippy's reaching for the handle on the outer door when his cell begins to ring. He glances at the screen: Petersburg Industrial Laundry. Arkady Alebev owns the company and it's where he spends most of his days posing as an honest businessman. This is a call Skippy has to take.

"Hey, Skippy, my condolences I'm offering."

"What?"

"The robbing, yes? Your cigarettes."

Skippy rubs the corners of his eyes. He knows the answer, but still has to ask the question. "How'd you hear about that?"

"Mike called me, your pal. He tells me of your loss and asks that I give you a little more time. I tell him, like I'm telling you, Skippy. You can have all the time you need as long as you pay the vig. Like tonight when the vig is due."

"Look . . ."

"Please, I am man of peace. Never do I need aggravation. No, I am man who is wanting simple life, so I tell you in most simple words I know. Tonight I am coming to your place of business at seven o'clock after workers have gone home. You will please to be present, Skippy. I have placed big bet on you."

And that's true enough. Skippy had been in the hole to three bookmakers and a loan shark when Arkady bought up his debts. Consolidating bad debt and finding a way to collect is Arkady's specialty.

Skippy's draws a breath. "Consider it done," he tells Arkady. "And now you'll have to excuse me because I gotta deal with this robbery thing."

"Yes, very sad. Goodbye, Skippy."

As Skippy reaches for the door, he's thinking it can't get any worse. This has to be the bottom. But then he pulls the door open to find Cepeda, the cop, standing on the other side, one hand extended as if to shake hands.

"Hey, Mr. Legrand, are you off somewhere?"

"Home," Skippy says, his tone barely civil. "I gotta change my clothes."

"Your home, it's way out on Long Island somewhere?"

"That's right."

If anything, Dante Cepeda's own clothes are even wetter than they were up on the hill. Skippy's always figured cops for suckers, all the bullshit and for what? You make a mistake and the public turns on you like wild dogs on a crippled deer.

"Well, I won't keep you long. First thing, I'm gonna need a list of your employees."

"You can get it from my bookkeeper. That would be Martha. Tell her I said it's OK. Anything else?"

Cepeda's eyes narrow, perhaps in amusement, Skippy's not sure. Then the cop smiles and says, "Now, tell me who didn't show up for work this morning."

SEVEN

Mike Tedesco has a bottom line: better dead than caged. He's not going back to prison, even if it means waking up on the wrong side of the grass. He made that vow to himself—never again—on the day he left Attica. Of course, he might have avoided prison by walking the straight and narrow after he was released, but that particular solution, obvious as it was, never occurred to him.

It occurs to him now, though, as he drives Daniela's ancient Honda over the 59th Street Bridge, from Manhattan into Queens. If only . . .

According one of his cellies, a sixty-year-old man who died in the prison hospital a year later, there are three words a man in the game must learn to avoid: shoulda, woulda, coulda.

"Fuck second-guessing. Keep your eyes on the road."

Tedesco taps the brakes. There's a massive eighteen-wheeler in front of him, another to his left, another behind. He feels like a cockroach on Fifth Avenue during the Saint Patrick's Day Parade. Pay attention or be crushed.

The traffic eases when Tedesco comes off the bridge at Queens Plaza. He's wearing faded jeans and a tan polo shirt, left behind when he first quit Daniela's apartment. Pug sits next to him, his face pressed to the window, tongue lolling as he watches the world go by. Pug took to Daniela right away, licking her hand when she offered it, never considering that he might be the animal sacrifice at her next tambor.

Daniela made her claim to be a *palera*, a priestess in an Afro-Cuban religion called *Regla de Ocha*, early in their relationship. Her life, she explained, was dedicated to an orisha named Oshun, goddess of love and mercy. It always would be, so he could get used to it or get out. Further, she headed a little congregation and held regular tambors in the basement of her apartment house.

Tedesco wasn't any more turned off by the tambors, than by the altar. Half the foster homes he lived in had a crucifix in the bedroom. Jesus nailed to the cross. Papi and Mami bouncing on the bed. Tedesco figured that if he could hear the mattress squeaking, Jesus could too. Jesus was a lot closer to the action.

Eventually, Tedesco came to enjoy the tambors, especially when the drums began to pound. Daniela spoke of them as voices, calling out to Oshun, demanding that she enter the body of one of her worshippers. The singing, a call-and-response with the same phrases repeated over and over again, was designed for the identical purpose. And it generally worked. Sooner or later, impelled by the drums and the chanting, lured by the offerings, Oshun would jump into someone's body and they'd dance around the room, or fall to the ground, or just stand there and howl.

The drums touched something in Tedesco that he couldn't resist. They rippled through his muscles, buzzed through his nervous system, flowed through his veins. Likewise for the chanting, though he didn't understand a word, the language being an ancient form of the Yoruban tongue. But Tedesco wasn't all that impressed.

Hip-hop rhythms had much the same effect on him, and while the possession part did take him by surprise—the possessed usually danced one of Oshun's many dances—his surprise had faded after a few minutes. After all, you could visit any Pentecostal church on any given Sunday and watch a dozen people speak in tongues while they rolled around on the floor. Possessed by the Holy Spirit.

Tedesco's blasé attitude ended abruptly one Friday evening when Oshun came for Mike Tedesco, grabbing hold of him and spinning him around the room. He'd resisted, every neuron in his brain screaming: not me, not me, not me. But whatever had hold of him wasn't letting go. The Bembé drums took charge of his body, and he danced on until he fell to the floor, exhausted.

As a general rule, fear didn't play much of a role in Tedesco's life, but the next day, before sunrise, he packed a bag and moved the fuck out. Running, as he understood it, for his life.

EIGHT

Tedesco reaches out to stroke Pug's incredibly broad head. He needs to get his priorities straight. There are no tambors or *paleras* in Attica. Just a cage and a few thousand violent criminals. Funny thing about prison: 90 percent of the prisoners just want to do their time and get out. Unfortunately, the other 10 percent are not only crazy violent, but completely unable to control their impulses. They keep the joint in chaos.

A few minutes later, Tedesco pulls to the curb in front of a large vacant lot and lets Pug out of the car. He's on 46th Road in Long Island City, a neighborhood conveniently close to Sunnyside where José Sepulveda lives. As Pug charges into the lot, Tedesco slips the burner and the gun into an open storm drain. Tedesco's already cleaned the gun and the burner with bleach, as he's removed the batteries in the burner and his personal cell phone. Powered cell phones are like having a personal snitch in your pocket. Here I am, over here, the guy with the pit bull.

It's time to call the dog and get moving, but Pug's out in the middle of the lot, taking a gigantic crap. Tedesco has a couple of plastic bags in the car, and he'd probably use them if there were any witnesses about. Now, he leans against the car and waits for the dog to finish. He's thinking about the call he made to Arkady Alebev. Alebev will ratchet up the pressure on Skippy, which is all to the good, but Tedesco's thinking further ahead. If Skippy goes down, Tedesco will need to find work. With a grateful Arkady? The real issue is whether Tedesco has the stomach for the level of violence Alebev routinely employs. His clients are among the most hardcore deadbeats in the city.

Pug's needs met, he runs back to Tedesco's side and offers his scarred head for another scratch. Tedesco looks down into a pair of dark eyes that are little more than narrow slits, the better to avoid the slashing teeth of an adversary. Tedesco's witnessed a dog fight. Neither excited, nor sympathetic, he'd only been there to meet an acquaintance and left with no desire to return.

On the road again, Tedesco's focus returns. Handling the gun, even for those few seconds, has sobered him up. He drives south, to Jackson Avenue, then over the Pulaski Bridge into Brooklyn. An hour later, he's parked on Flatlands Avenue in front of a pet store. He takes Pug inside, much to the consternation of a middle-aged woman with a Pekingese on the end of a shiny blue leash. Her face curls into a disapproving grimace as she snatches her dog up and cries, "Oh."

Pug ignores the other dog and the woman. He stands patiently while Tedesco fits several collars around his neck. Tedesco's tempted to go with one of the spiked collars, but finally settles for a plain brown collar and a six-foot nylon leash.

"That a rescue dog?" the teenage girl behind the counter asks when Tedesco steps up to pay.

"I think he kind of rescued himself," Tedesco says before walking out the door. "At least temporarily."

Tedesco leads Pug around the block and up two flights of stairs to a storage unit, one of hundreds in the building. The unit is tiny, with barely enough room to close the door behind him, but Tedesco's not concerned with privacy. There's only one item in the room, a military-style duffel bag. Tedesco slings the bag over his shoulder. He knows what's inside. A .45 caliber Colt Defender and five extended-capacity magazines, a .12 gauge sawed-off shotgun and four boxes of shells, and eight thousand dollars in fifty-dollar bills.

Tedesco was never a Boy Scout, but he began preparing on the day he left prison. Now he's as ready as he can be, though for what remains to be determined.

Pug shivers when Tedesco picks up the leash and heads off, but doesn't pull on the leash or hold back. He follows Tedesco to the Honda, watches him store the duffel bag in the Honda's trunk, then jumps into the front seat and stares out through the windshield. Good to go.

Tedesco drives to a McDonald's near Flatlands Avenue. He feeds Pug small pieces of meat as he works his way through a pair of bacon burgers and a large coffee. The first part, the emergency part, is done. He's got more time now, time to review, time to consider his next move, time even to note Pug's delicate touch as he takes the food. There's no threat, not even the hint of a threat, only a quick sweep of the tongue as he pulls the food between teeth that could break every bone in Tedesco's hand.

By now, Tedesco knows, he's definitely a suspect. The inside man or woman is the first person cops look for in a hijacking. Who knew the route? Who knew when the truck would leave the warehouse? Who knew the security precautions taken to protect the cargo? Trucks that haul cigarettes and liquor are marked only with the name of the trucking company, which pretty much eliminates a random event.

You don't have to be a genius—and most cops aren't—to know what question to ask first: Did all of your workers show up this morning? And Skippy won't lie to protect Tedesco because he, Skippy, is the ultimate insider and also a suspect. In fact, given the insurance, he'll most likely be suspect number one until he tells them about Mike Tedesco's absence.

OK, fine, Mike Tedesco's a suspect, but the road from suspect to convict is a long one. Tedesco knows this because he's traveled that road several times. And then there's José Sepulveda, who left the scene. Tedesco's hoping that José's on his way to his brother in Los Angeles, but even if he decides to stick around, he'll be hard to find. José's in the country illegally, as he foolishly confessed to a sympathetic coworker named Mike Tedesco. His social security number and driver's license were both purchased from a Mexican shipping agency in the Bronx. José Sepulveda is not his real name.

Suddenly, as he pushes the last of the burger into his mouth, the face of the woman in the window, visible for just that instant when the lightning flashed, jumps from Tedesco's short-term memory into the forefront of his consciousness. He'd almost forgotten her. Now he asks himself what she saw through all that rain. Better yet, what *could* she have seen, given the conditions?

Tedesco ticks off the items. She saw a man sitting on the curb, a man driving a truck and a man arriving in a car. She saw the truck driver pulled from the truck. She saw the driver of the car get out and open the hood of the truck. She saw the man on the curb shoot the man from the car, then hold a brief conversation with the truck driver, after which the truck driver—the *uninjured* truck driver—took off. Finally, she saw the shooter jump into a car and drive away.

There's good news and bad news here. The good news, assuming the witness was still at the window when José's truck rolled up, is that the sequence makes José look like a co-conspirator, exactly as Tedesco hoped. The bad news is that it establishes the presence, if not the identity, of a third man at the scene. The one who pulled the trigger. Twice.

"Is that a rescue dog?"

Tedesco looks up to find two women standing a few yards away. The women are young—college age—and reasonably attractive. Ordinarily, he'd jump at the chance to start a conversation. Not today.

"Nah, he's not a rescue. I'm gonna pit him tonight, but if he loses again, I'll pull his teeth and use him to train my younger dogs."

The taller of the women cocks her head to one side. She stares at him for a minute, then raises a middle finger. "Fuck you very much," she says.

Tedesco watches them walk off, then glances at Pug. He's staring back, his head cocked at almost exactly the same angle as the woman who gave Tedesco the finger. Tedesco wipes his forehead. The sky is rapidly darkening and the air, stirred by a faint breeze, smells like the breath of an animal. The day will end as it began, with thunder and rain.

"C'mon, let's get out of here." Tedesco dumps his trash in a basket at the corner, then loads Pug into the Honda. His thoughts return to his problem as he puts the car in gear and pulls away from the curb. He can't, he knows, be convicted solely on the testimony of a single co-conspirator. The prosecutors need some physical evidence tying him to the scene. The burner and the gun are both gone, but Asher's Lincoln is still out there. Tedesco was only inside the Lincoln for a short time, and he'd wiped it down as best he could. That won't necessarily protect him. The ME's office has a lab, able to recover miniscule amounts of DNA. Will they recover his? Will they find the Lincoln? Probably not, but he still has work to do.

Ten minutes later, Tedesco again pulls to the curb. He takes his cell phone from a small case attached to his belt and punches in a familiar number.

"Hello?"

"Sanda?"

"You were expecting someone else?"

Tedesco ignores the question. "I got troubles, Sanda, and I won't be home for a while."

"What troubles?"

"I'm not gonna tell ya that, and I'm not gonna tell ya where I'm stayin', either. But you're gonna get a visit from the cops, for sure, and probably from somebody else who you should definitely avoid. Somebody who won't believe you when you claim that you don't know where I am. If I was you, I'd get lost for a few days."

"I have lived in an apartment for fifteen years, Mike. And I am making career, in case you didn't notice. You expect for me to run away?"

"Suit yourself, Sanda. You always do."

NINE

Dante Cepeda's seated in a little cubicle, hunched forward, staring at a computer monitor. He's smiling a bemused smile, just a little tug at one end of his mouth that might easily be mistaken for a sneer by those who don't know him. But there's also a twinkle in his eye because he's just recognized the man on the screen, Mike Tedesco.

Back in the day, he and Tedesco had both served time at the Youth Hope Center, a group home in the Bronx. Dante can't speak for Tedesco, but whatever hope he experienced at Youth Hope, he'd manufactured on his own. And not in the center, either. Early on, at age thirteen, he'd taken up the fine art of boxing, reporting to a gym every afternoon. Supremely untalented, he served mainly as a sparring partner for brighter prospects, absorbing punishment willingly. That's because the only alternatives were the mean streets of the South Bronx, or the confines of a group foster home dominated by knuckleheads destined to pass their lives in prison or die an early death.

Mike Tedesco, a white boy in a people-of-color world, chose a fourth strategy. Smarter than most—*much* smarter—he made himself indispensable by smuggling drugs into the center. At one point, according to rumor, he was even dealing coke to several counselors, one of whom he was probably screwing.

"What's the smile for?"

Dante looks up to find Patti O'Hearn leaning over his chair. He's tempted to explain, but decides to keep his background to himself. Most of the cops he's known— all of them, actually—grew up in relatively normal families. Their lives might not have been perfect, but at least they were wanted. No one had wanted Dante Cepeda, not the several families who considered adopting him, but chose someone else, or the temporary foster families who profited from his plight.

"This guy didn't show up for work today at Legrand Transportation. His name's Mike Tedesco."

"That his mug shot?"

"Yeah, he did three years in Attica. Grand larceny, his second conviction. The first time he got probation."

Patti lays a hand on Dante's shoulder, unleashing a little jolt of electricity that runs up and down his spine. Dante's on the back side of an on-again, off-again relationship with an on-again, off-again hooker. The relationship was stormy from the outset, but at least he and Sarah understood each other well enough to know they needed to put space between them. Sarah was currently seeking employment in Seattle.

"You think he's good for the murder?"

Dante swivels his chair around to face Patti. Now her breasts are within a foot of his face, not exactly what he had in mind. Nevertheless, he reviews the case, what he's done and what remains to be done, before he responds to her question.

"Two things. First, the driver, José, was held at gunpoint while an attempt was made to disarm the GPS tracker. Second, José didn't walk down the hill, like he would if he was part of the hijacking. He ran full out, at least according to Myra Cuffee. If you remember, she was pretty clear on that point."

"José is the truck driver?"

"Right."

"So why didn't he come forward and report the hijacking?"

"Best guess?"

"Sure."

"First, because whatever the shooter said to him was enough to keep him on the run. Second, because according to Legrand's bookkeeper—her name's Martha Proctor and she likes to talk—José's probably illegal."

"OK, got it. But you still didn't answer my question. Do you think this guy, Tedesco, was the shooter?"

"Don't know, but I'll be sure to ask the question when I find him."

"Not, *if* you find him? You seem pretty sure of yourself."

Dante looks into Patti's tired eyes. What with all the summer vacations, she's working a double shift. But there's no turning down overtime and she's stuck until four.

"An investigation has to start down the most likely path," he says. "Otherwise you just turn in circles."

"And if the path turns out to be a dead end?"

Dante considers the question for a moment before smiling. "Then you're most likely screwed because too much time has gone by and other cases are piling up on your desk. By the way, thanks for putting out a heads-up on the Lincoln."

"No big deal." Patti shifts her weight slightly as a blush rises into her cheeks, heightening the spray of freckles beneath her eyes. "Ya know, I tried like hell to make the detectives when I first came on the job. In fact, I only took the sergeant's exam because it didn't work out." She shrugs her shoulders. "I do have a rabbi, but she and the chief of detectives are on the outs. My bad."

Dante nods sympathetically as he rises to his feet. At six-two, he towers over Patti O'Hearn. "You'll have to excuse me, Patti. I gotta hit the road. The way I figure, I've got seventy-two hours before Manhattan North transfers the case to Homicide."

Dante again reviews his morning's work as he sits in his car with the engine running. He's in Queens County, in the neighborhood of Sunnyside, about to approach the nondescript, redbrick apartment building where José Sepulveda lives. The air conditioner in the Impala is running full out, a matter of luck. Detectives aren't assigned units. You take whatever's available when you number's called, including behicles in which air conditioning is a distant memory. Now the cool air creates a little island of comfort surrounded by a perfect summer storm. It's raining as hard as it was in the morning, and Dante hasn't got another change of clothes. He doesn't have an umbrella, either.

The still-unidentified victim, he tells himself, *carried a cell phone, a burner.* Dante has already tried the single number in the call directory, only to be informed that the subscriber was unavailable. Please try again later. Dante then put in a request to his squad commander, Lieutenant Barnwell. Would the NYPD ask the manufacturer of the burner, PrivacyFones, to ping the unit, thus revealing its location? The request was little more than due diligence and his expectations were—and remain—too low to be measured.

Dante's time at Legrand Transportation was better spent.

Middle-aged and motherly, Martha Proctor liked to talk. And why not? Her employer had just been ripped off, she was a loyal employee and she supported her local police.

Mike Tedesco, she told Dante, was a kind of shop manager. He ran the show when Skippy was out of the office, which was pretty much every afternoon.

"Every afternoon? Where does your boss go?"

"To the racetrack." Martha's tone was conspiratorial. "But you didn't hear it from me."

"So, Tedesco was familiar with the entire operation?"

"He did most of the scheduling."

"And what about security? Did the trucks have tracking units installed?"

"Of course. In fact . . ." Martha worked the mouse on her computer for a moment, then said, "Right now, the truck you fellas towed is in Long Island City near Vernon Boulevard."

"Exactly." Dante nodded agreeably. "At our impound yard. Now tell me about this driver, José Sepulveda. What was he like?"

"A mouse, believe me. And maybe he had a driver's license and a social security number, but I guarantee he was an illegal. This city . . ." Martha sucked in her breath and rolled her eyes. "Nobody gives a damn. Not the cops, for sure. And not the bosses, either, especially my boss. José's on salary, OK? Four hundred dollars a week? That means he works fifty hours and gets paid for forty. Skippy loves him because he shows up every morning and doesn't complain."

Dante glances out the window at a woman passing by. The rain has slowed, but the humidity is thick enough to support aquatic life. The woman is plodding along, head down, a shopping bag dangling from either hand. She looks, to Dante, as if she'll give out before she reaches the corner. Not so the little girl beside her. The girl's hair is plastered to the side of her head and rivulets of sweat run down her face, but she skips along, her little mouth going a mile a minute.

As he climbs out of the car, Dante experiences a moment of regret. He tells himself that he's going to play the role of hard-ass cop only because there's a body involved. And because little José, Martha's mouse, is the key to closing the case. If only Dante Cepeda can find him.

TEN

The elderly man who answers Dante's knock stares at Dante's badge for a moment, then explains, in rapid-fire Spanish, that he doesn't speak English and even if he did, he's only a boarder and doesn't know anything. His eyes narrow when Dante replies in Spanish. Maybe it's the blue eyes, but he's clearly mistaken the cop for an Anglo.

"*Estoy buscando a José,*" Dante asks the man as he pushes past him. "*¿Donde esta el?*"

The old man doesn't reply, and Dante strides down a short hallway and into a living room that reeks of tobacco. Seated on a faded couch, a much younger woman is folding laundry. A girl and a boy, barely out of the toddler stage, play on the rose-red carpet.

"*Estoy buscando a José,*" Dante says to the children.

They stare, not at him, but at the badge he holds up, eyes wide. Then they look to the woman. "*Mami, Mami,*" the girl half-whispers.

Dante steels himself. There's nothing in the patrol guide about bullying little children, but . . . "Are you gonna talk to me?" he asks the woman in English.

"I don' know what . . ."

"Let's start with your name. No, wait, show me some ID. Right now."

The woman drops a blouse into the laundry basket at her feet. "José is not here," she says, ignoring his request. *"Por favor."*

Dante waits for the old man to shuffle across the room and drop into a rocking chair. He shakes his head when the man starts to light a cigarette.

"I asked you to show me some identification," he finally says.

Assuming this woman is here illegally, the demand is a double-edged sword. Illegals can't get driver's licenses, aren't eligible for social security or for any city services. Most compensate by carrying some sort of phony ID, but that's the rub. You can be arrested for showing false ID to a cop. Dante has only to glance into the woman's eye to know that she's fully aware of this trap.

"You're José's wife," Dante says.

The woman looks down. *"Sí,"* she says.

"What's your name?"

"Sofia."

"What's José's real name?"

"Herrera . . . José Herrera."

"Where is he?"

She shakes her head. "I don' know."

Dante questions the woman for the next fifteen minutes. At one point, he turns to the old man and they go back-and-forth in Spanish. But he can't shake either one, though he's certain both are lying, and he eventually settles for a quick search of the apartment before dropping his card into Sofia's lap.

"You tell José that I know he witnessed a murder and he's gotta call me. I'm serious, Sofia. Don't make me come back here, because if I have to come back, I'm gonna bring ICE with me."

* * *

The threat is seriously bullshit. New York is a sanctuary city, and cops are prohibited from working directly with Immigration and Customs Enforcement unless the illegal immigrant in question has committed a felony. And sometimes not even then. But José and his family hail from a country where the police can drag you into the boonies, put a bullet through your head and walk away. Maybe they've been told that New York cops are different, but old habits die hard and deportation would present the family with a number of painful choices, especially if the kiddies were born in the good old USA.

I handed them a carrot, Dante tells himself, as if the gesture somehow absolves him. I referred to José as a witness, not a perpetrator. Now it's up to them.

Ahead of him, a thin mist rises from a wet sidewalk fully exposed to a glaring sun. His department Impala, parked down the block, is also in full sun, so whatever's inside has already been cooked. The temperature has to be well over a hundred degrees, and his clothes will be saturated long before the air conditioner cools down the interior. Well, maybe he'll drop by his apartment in Brooklyn, change his clothes for the second time before he returns to the Three-One and several hours of paperwork.

The Honda's interior, when he finally slides behind the wheel, is as hot as Dante expects, and sweat instantly jumps from every pore in his body. It runs in little streams, from his scalp and face and neck, down under his armpits and along his ribs, then finally drips into a puddle beneath his bony ass.

This is why I don't go to church, he tells himself as he starts the engine.

Dante's still adjusting the air-conditioning vents when his cell rings. He glances at the screen: Patti O'Hearn.

"Hey, Dante, how's it goin'?"

"Slowly. Very slowly."

"Well, I have some good news for you. I'm pretty sure we found your Lincoln parked on Riverside Drive."

"Anything interesting inside, like maybe the murder weapon and a wallet?"

"Sorry, Detective, but I won't be able to answer that question until they put out the fire."

Patti's laughter echoes in Dante's ears even after he hangs up and puts the Impala in gear. He doesn't find her laughter mocking, not this time. She appears delighted instead, a young girl thoroughly pleased with her little joke and with herself.

ELEVEN

Paulie Bancroft isn't the brightest bulb in anyone's chandelier. In truth, his intellect barely flickers. But he's a large man and very strong, and his features are devoid of affect. You put him behind the wheel of a truck, you don't have to worry about rip-offs. Say when you're transporting a load of hot TV's from one warehouse to another. Even better, if you put Mike Tedesco in the passenger's seat to give direction—which you have to do because Paulie confuses about as easy as a human being can possibly confuse and still be said to function—you could pretty much guarantee success.

Skippy Legrand and Paulie Bancroft first became friends at age nine when Paulie's mother emigrated from a Minneapolis suburb to Bensonhurst, in Brooklyn. Paulie never saw his father again, but since he'd only seen his father three times, and those in a visitors' room at Stillwater Prison, he never actually missed the man.

Little Paulie's transition was anything but smooth. The boy arrived in the Big Apple devoid of the social skills necessary to survive an urban childhood. Still mostly white at the time, Bensonhurst was nevertheless a rough mix of Irish, Italians, and Jews dedicated to protecting their turf, whether it be the entire neighborhood of Bensonhurst or the east side of New Utrecht Avenue.

But if Paulie was socially inept, if the ways of his peers were and remained opaque, he did possess two virtues, and those in abundance. He was a strong kid and dead game in a fight.

Skippy Legrand, by contrast, was street smart to a fault. He knew the rules, and how to use them to his advantage, but lacked the means to accomplish his goals. Small for his age and easily intimidated, a pair of older boys regularly took his lunch money. Talk about agony. Every time the boy reached into his pocket and forked over the two dollars, it felt like his heart was being torn from his chest. He just had to find a way out.

Enter Paulie Bancroft.

Desperately grateful to his new pal, Paulie didn't have to be instructed at the critical moment. He tore into both of Skippy's tormentors, suffering two black eyes and a bloody nose, yet still managing to inflict enough pain to ward off future battles. Skippy could now pursue his ends in peace.

For the next couple of weeks, Skippy treated his pal to a chocolate milk and a Mars bar on the way home from school. Nothing for nothing is a maxim that's governed much of Skippy's life, Paulie being the ultimate proof. Skippy's been carrying the man for the better part of four decades.

Having taken a shower, medicated his psoriasis and changed his clothes, Skippy's now seated in the living room of a single-family house in Valley Stream, a town in Nassau County only a few miles outside the city. He's watching his twin girls, Ally and Carla, ten years old, work an iPad. They're watching YouTube videos, mostly boy bands with effeminate lead singers. Every few seconds, they squeal, always together, then look into each other's eyes and giggle.

Skippy's provided his girls with a pampered life, a life in sharp contrast to his own. He was just starting eighth grade the first time his dad brought him into the warehouse. From that day forward, he worked every Saturday at Legrand Transportation during the school year, and full-time in the summer. No aspect of the trucking business was excluded from his training. He loaded and drove trucks and called on customers with his dad. Booking, maintenance, scheduling, basic accounting, and collections all took a piece of his adolescence. By the time he finished high school, broken to harness, he was prepared to manage day-to-day operations while his father built up the business.

By contrast, Ally and Carla, ten years old, have never been asked to work, not even around the house. Instead, ferried from their swimming classes to the soccer field to their dance classes by a mother as ambitious as she is diligent, they're obsessed with their peers and their place in the pecking order. The larger world, with all of its many dangers, they simply ignore, certain that dear old dad will iron out life's wrinkles.

Far from resenting the situation, Skippy loves to spoil his daughters. His job, as he understands it, is to provide the money that makes their innocence possible and he's mostly accomplished that goal. No more, though. Gabriel is about to blow his horn, after which the walls of Skippy Legrand's city will come tumbling down. Ally's and Carla's city, too, if Daddy has to spend the next twenty-five years in a cage. Fay Legrand was a dispatcher for a car service when she and Skippy met, her pay only a few steps removed from minimum wage. That was fifteen years ago and she hasn't worked since.

Skippy's attention shifts to the tablet in his lap. He's wondering if his life can get any worse, but he already knows the answer. Like if he doesn't come up with five grand for Arkady Alebev by tonight. Arkady's been known to cut off fingers.

Well, Skippy still has a chance. He can win the race about to take place at Aqueduct Racetrack, a six-furlong sprint for thirty thousand dollars claimers. He's got a hundred dollars, his last C-note, spread out in exacta bets with the number-three horse, Shoeless Joe, on top. Shoeless Joe is currently nine-to-one and the smallest exacta payoff, should he come in with the favorite, is thirty-one dollars.

Skippy's bet is with an offshore gambling site. Payment on these sites is always in advance and the C-note has pretty much drained the balance on his debit card. The family won't be going out to dinner tonight. But Skippy thinks he has a decent chance here. Shoeless Joe is trained by Frederick Smead who runs a notorious betting stable. Smead's horses never win at short odds. Never.

Shoeless Joe's last four races, watched by Skippy through self-focusing binoculars, were typical Smead tank jobs. The gelding is a one-run horse that only wins—a rare enough event—when he comes from the back of the pack. Sent to the front, as he was in the four races Skippy witnessed, the gelding had collapsed after a half mile, finishing well out of the money. The bettors had made him a five-to-two co-favorite in the first race, a seven-to-two third choice in the second, and four-to-one in his last two. Now his odds have jumped to eleven-to-one in a barely competitive race.

Skippy watches the horses as they're loaded into the starting gate, a familiar tension rising through his body. This is what he lives for, what his life is all about, everything on the line, his very existence hanging in the balance. He feels sorry for all those people who play it safe. Maybe there's no agony in their lives, but there's no ecstasy, either. Meanwhile, if he loses . . .

* * *

As his horse is led into the four hole, Skippy memorizes Shoeless Joe's silks, blue blouse with a diagonal white stripe and a red cap. Then he closes his eyes for a moment, his expression as fervent as that of a martyr tied to a stake. "Please," he mutters to any god willing to listen. "Please, please, please."

When the starting gate finally opens, Skippy hears the bang, even though he's muted the tablet's small speakers. His heart drops when Shoeless Joe breaks alertly and stays with the pack for a few strides, but then Angel Cruz takes the gelding to the rail and lets the front runners go by.

As the field approaches the quarter pole, Skippy's grip tightens on the arm of the couch and his heartbeat ratchets up. He can feel his pulse in his temples, the veins swelling. Shoeless Joe has settled into an easy gallop, eight lengths off the pace. The gelding's not going in the tank, not this time, it's a full go. That doesn't mean that he'll win the race, but at least he's trying.

"Please, please," Skippy repeats, this time loud enough to draw the attention of his daughters. Neither speaks because they've witnessed similar scenes many times in the past and know their father wouldn't hear them if they screamed in his ear. But they look at each other, their expressions wary. Here we go again.

Shoeless Joe maintains his position on the rail throughout the backstretch and into the turn, his stride effortless. It's only as the field straightens for home, with the finish line a quarter mile away, that Cruz takes him to the outside, away from traffic, and applies the whip left-handed. Shoeless Joe responds immediately, as if he's been awaiting this cue for the entire race, first passing tired horses, then closing in on the race leader.

Skippy jumps to his feet, holding the tablet out in front of him with both hands. He looks back up the track as another horse—the favorite, Morning Gold—makes a similar move. Morning Gold's jock is beating the crap out of him, shaking the reins, leaning far forward in the stirrups. Skippy watches the horse respond, watches Morning Gold's stride lengthen.

"Please, please, please, please, please."

It's all over by the time they reach the eighth pole. Morning Gold might be the better horse, but his jockey miscalculated. Shoeless Joe staggers across the finish line two lengths in front of an eight-to-one shot named Empty Promise. Morning Gold finishes third.

Skippy lets out a breath he's been holding for the entire race, then looks down at his fingers. Still there, all ten, and they're gonna stay that way.

I knew it, he tells himself. I knew my luck was about to turn. I felt it in my bones. Now all I need is a little time, a little space. And for the cops not to put that murder on me, and for me to find that prick, Tedesco, before the cops find him.

"Please, please, please, please, please."

When he finally becomes aware of his twin daughters a few second later, they're staring up at their father, still unsure of what actually happened. Skippy glowers at them for just a moment, then grabs his belly with both hands and shakes it up and down, a September Santa Claus.

"Pizza time," he announces, much to their delight. "With ham and pineapple."

TWELVE

Paulie Bancroft parks his car in front of Sanda Dragomir's townhouse at one o'clock in the afternoon. He shuts down the engine, slides the seat back, and settles in. He has no idea what Sanda Dragomir looks like. He doesn't even know her age. Plus, he has to get through two doors, not one. The outer door first, then the door to her apartment, all without instigating a call to 911. And not only from Sanda, who lives on the second floor, but someone living on the first.

Problem solving isn't Paulie's specialty, but there's no telling Skippy that he failed. He has to do something or Skippy . . .

Paulie doesn't know what Skippy will do. He only knows that he can't make it on his own. On his own, he'd be lucky to get a job at a car wash. Skippy's the meal ticket. Skippy's why Paulie eats steak instead of sawdust.

The row house that commands Paulie's full attention is one of six attached, two-family houses on the south side of 45th Street in the Brooklyn neighborhood of Sunset Park. All six bear identical facades of pale, creamy brick and run to a thousand square feet per floor, which makes for a pair of relatively large apartments in each house. Probably two bedrooms with an eat-in kitchen.

Sanda Dragomir lives on the second floor of the last house in the row, and she's at home. From time to time, while he considers his options, Paulie sees her move across one of the open windows. The lower apartment is also occupied, but here Paulie catches a break. Fifteen minutes after he arrives, the front door opens and an elderly woman emerges. Paulie senses opportunity as he watches her drag a folded shopping cart down the steps to the sidewalk. She's some kind of dumpy slanted eyes, which comes as no surprise to Paulie because the city's overrun with chinks. And not just Chinese. Vietnamese, Koreans, Japs, Filipinos, even goddamned Cambodians. Swarming like flies. Taking over. On Eighth Avenue, which he just drove down, the signs on almost every store are in some kind of chink language. Like they don't even *want* your business. Still, there's good news here. If she's illegal, she won't call the cops if he makes a little noise.

Sunset Park is a low-rise neighborhood, the tallest buildings no more than eight stories, and there's a lot more sky here than in Manhattan. Enough for Paulie to mark the dark clouds streaming up from the south and the odd bolt of far-distant lightning. Paulie's fascination with lightning began on the day his mom read him a story about Zeus hurling thunderbolts from the sky. Paulie liked to imagine himself inside the clouds, liked to imagine being Zeus, liked to imagine the lightning bolts as they slammed into the ground or set whole forests ablaze. To this day, if he's outside, he tries to retain the image revealed by the sudden burst of light. That he's never succeeded, not once, doesn't bother him in the slightest.

Paulie's not so taken up with the electrical display that he forgets his assignment. Hurt, not kill. He knows the storm has come along at the right time. The flow of pedestrians, everyone a potential witness who might call 911, has been steady since his arrival. But the thunderstorms are sure to clear the sidewalks and mask any sound, say a scream, if he has to hurt (not kill) Sanda. Good news, assuming he gets inside. The building's outer door, as he noted when the chink opened it, is of thick wood, probably oak, and the deadbolt lock strong and heavy. Big as he is, he's not getting through that door without making a lot of noise, without alerting Sanda. The alternative, to ring her bell and claim to be a cop, hoping she'll open up, seems almost as risky. Suppose she doesn't? Supposed she tells him to fuck off?

Paulie watches the clouds darken as they lower. He watches the lightning bolts become more frequent and more intense, exploding in jagged lines. The glare primes him for what's to come. There's thunder now, explosions loud enough to mask a gunshot. Good, good, good. He's going to go with plan number two. He's a detective investigating a homicide-robbery, looking for a man named Mike Tedesco who resides at this address. Please open up.

Paulie touches the 9 mm Sig-Sauer tucked behind his belt, seeking comfort, but then his eyes snap to the rearview mirror. There's someone coming up the block. It's the old lady, pushing her shopping cart, now full. As the first raindrops, fat and heavy, begin to fall, she picks up the pace until her chubby legs are going a mile a minute. Watching her, Paulie's lip curls, his eyes narrow, and his brain finally stops spinning.

Paulie jumps out of the car as the old lady climbs the steps to her front door and slips her key into the lock. He's on top of her before the door closes.

"I'm a cop." Paulie waves the badge in front of her face. "My business don't have nothin' to do with you."

The old lady answers in a language Paulie doesn't understand. Maybe it's Cambodian. He taps her chest, a gesture that leaves her slack-jawed. Then he points to her door. Next, he touches his own chest before gesturing up the stairway.

"Go inside," he says, "or I'll put you under arrest."

The old lady, suddenly bilingual, complies without a murmur of protest. That's another thing that irritates Paulie. The aliens like to pretend they don't understand a word you say, as if you were the aliens and not them. Paulie looks at the badge in his hand. He's thinking there might be someone else upstairs, maybe even Tedesco. Paulie's never liked Tedesco, but he's ridden alongside him often enough to know that Tedesco's not a punk. If he's in there, he'll fight.

Paulie's reaches for the Sig-Sauer. He starts to pull the weapon free but then changes his mind. Tedesco knows the cops will be along . . . and pretty soon. He won't be upstairs, not after killing someone, not after robbing Skippy. He'll be holed up someplace, figuring his next move.

Despite Paulie's bulk, his steps are light as he climbs to the top of the stairway. The door in front of him appears flimsy. If worse comes to worse, he's certain he can break out the lock with a well-placed kick. One thing sure, having come this far, he's not prepared to back off. As he pins the badge to his jacket and knocks lightly on the door, he again repeats what Skippy told him. Hurt, not kill.

"Come on in, Mrs. Jiang," a woman's voice calls. "The door's open."

Paulie doesn't bother to count his lucky stars. As he twists the knob, opens the door, and steps inside, a grin he can't control spreads across his face. He's completely forgotten the first part of Skippy's instructions, to start out by asking nice.

The grin fades quickly. Paulie's looking down an empty corridor leading to the back of the house. To his right, a living room is unoccupied. There's a second room perhaps fifteen feet ahead, probably a kitchen though he can't see into it. A third room at the very end of the corridor is undoubtedly a bedroom. Paulie takes a step, again checks the living room to his right, then takes another. Something's wrong here, but he can't put his finger on exactly what it is until Sanda Dragomir steps into the corridor to face him. She's holding a semi-automatic in a two-handed grip, standing with her legs apart, her weight thrust forward to accept the recoil should she pull the trigger.

Paulie taps the badge with his left hand. He tries to smile, but misses the mark by a good deal. "I'm a cop," he says as his right hand inches toward the gun in his belt. "Put the gun down." After a few seconds, he adds, "Please."

The gun doesn't come down, but remains unwavering, the barrel pointed at the center of Paulie's massive chest. The woman has one eye closed, the other is fixed on the gun's sights. That she's prepared to pull the trigger, that maybe she's already *decided* to pull the trigger, is obvious.

"You are Paulie, right?" the woman says, her accent heavy. "Tedesco has told me about you."

"Yeah, see, Tedesco's who I'm lookin' for. Is he here?"

Isabell ignores the question. "Tedesco says that you are stupid man and now you are proving this," she explains as she pulls the trigger, pumping a round into Paulie's chest.

It takes Paulie a second to realize that he's not dead. Then he grabs at the gun in his belt. The gun is his only hope, but he's barely cleared his belt when Sanda fires twice more. The first round smashes into his left shoulder. The second cuts his descending aorta in half. The net effect is virtually instantaneous. The Sig-Sauer drops to the floor and Paulie collapses, pitching forward onto his face. He's unconscious before Sanda kicks the gun away. He's dead before she unlocks her cell phone and calls for help.

THIRTEEN

The interior of the Lincoln is little more than a pile of sodden charcoal by the time Dante Cepeda pulls up. Every scrap of plastic and fabric has been consumed by the fire and soaked by the firefighters' hoses. The exterior isn't in much better condition, and the odor of gasoline pervades the motionless air into which he steps for a cursory look. *DNA*, he thinks. *Yeah, right.* The Lincoln doesn't even have license plates.

Dante leans over the fender, careful to keep his jacket away from the charred metal, and copies down the vehicle identification number inside the engine well. Patient, as always, he calls back to the precinct, locates a civilian tech, and passes on the number. He'll have the name of the registered owner within an hour, which won't do him the slightest bit of good because the car's sure to be stolen. That's another thing about Dante Cepeda. He's as committed to Murphy's law as he is to drawing his next breath.

The fire department personnel are wrapping it up. There are three vehicles on scene, two pumpers and a tomato-red SUV. They've done their job, restricting the fire to the Lincoln although cars are parked in front and behind. Dante looks around, hoping for a nearby surveillance camera, only to be disappointed. He's standing on a causeway that looks west over Riverside Park and the Hudson River, north to the George Washington Bridge, and south toward the heart of Manhattan's commercial district. Behind him, on the far side of Riverside Drive, the mausoleums, gravestones, and mature trees that mark Trinity Cemetery rise from a steep slope that runs toward Broadway. Dante doesn't know if the trustees who operate the cemetery concluded that dead people don't need security, but there are no cameras here either.

"Funny thing, Dante." The voice belongs to Patti O'Hearn. "You can never find a security camera when you need one."

Dante manages a smile as he turns. "I like it," he explains. "Smart criminals motivate me."

"Can't get it up for the morons?"

OK, enough, Dante tells himself. What are you waiting for? Does she have to rub her panties in your face before you take the hint? "Too easy," he tells her. "I relish a challenge."

Patti's smile fades before Dante realizes that his comment can be taken the wrong way, a dagger with a two-edged blade. "Of course," he adds, "there's something to be said for the mope who kills somebody in front of fifteen witnesses."

"Those are the ones that get you promoted. It's a numbers game."

That was true, a fact of life made abundantly clear by Dante's commanding officer, Lieutenant Kelly Barnwell. A real go-getter, Barnwell conducts monthly meetings with each of her detectives, making the same point each time. The road to promotion—to detective, second grade, in Dante's case—is paved with arrests. At some point, the desk jockeys at the Puzzle Palace will compare the stats generated by her squad with the stats of other squads in New

York City. And it isn't about superstars, either. It's about hitting .280 when your competition's batting .250.

A fanatic Yankee fan, Kelly Barnwell works the team's fortunes into almost every conversation.

Dante nods to Patti, then glances to his left, across the Hudson River, at the apartment buildings that rise from the bluffs. Softened by mist and summer haze, they remind him of the tombstones in the cemetery behind him.

"Actually, I don't have to worry about that," he says. "About the numbers. Not in this case."

"How so?"

"Because at any moment, and surely within seventy-two hours, Manhattan North Homicide will take the case away from me. Once that happens, whether it's cleared or remains open falls on them. Meanwhile, we're shorthanded due to vacations and I'm workin' without a partner." Dante stares into Patti's eyes for a moment. He wants to ask her, all casual, if she'd like to meet him for a drink after work, but that's really stupid. And not only because they both drink at a local cop bar on St. Nicholas Avenue. Dante won't stop working this case until he runs down every lead. More than likely, he'll labor into the early morning hours, catch a nap on a precinct cot, and head out again in the morning. "I could play it by the numbers, of course, maybe spend my time running down the owner of the car. Clock out at the end of my tour."

"But you won't?"

"Three things need doing right away. Find Mike Tedesco, the missing employee. Find José Sepulveda, the missing truck driver. Identify the victim and tie him to Tedesco or Skippy Legrand, the boss at Legrand Transportation. Not necessarily in that order, of course."

Patti smiles that knowing smile of hers. "You really want this shooter," she says.

"Yeah, exactly. I wanna cuff the asshole behind his back, read him his rights, and watch his reaction. He knows he lost. He knows I won. Sometimes they curse me, but the assholes mostly fold their cards. That's because they're lookin' into their long-term futures and seein' a cage."

Patti's blue eyes light up as she runs the sleeve of her regulation blouse across the sweat on her forehead. "If you wanna get a head start on that project, I'll have the car towed to an impound yard. Also, I can spare a couple of men to canvass those buildings just in case somebody was lookin' out the window when the Lincoln was torched." She gestures to a pair of apartment buildings on the far side of the cemetery. They're at least a hundred yards away. "Maybe we'll get lucky."

FOURTEEN

We? As in *we'll* get lucky. Dante considers the implications on the long drive to the south Brooklyn neighborhood of Sunset Park, a drive made even longer by a fast-moving thunderstorm that reduces visibility to a few feet beyond the hood. Having several times been rejected by parents out to adopt, Dante usually avoids emotional risk. The women in his life, and there have been many, have all come from a background similar to his. They've had a hard-ass approach to life and a manner easily read. As a general rule, Dante admired their pragmatic approach, but mysterious was not on their agenda. Quick to confront, they spoke their minds.

Dante's driving one of the precinct's newer vehicles, with the air-conditioning turned up full blast, half-listening to the emotionless drone of a bored dispatcher. He's not expecting to find Mike Tedesco at home. Not only did the man not show up for work, he didn't call in with an excuse and he's not answering his phone. Will his girlfriend lie for him? Probably so, but she can also name Tedesco's friends and hangouts, priceless information if it comes down to a manhunt. How to approach her? That's the question, and one he can't answer until they meet, which might not happen on this run. Sanda might not be at home, or she might not answer the door, or . . .

The possibilities narrow considerably when he turns onto her block and finds it clogged by vehicles parked in the middle of the street. Police cruisers, four of them, an unmarked Ford the same shade of midnight blue as his own, a white morgue wagon, the death investigator's SUV and a Crime Scene Unit van present an impassable barrier. Three uniformed cops, a sergeant among them, huddle outside a row house further up the block. Dante reads the address as he approaches on foot. Sanda Dragomir lives on the second floor.

The cops nod hello even before Dante pulls his gold shield. He has cop written all over him. "We got a body upstairs," Sergeant Diem, a slight Asian who can't be more than five-seven, explains.

"Is she dead," Dante asks as he steps through the outer door.

"Who?"

"Sanda Dragomir."

"Dead? Man, have you got it wrong. Dragomir's the shooter."

Dante finds a detective at the head of the stairs. He's standing as close as possible to the door while a death scene investigator from the ME's office examines the body and a CSU team processes the narrow hallway.

"Dante Cepeda, from the Three-One," he tells the detective. "I'm investigating a homicide. Took place early this morning in West Harlem."

"Walt, O'Brien," the detective replies. "From the Seven-Two. This homicide, does it involve Sanda Dragomir?" Well over six feet tall, O'Brien, with his ruddy complexion and tiny blue eyes, is a throwback cop. He's wearing a brown suit, black shoes, and a stained blue tie.

"I'm lookin' for her boyfriend," Dante says. "He lives here."

"What a coincidence."

The death examiner chooses that moment to roll the victim onto his back. Dante's smile, when he recognizes Skippy Legrand's employee, is as grim as smiles get.

"She say anything yet?"

"Dragomir?"

"Yeah."

"She told me her lawyer's *en route*. We recovered a second gun, by the way. Near the victim, unfired." O'Brien scratches the back of his neck, then glances at his fingernails. "So, tell me what's up with your case that brings you to Brooklyn."

Dante runs through the details, the hijacking, the murder, the simple fact that Sanda's boyfriend, Mike Tedesco, who knew the route of the hijacked truck, didn't show up for work. "I think my victim was supposed to disarm the trucks' GPS system. I think he was murdered because he failed."

An hour later, Dante sits at the kitchen table, O'Brien to his right, Sanda Dragomir and her attorney, a slender Black man named Jaylen Boyle, on the far side. O'Brien's already played his trump card. He told the lawyer that absent an on-the-record statement by Sanda, she'll be arrested for murder in the second degree with the probability of a bail she can afford near zero. That was the thing about dead bodies lying in a pool of dark arterial blood. Better to be safe than sorry.

Boyle had conferred with his client for a short time following O'Brien's threat before announcing, his tone triumphant, that Sanda was ready to answer any question related to the shooting.

"She has nothing to hide."

FIFTEEN

Dante's chair is pulled off to one side and he leans over an open notebook. This is O'Brien's case and he'll go first. The big cop takes a small digital recorder from his pocket and flicks it on. He speaks into it for a moment, recording his name and rank, the time and date, and the names of all present, including Dante Cepeda. Then he lays it on the table, raises his bloodshot blue eyes to meet Sanda's and recites a list of her constitutional rights. Just as if she didn't have a lawyer sitting next to her.

Sanda's eyes are clear, her expression composed, her manner almost serene. Dante finds the combination extremely attractive, especially her glossy black hair, which falls to her shoulders, every strand in place. Her eyes are slanted, almost Asian, yet her skin is the color of milk. And killing doesn't appear to have dented her self-possession. If anything, her mouth, turned slightly up at the corners, betrays contempt.

"Do you understand these rights as I've read them?"

"Yes."

"And you're voluntarily waving your right to remain silent after consulting with your attorney?"

"Yes."

O'Brien leans back in his chair, giving Sanda room. He gestures with an open palm, then says, "The ball's in your court, Ms. Dragomir. Tell me what happened earlier this afternoon."

"A man has broken into my apartment, a man with a gun. I have shot this man before he is shooting me."

"That's it? That's all you have to say?"

Jaylen Boyle speaks first. "You saw the gun."

"Second by second, Counselor. That's how I want to hear it. And without prompting. What we're doing here? It's a voluntary statement, not an interrogation."

Sanda lays a restraining hand on Boyle's shoulder. "All right, here is what happens. As you say, second by second. I do not know exact time, but near to two o'clock I hear knock on door. I think this is Jiang Chen, who comes up in afternoons for cup of green tea. We are taking break, Chen from housework and me from work on my job." She gestures to a drawing table in the living room. A computer workstation faces the wall alongside. "I am professional illustrator."

Sanda pauses long enough to fold her hands on the table, but does not turn her eyes away from O'Brien's, leaving Dante with the impression that she views the interview as a contest. Formidable is the word that comes to mind. Sanda Dragomir is a formidable woman. And what does that make her lover, Mike Tedesco?

"I am in the kitchen where I hear knocking. I say 'come in' because I am thinking it is Chen, but when I look into hallway, I see strange man, very large, holding up phony badge that is not like New York police badge. When I jump into kitchen, he says 'come back here, bitch.' I come back, yes? With Glock gun I have in drawer. I tell him to stop, but he has gun of his own, which he takes from behind belt. Then I am firing, one, two, three times, and man falls to ground. He says 'help me' and I call police and here you are."

"The Glock," O'Brien asks, "where did you get it?"

"I have purchased from dealer." Sanda lifts her chin slightly. She's been waiting to deliver this particular tidbit, a saleswoman closing a deal. "I have permit for gun from city. I practice at Metropolitan Gun Club on Pacific Street. I am not good shot from fifty feet, but here is twenty feet. I do not miss."

"And where is that permit now?"

"In same drawer where gun is kept. Should I fetch this?"

"Later will be fine."

Dante scribbles away in his notebook. The interview isn't about deciding whether or not to arrest Sanda Dragomir. The assistant district attorney assigned to the 72nd Precinct will make that call. This is about getting Sanda on the record in the hope of discovering inconsistencies. Unfortunately, there are none here. Paul Bancroft was inside Sanda Dragomir's dwelling, waving a phony badge, in possession of a weapon. Even Sanda's claim that she fired from twenty feet away is consistent with the death examiner's findings. An initial examination of the victim's white shirt revealed no powder burns and no evidence of gunshot residue.

"Ms. Dragomir, you say that your door was open because you expected your downstairs neighbor and that's how the intruder got into your apartment. But how do you think he got through the outer door."

"He follows Chen inside when she comes back from shopping."

"And how do you know this?"

"I am speaking to Chen before police arrive."

"Did you discuss the bit about her coming up every afternoon for tea?"

Sanda refuses the bait. "Except on weekends. She does not come up when her family is home."

"And she'll confirm that when we ask her? That she visits you every weekday afternoon for tea?"

"I would not say this if it was not true. I am not here for lying. Man has broken into my house and I am in self-defense. If you were woman from Romania, you would understand this. But you Americans, you are all babies in the world. You know nothing."

After establishing that Sanda's a legal resident of the United States, O'Brien turns the questioning over to Dante. By then, both detectives know that her claim of self-defense will stand, at least in the absence of new evidence. But this is O'Brien's problem, not his. Dante had made Paulie Bancroft for muscle the minute he laid eyes on the man. That Skippy Legrand would set him on Tedesco's trail comes as no surprise. That he got what he deserved is also beyond dispute.

"Ms. Dragomir, would you describe your relationship with a man named Mike Tedesco?" Dante asks.

"No, no, no." Jaylen Boyle lays a restraining hand on his client's shoulder. "I'm instructing my client not to answer that question."

"Why not?"

"Because it's not germane." He pauses long enough to shake a bony finger in Dante's general direction. "Specifically, it has no bearing on whether or not my client acted in self-defense."

"True, enough." Dante leans back and crosses his legs, the picture of calm. "But I'm appealing for her assistance with an unrelated case, a homicide that occurred in Manhattan this morning. Naturally, I can't compel her to cooperate. I'm just hoping she turns out to be a good citizen."

Dante's playing the part of the executioner who smiles as he slips the noose over your neck. Self-defense or murder, a judgment call if there ever was one. You don't want to help us out, you must be a bad guy. Cops arrest bad guys and if we arrest you, given the severity of the charge, you'll spend quite a bit of time behind bars. Even if you eventually walk away.

But Dante's not really expecting Sanda to give up her lover. He's just having a little fun. The case Dante's investigating, despite his claim, is obviously related to the death of Paulie Bancroft, whose body is now on its way to the morgue. "And by the way, there's no Fifth Amendment issue here because your client's not a suspect. She'll either help us out or she won't."

Boyle makes a show of it, leaning over to whisper in his client's ear. Sanda merely nods as she meets Dante's gaze. Her eyes are as dark as her hair.

"Mike has life and I have life," she tells him. "Separate lives. I know only that he works for Legrand Transportation, that he is going off to work in morning and coming home at night."

"Every night?"

"No, sometimes he stays out."

"Does he call to let you know?"

"Yes, he is calling. This is rule we have. My apartment is not hotel."

"Did he tell you he wasn't going to work this morning?"

"Only you are telling me now."

"So, when he left this morning, you thought he was going to work as usual?"

"This is truth."

"Have you heard from him, Ms. Dragomir? Since he left for work?"

It's a trick question that Dante hopes to slip in. If Sanda lies, her phone records will give the lie away. But Sanda reacts a little too fast and Dante knows she's anticipated the question.

"Yes, Mike calls before noon. He tells me he will not be coming home for a time. How long, he does not say, or why."

"And that was fine with you?"

"Yes, I have own life."

"And they don't overlap? No, scratch that." Dante smiles. "Here's where you can really help us. I need a list of Mike's friends and the places where he commonly hung out. That only makes sense, right? If he wasn't here with you, he must've been someplace else."

Sanda's eyes flare briefly. With pleasure? With annoyance? Dante's not sure, but she nods once before speaking.

"I am not friends with Mike's friends, but there is bar in Queens called Tasso's where Mike goes. Owner is named Freddy Tasso, but everyone calls him Tasso. He is friends with Mike from childhood."

"Where in Queens? Do you know?"

"Yes, Long Island City. Mike goes there almost every night after work. I have phoned him there many times."

SIXTEEN

She's gonna walk," O'Brien says. He and Dante are standing together on the sidewalk outside Sanda's townhouse. The passing thunderstorms have left the air saturated and both men are already sweating. "That woman's full of shit. She doesn't know the names of Mike's friends? I really hate it when they throw their lies in your face."

It's too early to make that judgment, but Dante declines to argue the point. He shakes hands with O'Brien and promises to keep him abreast. Then he walks over to his unmarked Ford, opens the trunk, and takes a small tablet from his briefcase. The Ford's been parked in the shade, so the interior isn't quite a furnace when Dante slides behind the wheel. More like a steam bath.

From time to time in the course of an investigation, Dante's used his tablet to go online, especially when looking for addresses and telephone numbers. Now he tries again, tapping his finger on the Chrome icon. There's a bit of luck involved here because he needs to access a Wi-Fi signal that isn't locked. But there are hot spots all through the city, every Starbucks, every McDonald's, along with thousands of other stores. The signals leak out, of course, there to ricochet in unpredictable patterns from building to building. Dante scrolls through several screens before finding an unlocked signal, not the strongest, of course, but he perseveres.

Dante's reasoning is simple enough, though based on several unproven assumptions. First and foremost, that the victim, still unidentified, was killed because he failed to disable the GPS unit. Then, that he knew how to disable the units because he works, or worked, for a company that installs them. Finally, that his partnership with Mike Tedesco came about only because their daily lives intersected at some point.

Dante's first search, for GPS units, produces several million hits, as Dante expected. He adds "tracking" and "trucks," then gives it another go. That reduces the number to a few thousand, including online companies that leave installation to the consumer. After a moment, Dante includes "installation" and "near 10031." Now, he's looking at a few hundred possibilities, with only the first four being viable. Three are for truck-repair shops in New Jersey, one for a company in Long Island City, Thurman Security Systems. A tap on the screen takes him to Thurman's single-page website where Dante finds a list of the company's services, including the installation and maintenance of "GPS tracking systems."

A moment later, Dante's on the phone, speaking to the company's owner, Maury Thurman. After identifying himself as a police officer, he asks, "When do you close?"

"At six."

Dante glances at his watch. It's ten minutes after five and the trip to Long Island City involves two of the most notorious roads in New York, the Gowanus and Brooklyn-Queens Expressways.

"I need to ask you one question . . ."

"Hold it right there. You wanna ask me any questions, you gotta prove you're a cop. Say by standin' right in front of me with a badge in your hand."

Dante makes the trip in thirty-five minutes, siren blaring, lights flashing, along the Gowanus Expressway into the Brooklyn-Queens Expressway and over the Kosciusko Bridge. In places the rush-hour traffic creeps along, starting and stopping, and drivers give ground reluctantly. They glare at him as he passes by, and several present him with an upraised finger, which he ignores. Nobody likes cops and this is one of the reasons. For all they know, he's on a doughnut run.

Thurman Security Systems, as it turns out, is as homely as the surrounding industrial neighborhood and smaller than Dante expected, a concrete, single-story building painted a dull gray he associates with backed-up sewer lines. There's a single door, painted blue for some reason, and a small yard containing the company's fleet of vans. The yard's gate is locked, as is the door, and Dante's first thought is that Maury Thurman left early, despite the man's assurances. Still, he pounds on the door with the side of his fist, hard enough to produce an echo inside the building, waits a minute, and tries again. The second attempt pays off.

"We're closed," a man shouts from inside.

"Police," Dante responds.

The door opens a few seconds later and Maury Thurman steps out. He's a short, nearly bald man with a broad back and a gut to match. As he closes the door behind him, he takes the stub of a cigar from the pocket of his shirt and lights up.

"You the cop I spoke to on the phone?"

Dante flashes his shield. "That's me."

"Well, here I am." Thurman blows a cloud of smoke into the steamy air and folds his arms across his chest. The interview is to be conducted outside. "You wanna tell me what's happening here?"

Dante wants to say that it's about hope being eternal. Instead, he says, "I'm investigating a homicide that took place early this morning. My interest now is with GPS units, the kind they put in trucks."

"OK, so what about 'em?"

"Do you install these units?"

"Install and maintain, we do both. Only it's not that big with us. Most of our work is in commercial security. But tell me what this murder has to do with Thurman Security Systems? Am I some kind of suspect?"

The term *suspect* being a legal term of loosely defined art, Dante feels he can reassure Thurman without compromising the investigation. "No, but the homicide occurred in the middle of a failed hijacking, and we have reason to believe that the victim tried to disable a tracking unit. He was probably killed because he failed."

"Failed?"

"The unit was concealed behind the . . ." Dante snaps his fingers and glances to the left, but his memory fails him. "The thing that makes regular brakes into power brakes."

"The hydrovac?"

"Yeah, the hydrovac."

"That would be K and S Truck Services. They're in Jersey City. We don't do that because you have to extend the linkage connecting the brake pedal to the hydrovac. If something goes wrong, we'd be liable." Thurman shifts his weight as he puffs on his cigar. "Tell me if I have this right. The unit in question was installed on a vehicle transporting cigarettes or liquor."

Dante's smile is encouraging. "Cigarettes."

"Yeah, makes sense. See, most companies don't use GPS units for security. They only wanna keep track of their drivers. But when it comes to trucks haulin' valuable cargoes, they'd be hijacked every day if they didn't take precautions." Thurman glances at the door. "Look, I gotta go back inside, but get this. With the installation you're talkin' about, you have to remove the hydrovac if you wanna defeat it. That means disconnectin' the linkage, which also means the truck ain't goin' anywhere till you reconnect. The job would take a half hour, minimum, even if you knew exactly what you were doin'."

"Got it, and thanks for the education, but I only have a few more questions."

"Let's hear 'em." Thurman takes the stub of his cigar out of his mouth, stares at it for a moment, then tosses it into the street.

"First thing, I want to know if an employee with a knowledge of GPS installations failed to show up for work this morning."

Thurman's eyes widen as the truth settles over him. "That prick," he says. "That little prick."

Dante's careful to mask his excitement. "And the little prick in question would be?"

"My nephew, my wife's sister's kid, Asher Levine."

"He didn't show up this morning?"

"He called me last night, at home, said he thought he had the flu."

"What were Asher's duties?"

"We don't do installations here. We go to the customer. First, because we don't have room. Second, because we have to set up the electronics so the trucks can be tracked from the customer's office. Asher, he did the job from top to bottom, the installation of the units and the installation of the software. I mean, the kid had talent, don't get me wrong. He had ambition too. What he didn't have, unfortunately, is a work ethic. The asshole asked for a raise every other week."

Dante has no interest in the work ethic of a man who's already dead. Or probably dead. Still, he continues to nod agreeably. "Would you have a picture of your nephew anywhere?"

"On my cell phone. In the office. We took it at a company picnic." Thurman jams his hands into his pockets and looks away for a moment. "I'm gonna be straight with you, Detective. I got someone inside and she don't wanna be seen. Excuse me for livin'. But I'll get the phone and bring it out to you."

Five minutes later, Dante's staring down at a face he instantly recognizes. Though he's careful to maintain a neutral expression, he's thrilled. He wasn't kidding when he told Patti how much he loves the chase and the capture. He wasn't exaggerating, either.

"That's him, right?" Thurman says, pointing to a young man standing at one end of a long line of men and women. "That's the kid got killed this morning?"

"Yeah, that's him."

Thurman's brought a fresh cigar from inside. He puts it in his mouth and lights up. "This is really fucked-up. Like Stella's husband pulled out ten years ago and except for Asher, the woman's all alone. So, what exactly am I gonna tell her? I mean, the kid's all of twenty-five years old. He's a fuckin' baby. No, he's *her* fuckin' baby."

"You could wait, if you want. Where does Asher live?"

"In Whitestone, near the water. And that's another thing. Stella's got money up the wazoo and Asher's a smart kid, or at least he was. So how come he's not in college?" Thurman answers his own question. "Because the kid's a fuck-up who barely graduated high school. Me, I blame Stella. No matter what, she defended him."

Dante finds himself growing impatient. Asher's mother has to be formally notified—not by Dante, not necessarily—but it has to be done. "Give me Asher's address and I'll see that she's informed. But if you really want to help your sister-in-law, come down to the morgue tomorrow and make the ID. If not, she'll have to do it herself."

SEVENTEEN

Set on a narrow, elevated plot, Stella Levine's relatively modest home is surrounded on both sides by reverse-engineered McMansions. A low brick wall and a series of concrete steps and landings rise to a tiny porch. The porch overlooks an equally tiny yard of browning grass and recently trimmed hedges. Dante takes it in as he pulls to the curb behind a police cruiser driven by a female patrol officer he recruited at the 109th Precinct. He's hoping to get a look at Asher Levine's room and he'll need Stella's approval. If he doesn't get it, he plans to offer his condolences and leave. Dante could have phoned the One-O-Nine and asked them to make the notification without his assistance. Instead, he came all the way to Whitestone, fighting rush hour traffic every inch of the way, an investment of his precious time from which he hopes to profit.

The woman who answers the door is almost as tall as Dante and outweighs him by a good thirty pounds. She's wearing an emerald-green dress secured by a yellow belt that has to be six inches wide. A pair of golden pearls dangle from her ears. They neatly match her glistening eye shadow and lipstick. As she looks from Dante to Sergeant Alyssa Mercado, a diminutive Filipina, her dark eyes reveal a touch of defiance.

"I'm Detective Cepeda," Dante says, "This is Sergeant Mercado. Are you Stella Levine?"

"Yeah, I am. So, what'd the kid do this time?"

"I'm very sorry to have to tell you this, Ms. Levine, but your son was killed in the course of a robbery that took place in West Harlem this morning."

Stella's eyes shift from defiance to despair in the space of a heartbeat. Whatever she expected to hear, it wasn't this. "I, I, I . . ." She collapses before she can manage a second word.

Dante and Alyssa catch the woman before she hits the ground. They haul her into the house and kick the door shut. Stella, all the while, staggers backward, one hand clutching her chest, gasping.

"You wanna call for an ambulance?" Mercado asks Dante once they've eased Stella onto an oversize couch.

Stella waves the suggestion off. She's breathing more deeply now, though her voice is little more than a whisper. "This can't be true," she says.

"I'm sorry, Ms. Levine, but I'm afraid it is." Two chairs face the couch, and Dante finds a perch on the edge of the one closest to Stella. He leans forward, eager, yet unthreatening. The woman needs space and time while she collects herself. Rushing her would be counterproductive.

"What was my son doing in Harlem?" Stella finally asks. "You say this morning?"

"Yes, ma'am, early this morning. And I don't know why your son was in Harlem. All I can say for sure is that he was unarmed. But we do have a suspect."

Stella looks up, her eyes hopeful, as if apprehending Asher's killer will bring him back to life. "Did you arrest someone?"

"No, no, but you can help us here."

"What do you want to know?"

"His friends, his girlfriend, where he went after work, anything like that."

"I don't know, really. He didn't have a steady girlfriend, at least not one he told me about. Mostly, he spent time with his two cousins—they're identical twins—only I don't know what they did. I mean, I'm Asher's mother, right? Not his pal."

"I understand, Ms. Levine. And I know this is hard for you, but do you think I could take a look at Asher's room? Believe me, if I connect him to this suspect, I'll have your son's killer in handcuffs by morning."

Dante weighs the facts, even as he makes his pitch. First, you have Mike Tedesco, who knew the truck's route and who didn't show up for work. Then you have Asher Levine who installed tracking GPS units for a living and who also didn't show up for work. Would merely connecting the pair constitute probable cause to make an arrest? In the absence of any physical evidence? Probably not, but it wouldn't be his call in any event. Most likely his squad commander would cover her ass by leaving it up to the riding DA assigned to the precinct.

"What if you find . . ." Stella breaks off suddenly. It doesn't matter what the cops find because her son can no longer be harmed. "Yes, all right. It's the bedroom at the back of the hall."

Dante's still processing his first reaction to the chaos in Asher's room when Stella Levine begins to wail. He listens to her for a moment, her grief carrying him far back into his childhood, carrying him to a place he hasn't visited in many years. Dante was fourteen years old, his birthday only a week in the past, on the night he was tested. Having smuggled a liter of Pepsi into the Youth Hope

Center on the prior evening, Dante now found himself in desperate need of a urinal. Still half-asleep, he'd stumbled out of the dormitory, down a short hallway and into the bathroom, totally unprepared for what he found.

Bent over the second of four sinks, his pajamas around his ankles, a boy named Paco Altoona gripped both faucets. Mike Tedesco stood behind him, grunting with each thrust of his hips. Tedesco's eyes were jammed shut, and he was unaware of Dante's presence. Not Paco Altoona. Paco stared at Dante's reflection in the mirror, his mouth tight with pain, his brown eyes pleading. *Help me, help me, help me.*

Initially stunned, Dante turned away after a few seconds. Despite a burning rage that rolled across his skin like napalm, he headed for a second bathroom, this one reserved for staff, where he took care of business before returning to his bed.

Welcome to the jungle. That's what he told himself. Only the strong survive. But the mantras didn't work. No, as the weeks and months went by, he recognized the incident for what it was. Dante Cepeda had come to one of those defining moments his counselors often spoke about and he'd failed the test. Simple as that. And Paco? One morning, only a few weeks later, Paco headed out to school, never to return.

Dante closes the bedroom door, but only succeeds in muffling Stella's cries. Still, it's back to work, and he quickly surveys the room, his eyes moving systematically over the chaos. Asher Levine had been a hoarder, not quite ready for a cable TV show, but well on his way. Boxes scattered haphazardly against the walls are filled to overflowing with junk of every description, from a Mickey Mouse doll with one ear to a tattered iridescent boa. Irregular columns of magazines and books rise from the floor, some tipped over, their volumes fanned out across a soiled rug. In one corner, a basket filled with clean laundry crowns an outdoor gas grill.

Dante searches the room's single dresser first, opening drawers, finding nothing of interest beyond a collection of colored jockstraps. Not his business, though, and he turns to a nightstand beside the bed, scanning the top, opening the single drawer. A notepad raises his hopes, but the pages are empty, and he moves to a single-drawer filing cabinet where he finds a collection of gay porn, both videos and magazines. Again, not his business.

Finally, now that he's exhausted the obvious, he turns to a laptop computer on a small desk. As he taps a key, he mouths a silent prayer. Let it be unlocked. When the Dell opens immediately, he acknowledges his thanks with a little nod, then goes online. He doesn't have time to examine individual files, but he has high hopes for Asher's emails. Downstairs, Stella's cries have diminished. Now she's merely sobbing.

Dante accesses Asher's email service and quickly turns to the boy's sent-mail page. He opens and closes the individual emails quickly, but finds none tying Asher to Mike Tedesco. An examination of deleted emails is no more fruitful. What he needs is Asher's everyday cell phone, but it's nowhere to be found. Or perhaps it is, tucked into one of the many boxes he hasn't the time to search. Or maybe none of it matters because one of the conspirators, probably Tedesco, was smart enough to avoid any traceable contact.

Dante stands and walks over to the door. As a matter of habit, he turns to give the room a last look. He begins at the wall to his right and tries to name the things he sees, a practice rendered nearly impossible by the chaos. But he continues on, past the outer wall, across the bed to the nightstand where a glass rests alongside a plastic coaster. Streaks of some pink liquid, now dried to a powder, coat the glass, inside and out. Dante's focus was drawn to this crud the first time around, but now his eyes come to rest on the plastic coaster. The coaster's essentially transparent except for the blood-red letters that run across its face to spell out a single word: TASSO'S.

Ten minutes later, after reassuring Stella once again, Dante's asks for a recent photo of her son. That secured, he's out the door, on his way to Tasso's Bar and Grill in Long Island City. Feeling good about the case, feeling good about himself, feeling good about the rapidly cooling air.

EIGHTEEN

Restless, Skippy Legrand traces an irregular circle in an open space that fronts one of the two roll-up doors leading into the Legrand Transportation warehouse. Like Thurman Security Systems and thousands of other small, city businesses, Legrand's housed in a plain-as-mud building with a fenced yard attached. Skippy's trucks—unloaded, of course —are parked in the yard, gassed up and ready to go in the morning.

Skippy's jitters have nothing to do with Arkady Alebev's imminent arrival. Shoeless Joe's win at Aqueduct netted Skippy nine thousand dollars, enough to pay the vig on his debt to the shylock, with four thousand left over. At least for now.

Skippy's nervous for two reasons. First, Paulie Bancroft is among the missing. Second, the baseball game he's watching on his cell phone isn't going the way he expected. The game's become a pitching duel, with Brooks Kriske up against Robbie Ray, Toronto's strikeout leader. The two players are on opposite career paths, with Kriske a fill-in before he heads back to the minors and Ray's star in ascendance. No contest, right?

When Skippy laid down his thousand-dollar bet, he'd expected Toronto's powerful hitters to drive Kriske out of the game in the early innings. That hasn't happened, unfortunately, as both pitchers have thrown up zeroes for the first four innings. Now the advantage has shifted, what with the Yankees shutdown relievers. If Kriske pitches into the seventh inning, the Yanks will probably win.

Skippy glances at his watch, a knockoff Rolex he bought after he hocked the real thing. Alebev was due at seven, but it's already ten after eight and Skippy's wondering how long he's supposed to hang out. He decides to call, but then looks down at his phone as Kriske strikes out Bo Bichette for the second time.

"Damn," he says. Kriske's been working the corners all night, tossing a mix of sliders, changeups and perfectly spotted fastballs that hitters as skilled as Bichette can't reach with a tennis racket.

Skippy jumps to attention at the sound of a horn outside, four sharp beeps in rapid succession. "Finally," he mutters as walks over to a small door, the main entrance for employees and visitors. He tucks in his shirt as he goes, and hitches up his pants. Skippy's got Alebev's money and there's nothing to fear. After a worst-ever losing streak, his luck has finally turned. He's on a roll.

Skippy steps onto the sidewalk, eyes the gray BMW facing the closest roll-up door, then ducks back inside. He pushes the button controlling the door, watches it curl into its casing, then presses the button again as Alebev's car rolls into the warehouse. Finally, unable to repress a grin, he turns. Skippy can't wait to see the expression on Alebev's face when the money's handed over.

A home-team roar from his cell phone's speaker draws his attention. Aaron Judge, the Yankees right fielder, has turned around a Robbie Ray slider and the ball is now ten rows back in the right field stands. What with Gino Urshela being on first base, the score is now 2–0.

Skippy's thinking maybe his luck hasn't turned after all, a

passing notion that locks into place, tight as a bank vault, when Mike Tedesco steps out of the BMW.

"Hey, Skip, whatta ya say?"

"What do I say?" Skippy's a large man, much larger than Tedesco, and probably stronger. He's game, too, although woefully out of shape. He starts toward Tedesco, jaw and fists clenched.

"Cool it, Skippy. I brought you a present." Tedesco's smiling, but his green eyes are as cold as ice. "Everything's changed, ya know. Between me and you, Skippy. Everything."

Skippy comes to a halt, reminding himself that Mike Tedesco committed a murder this morning and you had to respect that, him actually pulling the trigger. And not once, but twice, the second shot splattering the kid's brains all over the sidewalk. The cop, Cepeda, had made Skippy take a long look. Too long.

"You didn't have to kill the kid," Skippy finally says. "Even if he was a complete fuckup, even if he couldn't disable the GPS unit, you didn't have to kill him."

"C'mon, Skippy. I'm not sayin' I killed the kid, but if I did, it wasn't because he fucked up with the unit. No, if I did kill him, it's because he said my name. Twice."

Skippy shakes his head. He's got more questions, the most important being, If you killed the kid, how could you be stupid enough to cut José loose? But the words die on his lips when Tedesco opens the BMW's front door and the ugliest pit bull that Skippy's ever seen jumps out. The dog's face is a mass of intersecting scars.

"Watch this, Skippy."

Tedesco reaches into the car and pulls on a small lever beside the seat. The trunk pops open, rising slowly to expose two men, piled one atop the other. The man on top is Arkady Alebev. His legs are taped together, his arms are taped to his sides, and his mouth is covered with a strip of the same puke-green tape. The man beneath him is not taped, and while most of his body is concealed by Arkady's bulk, Skippy can see what's left of his head.

"Whatever ya do," Tedesco says, "don't touch the car."

Only now does Skippy notice the surgical gloves covering Tedesco's hands. "You're crazy, Mike. You're outta your fuckin' mind."

"Ya think so?" Tedesco approaches the BMW's open trunk. "Well, lemme show you somethin' that'll maybe change your mind."

As Skippy watches, Tedesco grabs Alebev by the shoulders, drags him over the lip of the trunk, and dumps him on the floor. Alebev grunts, but then rolls on to his back and looks up at Skippy. Not enraged, not defiant, but as a beggar. *Let me live, please, please, please.*

Alebev sucks in a long breath when Tedesco pull away the tape covering his mouth. He closes his eyes for a moment, then opens them to find the dog, Pug, sniffing his taped legs. The shylock jerks away, an unnecessary response as it turns out. Pug, his curiosity satisfied, wanders off to piss against the roll-up door.

"Arkady," Tedesco says, "I want you to look at me and Teddy while I'm talkin' to you. Turn around."

Skippy watches Arkady roll over. His mouth and one cheek are bright red where Tedesco yanked off the tape. It must hurt like hell, but Arkady, apparently, has other things on his mind. Like surviving.

"Why you do this?" he asks, his voice tight and weak. "I have not to hurt you."

"Money," Tedesco replies. "As in my boss owes you a whole lot of it and he doesn't wanna pay. You could hardly blame him, right? Because the truth is that he can't pay and you knew that when you bought up his debt. Sure, he might put the vig together. *This* week. But sooner or later, what with him being a degenerate gambler, the payments are gonna stop, and you'll have to hurt him. Tell me somethin', Arkady, were you lookin' forward to it? Maybe breakin' his fingers? Maybe an elbow?"

Skippy drops to one knee when Pug approaches. He scratches the dog's head as the truth finally dawns on him. Arkady's terrified, ready to make any deal, agree to anything. Down deep, he's ordinary. You look at him, you have to wonder what you were afraid of.

"I will forget these monies."

"What about your dead friend in the trunk? You gonna forget him too?"

"He is nothing. Men like him you can find anywhere." Alebev looks at Skippy, who looks away. The man has to die tonight. There's no cutting him loose.

"Ya know," Skippy tells Mike Tedesco, "Arkady's connected to the Russian mob."

"That's right, Boss, and it works to our advantage. His people aren't gonna think a connected man like Arkady got whacked by two assholes like us. They're gonna be checkin' out bigger fish. Meanwhile, you're fifty grand to the good. To my way of thinkin', that makes me eligible for a really big raise."

Tedesco doesn't wait for Skippy to agree, the matter, in his mind, apparently settled. He retrieves a roll of tape from the BMW and begins to wind it around Alebev's head, covering his mouth and his nose with layer after layer. By the time Tedesco rises, the gangster's whole body is vibrating, from his head to his toes, and his eyes are the eyes of a madman. Flecked with burst capillaries, the whites rapidly turning blue, they project a level of fear unknown to Skippy Legrand, a level he hopes never to face.

"No blood, right?" Tedesco explains. "Nice and clean."

NINETEEN

Skippy's adrenaline level has reached the point where his eyes are bulging almost as far as Arkady's before the gangster's heart gave out and he abruptly deflated. There are a million questions to be asked, about the past, the present, and the future most of all, assuming they have a future that doesn't include spending the rest of their lives in a cage. But Tedesco's mind is focused, for the moment, on their most immediate concerns. There's no time for questions.

"We gotta get rid of the bodies," he explains as he grabs Alebev by the shoulders and rolls him into the trunk. "Like pronto, Boss."

Skippy doesn't argue. He follows the Beamer in his own car, down the West Side Highway, through the Battery Tunnel, all the way to the Brooklyn neighborhood of Brighton Beach, a haven to Russian and Ukrainian immigrants for a generation. As he waits for Tedesco to park the BMW on Neptune Avenue, he can't help but think about how crazy he was to go for the original deal, the hijacking, and about how he totally misjudged Mike Tedesco. The guy seems all calculation, but inside he's as crazy as crazy gets.

"We need to stop somewhere, pick up some dog food," Tedesco tells Skippy as Pug jumps onto the back seat and immediately begins to slobber on the window. "But for now, let's get the fuck out of here."

Skippy puts the Lincoln in gear and heads for the Belt Parkway, a few blocks to the south. He's thinking about his entire world being turned on its head, about the good and bad news. His debt's gone. That's the best news. He can take Alebev's five thousand and use it to pay his mortgage and retire a decent chunk of his credit card debt. Or maybe not, because the second-best news is that Toronto pulled the game out, scoring three runs in the top of the eighth to beat the Yankees.

If I'm right, he tells himself, *if I'm on a roll, I can turn the five thousand into fifty thousand. I've done it before.*

Unfortunately, the bad news—three dead, three murders, with Skippy Legrand implicated in every one of them—won't be crowded out. And his best move? Go to the cops, tell 'em the truth, take whatever mercy they're willing to bestow.

"Hey, Skippy," Tedesco says, "you wanna hear the story?"

"What story?"

"The one about how I came to have Arkady Alebev and his bodyguard in the trunk of Alebev's car. And by the way, that Beamer, it's like ridin' on a cloud. Alebev could've paid twice as much and it'd still be worth every penny."

Skippy grunts. "You need to come off whatever you been smokin', Mike. This ain't about a celebration, like we won somethin'."

Tedesco rolls down the window halfway. It's still July in New York and the temperature's somewhere in the lower eighties, even at ten o'clock. But there's no humidity for once, a blessing. Behind him, Pug leans into the breeze, nostrils twitching.

"Does that mean you don't want to hear the story?" Tedesco asks, his tone on the edge of mockery.

"Stop with the bullshit. Say what you have to say."

"Right, got it." Tedesco straightens. "So, back up to this afternoon. I was like you are now, Skippy, my thoughts all over the place. I wanted to run away. I could feel it in my body, like when I was a kid and somebody caught me fuckin' up. I knew the cops would be after me as soon as you told 'em I didn't show up this morning. So, I just started movin'."

"Look, Mike . . ."

"I'm not blamin' you, man. I didn't punch in and my card was blank. You did the right thing. But the story, about Alebev and why I went to the laundry in the first place, that's what I'm gettin' to."

Skippy nods. Petersburg Industrial Laundry, LLC, is Alebev's front. Tucked into the Bronx neighborhood of Hunts Point, the business counts hospitals, nursing homes, restaurants, and hotels among its customers.

"I'm so crazy by the time I decide to go up to the Bronx," Tedesco continues, "that I'm actually thinkin' I need another job. I'm thinkin' I can't go back to Skippy's because the cops are lookin' for me and they've already told Skippy to call 'em if I show up. I mean, when I look at the situation now, I can't believe I was so stupid. But that's why I went up to see Alebev. I wanted a job, even it meant collectin' for a shylock."

Tedesco pauses to check on Pug, who's now slobbering on the opposite window. The pause allows Skippy enough time to realize that Tedesco's lying. Alebev knew all about the hijacking when he called Skippy early in the morning. He knew about it because Tedesco told him. And whatever Tedesco hoped to accomplish at Alebev's, the end result would not have been good for Skippy Legrand.

"So," Skippy says, his voice tight, "what changed your mind?"

"Security cameras."

"Gimme a break."

"Skippy, I'm not kiddin' you. Hunts Point? OK, first, you have the apartment houses near Bruckner Boulevard. Then you have the Hunts Point Market where most of the city's food comes in. That's east of Halleck Avenue. Last, you have an industrial area near the river, a rough place in a rough neighborhood and practically deserted at night. This is why every small business has security cameras. Except for one."

Skippy thinks it over as he crawls around a yellow cab stalled in the middle lane. "So, you're sayin' the laundry didn't have any security cameras?"

"*Nada*, Skippy, as in not a single fucking one. And we both know why. Arkady doesn't want any record of the people who visit. That's the connected part." Tedesco rolls up the window as Skippy accelerates. The road ahead is clear, at least until the bend leading to the Brooklyn Bridge on-ramp. He slides the seat back and stretches out, pressing his feet against the firewall.

"So what, Mike?" Skippy asks. "Why would that make you do . . . whatever it is you actually did? And why would you notice security cameras in the first place?"

"It's automatic, wherever I go, walkin' or in a car. The thing about prison is that everybody talks crime and cameras are what thieves and muggers fear most. The way they figure, if somebody rats you out, you can convince that somebody not to show up on trial day. But a camera? When the jury sees your face on the little screen, it's as bad as DNA. The good news is that you can avoid cameras altogether. See, there are no security cameras that cover an entire street and both sidewalks. The cameras only pick up little slices, so if you know where they are, you can work around 'em. That's why I picked 141st Street for the hijacking. There was only one camera and it was too far away to matter." Tedesco pauses for a moment, then waves at an off-ramp. "Do me a favor and pull off here. I gotta feed this dog."

TWENTY

They're standing, Skippy and Mike Tedesco, on a sidewalk in front of an Astoria pizza parlor, watching Pug eat three meatballs from an aluminum takeout container. The dog's approaching his dinner cautiously, sniffing, nibbling, looking up at Tedesco from time to time.

"Probably the tomato sauce," Tedesco says.

Skippy's not interested. What with the scars and the torn mouth stained red, the dog's uglier than ever. "Finish the story," he tells Tedesco.

"Yeah, the story. So, when I saw there were no cameras, I felt liberated. I know that's weird, right, but the whole day, ever since things went wrong, I'd been feelin' like I was under a microscope. Like I was bein' studied and I couldn't get away. Now I was in this place . . ."

"Enough, Mike. Enough with the psychology. Tell it straight or bottle it up. I can't listen to this bullshit all night."

"OK, whatever you want." Tedesco squats down. As he feeds Pug small pieces of meatball, he begins to speak, his tone surprisingly flat. "I come through the door and there's just Alebev and his muscle, a squat guy with a big chest and a gut to match. The muscle's got this little grin on his face, like I'm nothin', and right away I figure this is gonna go bad. I figure it's gonna go bad and I'm happy. Like the whole fucked-up day I just been waitin' for this minute. For the smirk, right, and the attitude? Meanwhile, I got a Colt .45 cal tucked into my belt, and when the scumbag turns to smirk at his boss, I crack the barrel into his head, three times before he hits the ground. I don't know, maybe he has a thin skull, because something gives way on the third shot and his eyes roll up in his head."

"What about Alebev?"

"Alebev froze, Boss, like he couldn't believe what was happening. Like he never even considered the possibility that an asshole like Mike Tedesco . . ." Tedesco pauses long enough to draw a breath. He's left a number of things out, including the drums, which began to pound inside his skull as he walked up the block. Daniela's work. "Once I realized the muscle wasn't gettin' up, I put the Colt on Alebev. I was thinkin' about killin' him right there, but then I thought about you and the debt and how we were doin' everything wrong. Splittin' up, each of us fightin' his own battle? That's not gonna work, Boss. No way, no how. Because if cops are good at anything, it's divide and conquer."

When Tedesco ushers Pug into Skippy's Lincoln, the dog rubs his muzzle against the leather seat, then turns its face to the back window. Skippy watches the sequence, thinking that the animal's fur and DNA are in his car, just like they're in Alebev's BMW.

Neither man speaks for the next few minutes as Skippy works his way onto the Triborough Bridge. Then Tedesco fiddles with the air-conditioning vents for a moment. "Here's how it has to go down," he says. "Tomorrow morning, I'm gonna show up for work like nothin' happened. I'm gonna show up on time, get the trucks out, and schedule tomorrow's deliveries."

"What are you gonna tell the cops?"

"Nothin', Skippy, not a fuckin' thing. I have a lawyer who knows me. I been carryin' his business card since I got out the joint. If the cops make an appearance . . ."

"*When* the cops make an appearance," Skippy says. "Remember, I'm a suspect too. And I'm supposed to call this detective the minute I see your face."

"Yeah, but you're not gonna do that. So, *when* the cops show up, I'm gonna tell 'em to call my lawyer because I got exactly nothin' to say. And when the cops turn to you and ask why you didn't call, you're gonna tell 'em the same thing. Call my lawyer. Now, if they have enough evidence, they'll make an arrest, maybe one of us, maybe both. If they don't, they'll walk away. Remember, once we lawyer up, they can't talk to us without our lawyers present."

Skippy's spent a good piece of his life trying to pick a winner. Now he has to pick a winner in a race where the stakes are as high as stakes get. He thinks of his children, Ally and Carla, and of his wife. If he's arrested, if Legrand Transportation goes belly up, if they have to depend on Fay, they're doomed.

Still, there's some good news here. The boy Tedesco killed, Asher Levine? Skippy's never met the kid, never spoken to him. They can't be connected. Plus, he has an alibi for the time of the hijacking. Skippy was still at home, thirty miles from Manhattan, going about his regular business.

"All right, I'll go along," he says. "But you gotta get rid of the mutt."

"Pug?"

"Yeah, fuckin' Pug. He's been inside Alebev's car and he's been inside my car. That's a connection I don't need to worry about. Dump the dog."

As he comes off the bridge, Skippy can feel Mike Tedesco sulking on his side of the Lincoln. Tough shit. Dogs have DNA, too, and this ain't the time to get sentimental. You want to tough it out? You want to stonewall the cops, throw it in their faces? It really doesn't pay to leave any loose ends. Like the dog, or for that matter, José Sepulveda.

"See, I'm havin' a hard time with one particular thing," Skippy says. "You told me you killed Levine because he said your name."

"I said *if* I killed him that would've been the reason."

"That doesn't make sense, Mike, because the only person who could've heard Levine say your name is José and you let him go. I mean, if you weren't gonna kill José, why'd you kill Asher Levine?"

Tedesco glances into the back seat, at Pug. "I admit the thing with José was stupid. Maybe I wasn't thinkin' straight at the time, what with the rain and bein' so pissed off with Asher. But José can't put you at the scene, so why don't you let me worry about him. He's my problem."

"Your problem?"

"Yeah, and if he still in New York, I think I know how to find him."

Skippy phone rings before he can offer an opinion on what his partner's obviously suggesting. He checks his caller ID and frowns. Detective Dante Cepeda.

"It's that fucking cop," he says.

"So . . . answer. See what he wants."

Skippy does exactly that, fully intending to tell the cop that he's lawyered up. But he shuts his mouth in a hurry at the news Cepeda brings. A minute later, without saying a word, he hangs up.

"What's the news?" Tedesco asks.

Skippy looks down at his feet for a moment, searching for a convenient lie, but the words don't come and he finally settles for the unvarnished truth. "This afternoon, I sent Paulie to your girl-friend's house."

"Sanda's."

"Yeah, Sanda's."

"Did he hurt her, Skippy?"

Skippy shakes his head. "Just the opposite, Mike. It turns out she shot him after he broke into her house. Paulie's dead. And the funny part? The cop thinks she was expecting Paulie. He thinks she suckered him."

Tedesco laughs. "Yeah, that sounds like Sanda. I warned her, by the way, that you'd be sending someone by." He claps Skippy on the shoulder. "But, hey, man. That's water under the bridge, right? Let bygones be bygones? Besides, you're better off without him. The guy was a fuckin' retard."

"That ain't funny, Mike." Skippy looks down at his feet for a minute. Paulie is his oldest . . . well, he wasn't actually a friend. Maybe a companion, or a follower. Still, at some point, Skippy's sure to miss the man. In fact, he's missing Paulie right now because the bottom line is too obvious to ignore. If Skippy Legrand decides that Mike Tedesco needs killing, which he very well might, he'll have to do the job himself.

TWENTY-ONE

By the time Dante Cepeda parks a block away from Tasso's Bar and Grill at eight o'clock, his narrow butt is seriously dragging. He's been at it for the past fourteen hours, nonstop, without pausing for lunch. Now it's past dinnertime, and he's not up for an all-out assault on the bar where Asher Levine and Mike Tedesco both hung out. That said, the hurdles facing him could be a lot higher.

Gentrification has come to Long Island City. The warehouses and factories that employed thousands of New Yorkers are gone, replaced by high-rise, high-end apartment houses with stunning views of midtown Manhattan. Ditto for the beauty parlors replaced by spas, the diners replaced by bistros and the liquor stores replaced by boutique establishments hawking wines and spirits. For these businesses, the ideal customer is an unattached twentysomething, male or female, with an advanced degree and a serious interest in the mating game. The resulting noise in the bars and restaurants commonly approaches near-deafening levels, every sound amplified by stone floors, brick walls, tin ceilings, and a sound system manned by a DJ/mixologist.

Heavy on the hip-hop, naturally.

Conducting an interview under these circumstances, even with a badge, isn't a challenge Dante's been looking forward to, but here he catches a break. Tasso's Bar and Grill is a throwback joint, a relic with smoked windows and a tattered sign hung below a green canopy stained with pigeon droppings. Inside, the floors are wood, the walls paneled and the lights dim. This is a joint where everyone knows everyone else.

Which means that Mike Tedesco and Asher Levine knew each other. Which means that most of the patrons Dante observes as he comes through the door know Tedesco and knew Levine.

Three people, two men and a woman, are seated at the bar when Dante enters. Engrossed in the baseball game running on a small TV above the cash register, all three wear paint-stained overalls. A dartboard to Dante's left has attracted a cluster of younger patrons, the tallest among them poised to throw. To Dante's right, two women, sisters by the look of them, shoot pool on an undersized table with a hole in the felt. A middle-aged man wearing a narrow-brimmed fedora perches on the stool at the end of the L-shaped bar. Huddled over tomorrow's racing form and a cup of coffee, he's the only one not to look up when Dante comes through the door.

As the door closes behind him, Dante quietly registers each of Tasso's customers, the task more or less automatic for any cop, but his focus quickly centers on two men seated at a table near the window. They're chomping on giant hamburgers topped with cheese, lettuce, tomatoes, and a pile of onion rings.

Dante fights an explosion of saliva, swallowing twice as walks to the bar and finds a stool. Before he can signal, the bartender deserts the glasses he's been rinsing and walks over. He approaches Dante slowly, his expression studiously neutral, yet somehow protective.

Standing well above six feet, the man wears a midnight-blue T-shirt over well-defined pecs. His forearms rival Popeye's.

"What could I get ya?" he asks, his voice so hoarse that Dante half-intuits the question.

"One of those." He points to the burgers. "Medium rare. And a beer, I don't care what, as long as it isn't lite."

"The kitchen's closed."

Dante ignores the challenge. "Look," he says, "I know that you know I'm a cop. I saw it in your eyes when you came over. But see, I've been investigating a murder that took place fourteen hours ago and I didn't have time for lunch or dinner and I'm really hungry. So, please, cook me a burger, medium rare, and pour me a beer."

For the next ten seconds, Dante simply endures the bartender's glare. Until the man turns to a pass-through behind the bar and calls out Dante's order.

"That's all we serve," he explains while he draws Dante's beer, "hamburgers, fries, onion rings. But we do 'em right." As he sets the glass before Dante, he offers a smile so cold it might have pulled from his freezer. "Name's Freddy Tasso, but everyone calls me Tasso."

Tasso's claim proves essentially true. The burger, when it's finally served ten minutes later, is juicy, the cheddar cheese luscious, the onion rings crisp. Dante eats slowly, savoring each bite, an act of pure defiance. Back in the day, in foster care, he'd fought over food more than once.

"So, Tasso," he says as he wipes his mouth, "how'd you make me?"

"Same way you made me, the look in your eyes. Like a wolf examining a meadow filled with sheep."

"That right? My look?"

Tasso laughs. "No, not really, but you shouldn't leave your jacket unbuttoned when you wear a shoulder rig. Only cops wear shoulder rigs."

After a final bite, Dante lays his napkin on his plate. "I wasn't exactly tryin' to disguise my true identity. And I didn't stop in for the burger, though I have to admit this one's high up on my list of all-time greats. I have business here."

Another hard look from Freddy Tasso only encourages Dante. He reaches into his pocket, withdraws the photo supplied by Asher's mother and lays it on the bar.

"You know this guy?"

"Next question."

"OK, next question. Did you know that Asher Levine, which is this guy here, and your school-days buddy, Mike Tedesco, were gonna hijack one of Skippy Legrand's trucks? Were you part of the conspiracy? Oh, and by the way, the two of us, me and you? We don't have to pretend about Mike Tedesco. See, I also knew Mike when he was a kid. We spent time in the same group home." Dante shakes his head and smiles. "Thing about Mike, he knew how to work a room. Other kids were always running his errands, taking his risks. Some of their own free will, others forced."

"Man, you need to move on."

"Or what, Tasso? What happens to me if I stay right where I am?"

Dante stifles a smile as he absorbs Tasso's anger. How many times has he been here, as a boy and as a man? Too many to count, for sure. "I have business in the bar, police business. I'll leave when it's finished. You want me out of here, you need to cooperate. That's because I know that Asher Levine drank here. I know he was a regular."

"What's that got to do with Mike?"

"Leave that for later. Right now, just answer the question I originally asked. Do you know the man in the photo?"

"Yeah, that's Asher. What of it?"

Dante goes back into his pocket for his cell phone. He pulls up a photo of Asher taken at the crime scene and lays the phone on the bar. Asher's lying on his back, staring up into the air, with an entrance wound above his left eye and an exit wound behind his ear. His hair and shoulders are soaked with blood.

"For your sake, I really hope Asher wasn't running a tab," Dante says. "Because if he was, you're gonna have to eat the loss."

Tasso bites at his lower lip as he glances to his left, at the men and women standing before the dartboard. "How'd he catch it?"

Dante follows Tasso's eyes, only then noticing that two of the men, even viewed from behind, are virtually identical. They share the same height, the same build, the same bald patch at the backs of their heads.

"Are those Asher's cousins?" he asks.

"Why don't you go ask 'em?"

Dante nods, then waves to the three painters standing at the bar. He and Tasso have already caught their attention and they respond without hesitation when Dante says, "Hey, check this out."

Not to be left behind, the two pool shooters lay down their cue sticks and join the party. Ditto for the dart throwers on the other side of the bar and the two men at the table.

Dante gets off his stool and steps away, giving Tasso's patrons as much time as they want to compare Asher alive to Asher dead. Only when they begin to turn for an explanation, does he finally display his shield. "Detective Cepeda," he announces. "I'm investigating Asher Levine's murder."

Dante glances at Tasso, registering the man's intense anger. Tough shit.

"How did this happen?" one of the pool players asks.

"Around seven o'clock this morning, two men attempted to hijack a truck hauling cigarettes. According to a reliable witness, Asher Levine was one of the hijackers. The man who killed him was his partner."

"Why did he do it?" Tasso asks, his hoarse tones almost wistful.

Dante addresses his response to the whole group. "Trucks hauling cigarettes are equipped with GPS units. If the truck leaves a programmed route, the unit notifies the base in the warehouse. Asher was supposed to disable the unit, which he was trained to do, but we think he failed and that's why he was killed."

Dante's not expecting anyone to come forward, not right away. He's making his pitch, as focused on his talking points as any politician.

"Now, here's the thing. The truck, the target of the hijacking, belonged to a company named Legrand Transportation. Mike Tedesco, who you also know, is a manager at the company, a manager who didn't show up for work this morning." Dante pauses briefly, then ticks the items off on his fingers. "You can't hijack a truck hauling cigarettes unless you know how to disable the GPS unit. Asher knew how to disable GPS units. You can't hijack a truck hauling cigarettes unless you know where it's gonna be and when it's gonna be there. Mike Tedesco knew where and when, plus he didn't show up for work this morning and he's nowhere to be found."

Tasso slaps the bar. "So, whatta ya want from us? You think one of us had something to do with this?"

"No, I don't." Dante sweeps the faces gathered at the bar. "Look, before I came here, I spent an hour with Asher Levine's mother. Asher was her only child and her husband's been gone for years. You understand? He was all she had and now she's alone." This isn't exactly true. Stella Levine has at least one sister living in New York. But accuracy's not the point here. "Stella broke down, of course. Alone in her apartment, her only child dead on the street. That photo you're lookin' at? The one of him on his back? I had to show it to her. I had to ask her to look at that photo and tell me that a dead body lying in the road was her son."

Tasso's the only one not buying. The rest, though wary, are processing the information. That's good enough for Dante. He takes a small stack of business cards from his pocket and begins to hand them out.

"I'm askin' the same question," Tasso says. "Whatta ya want from us?"

"Anything connecting Mike Tedesco and Asher Levine," Dante explains as he continues to pass out cards, making eye contact whenever possible. "Even if you just saw them together on occasion, say huddled over a couple of those burgers. Or maybe one of them, probably Asher, shot his mouth off in an unguarded moment. You have to admit, they make an odd couple. Tedesco came up in the foster care system. He's hard-core. But Asher?" Dante nods to the cousins. "You two know about his home life. Foster care it wasn't."

Dante ends the pitch by dropping several cards on the bar. He plans to head back to the Three-One, write up the day's activities, and nod off for a few hours on a sagging cot. He'll visit the cousins, one at a time, tomorrow. If Asher shot his mouth off, it'll probably be to one of them. There's José as well, the missing truck driver. His family knows where he is and if Dante leans on them hard enough, maybe they'll do the right thing.

Dante's already rehearsing his approach as he heads out the door. Maybe he'll display Asher's death photo, appeal to Sofia's conscience. Maybe he'll dig up Mike Tedesco's mug shot, show her that too. Maybe he'll point out that Tedesco and José both worked at Legrand Transportation, that Tedesco knows that José can identify him, that Tedesco's already proven himself a killer, that José and his family can never safely reunite until Mike Tedesco's arrested.

Yeah, Dante tells himself, *that's it. Appeal to self-interest. If Tedesco's arrested for murder, he won't get bail. If he's convicted, he'll spend the next twenty-plus years in prison. No . . .*

As Dante reaches for the doorknob, the door opens to reveal Sanda Dragomir. Sanda's wearing a white-on-white dress tied high up on her left hip with a series of indigo ribbons. She smiles when she sees him, a soft quizzical smile that reveals exactly nothing.

Dante returns her smile. Between the white dress and the white-on-white complexion, the inky-black hair and the dark ribbons, the red lipstick, and a red pendant, which might be a small ruby, he needs a moment to regain his composure. Finally, he poses the obvious question, "You here to meet Mike?"

"No, Detective, I am here for you."

"How did you know I'd be here?"

"Who is sending you here, if not me?"

TWENTY-TWO

As Dante watches, his expression mild, Sanda's eyes flick past his shoulder for a fraction of a second, inspiring possibilities that Dante files away. The only relevant fact, for the moment, is that he'll spend the night with Sanda Dragomir. He leads her up the street, pops the door locks on the little Ford, finally opens the door on the passenger side. Dante knows that Sanda's skirt will ride up when she slips into the car. He doesn't look.

"Where do we go?" Sanda asks when Dante pushes his key into the ignition slot on the steering column.

"Nowhere."

Dante rolls down the windows, slides his seat all the way back, then finally glances at Sanda's legs. She hasn't pulled her dress down and the hem now rides at mid-thigh. Under other circumstances, he'd already be flying down the BQE, siren blaring. As it is, he's content to stare through the windshield at Tasso's Bar and Grill. Dante's thinking that it's only a matter of days, or even hours, until he arrests Mike Tedesco. Assuming, of course, that Mike Tedesco's willing to be arrested. The man's killed at least once, and for no valid reason. He's been to prison as well, for the crime of robbery in the second degree. Will he go down easy? Time will tell, but murder committed in the course of a felony makes the offender eligible for a sentence of life without parole. This is a fact with which Mike Tedesco is surely acquainted.

"Are you not trusting me, Dante?" Sanda asks.

"Should I?"

Sanda sighs, then crosses her legs. "This is story of my life."

"Mine, too, but I don't give a shit. On the other hand, if you want me to trust you, tell me why you came all the way to Long Island City on public transportation. I know there's an N stop in Sunset Park, but even if the subway's running on time, we're talkin' about twenty stops followed by a half-mile walk. I'm not buyin' that you came all that way in the hope I'd be here when you arrived."

A long pause follows, a pause Dante barely acknowledges. The evening is cool, especially for July, and he leans toward the open window. There's enough of a breeze for him to pretend the air is free of the mingled odors of exhaust fumes and garbage set by the curb. It's not.

"I am creating a graphic novel," Sanda tells him, as if that explains everything. "Title of this novel is *Mirrors*. One year's work I am already putting into this book."

"Do you have a publisher?"

"Yes, Black Stallion Productions. They have given me advance, but I have already spent it."

Dante lays his fingertips on Sanda's knee. There's no reason to be coy here, to pretend, no need for courtship or seduction. If Sanda doesn't want him, she'll say so. When she doesn't, he kisses her beneath her ear, the touch of his lips, like the touch of his fingers, gentle, patient, confident, safe. Nevertheless, his eyes never leave Tasso's doorway.

"What's it about? Your novel."

"About Alexander Litvinenko." She lays a hand on his shoulder and flicks at his earlobe with the tip of a manicured nail. "Very . . . seductive, this story. For cops, yes? This is porno for cops."

"Are you good at telling tales, Sanda?"

"Yes, very good. My whole life is made up."

Dante slides forward on the seat. He presses his feet into the firewall and smiles. "All right, let's hear the story."

"Of my life."

"Of Alexander what's his name."

"Litvinenko." Sanda turns her head to face Dante. "Alexander Litvinenko is spy for Russia. He works for KGB under Soviet Union, then with FSB after the fall. He is lieutenant colonel with Vladimir Putin for a boss. Alexander is ambitious, yes? But Putin is thug and Litvinenko is patriot, so what to do?" Sanda shrugs, again by way of explanation. "After revealing plot to kill Russian tycoon Boris Berezosky, Alexander leaves Russia and comes to Britain where he takes up profession of journalist. Russia is favorite topic and Alexander is very critical. Just before he is poisoned, he is investigating the murder of Anna Politkavskaya. Anna is journalist who stayed too long in Russia."

"Was anyone charged with her murder?"

"Five men, all convicted. Two have been sentenced to life. But they are not telling who ordered this."

"Sanda, there's an old saying in American politics. Reward your friends, punish your enemies. Vladimir Putin's taken the message to heart. You fuck with him, he'll definitely kill you. But this isn't exactly news."

"True, but here there is . . . is what my agent calls hook. Litvinenko was poisoned by a spy named Andrei Lugovoi who put radioactive element—Polonium-210—into Alexander's tea. This dying is very slow, very painful, six days of agony with whole world watching because Alexander speaks to press from his hospital bed. In last photos, flesh is yellow, hair is gone, his bones show through his skin."

"Yeah, that's good. Radioactive poison? Murdered by another spy? In fact, I'm already hooked."

"Yes, this is enough for big-time drama, but there is final twisting of plot. Alexander Litvinenko, all the time he claims to make his living as journalist, is really being paid by British Intelligence Service, MI6."

Dante lays a restraining hand on Sanda's shoulder as Tasso's door opens. He leans forward, now intensely focused, a predator on prey. The man who steps onto the sidewalk had been seated at the end of the bar when Dante left Tasso's. He was the only one who didn't look up when Dante entered or examine Asher's photos when Dante laid them on the bar. A small man with a narrow mustache and a soul patch, which in no way makes him soulful, he's pulled his fedora low over his forehead. A tooled shoulder bag hangs from his right shoulder, leather from the look of it, and expensive.

"Wait here," Dante tells Sanda as he opens his door, gets out, then circles around the back of the car and steps onto the sidewalk. The man is walking toward Dante, head down, but they're still twenty feet apart when he finally looks up. Startled, he glances to his left, out into the street, but it's a hundred yards to the corner with no rabbit holes in between.

Left without a viable choice, the man sucks it up and continues forward, his startled expression gradually softening. By the time he reaches Dante, his gaze reveals only mild curiosity.

"What's your name?" Dante asks.

"Ralph . . . Musetta."

"OK, Ralph, I want you to turn around and put your hands on the wall. I'm going to search you."

"Hey, Detective, you got no cause here. I'm just walkin' down the street."

Mildly curious no more, Musetta's eyes reflect oncoming panic. Evidence of a guilty mind, no doubt. Again, he looks into the street, but there's nowhere to go and he doesn't resist when Dante shoves him into the front wall of a brick apartment building. Not hard enough to do damage, but hard enough to make a point.

"Hands on the wall, Ralph." Dante waits until Musetta complies, then lays his own hands on the man's shoulders. "You carrying any weapons?"

"In my back pocket. On the right side."

"What am I gonna find?"

"A razor."

"You gotta be kiddin'." Dante removes the straight razor, a vicious weapon with a four-inch blade that gleams along the edges. "Aren't razors a bit on the retro side? Like the mustache and the hat? But I guess it's all about the image. Gotta look cool, right?"

Dante hands move over Musetta's body, his touch firm, yet patient. He knows that a large majority of the bars in New York, from the most exclusive clubs in Manhattan to hole-in-the-wall Brownsville dives, have at least one resident drug dealer. Exchanges are not done in plain view, and usually not in the bar itself. But if you find yourself in need of a few lines or a fat joint to augment the booze you're buying, there's usually somebody around to serve your needs. Dante made the man whose pockets he now turns inside out to be that dealer, his failure to acknowledge the presence of a cop in Tasso's another example of a guilty mind.

"What you're doin' ain't right." Musetta finally rediscovers his voice. He even manages an indignant tone. "You need probable cause to search someone. I'm not a fuckin' idiot. I swear, once this is over, I'm gonna sue you."

Dante ignores the threat. He doesn't mind backtalk, so long as it remains talk, and he has a job to do. Once he's satisfied himself that Musetta's not carrying contraband or another weapon on his person, he turns to the man's shoulder bag where he discovers a pair of one-quart baggies. The first contains a dozen tiny vials filled with a white powder, either cocaine or heroin. The other contains a larger vial filled with little blue tablets that Dante knows to be oxycodone.

"I want a lawyer."

"Are you serious?"

"Yeah, I know my rights."

Dante slaps him in the head. "Ralph, you're exactly as fucked as I want to make you. And we both know it. So, whatta ya say we cut the chatter and find common ground?"

TWENTY-THREE

Dante's in Sanda's bathroom emptying vials of cocaine into the toilet while Sanda luxuriates in a steaming tub, the water fortified with bath oil beads. It's very late now, past midnight, and Dante's doubly tired, from the long day and by Sanda's hauling his ashes so completely that he's convinced she was once a high-end hooker. Or still is.

"I will tell you if Mike contacts me," Sanda announces. "I promise this."

"Good to know."

In fact, at this point it doesn't matter. According to Ralph Musetta, Asher and Tedesco had spent a considerable amount of time in each other's company over the past few weeks. One example, Asher commonly left the bar several times in the course of an evening for a quick smoke. Tedesco, a nonsmoker, joined him as often as not. Further, half-drunk one night, Tedesco confided that he had a big job coming up.

"A slam dunk," he'd informed Musetta. "A can't miss with a big-ass payoff."

Unfortunately, Tedesco hadn't been drunk enough to mention Legrand Transportation or Asher Levine. Plus, Musetta would make a poor witness.

"What am I gonna say," Musetta had asked Dante, "when Tedesco's lawyer asks me why I spend my entire waking life drinking coffee in a bar? Which is not even to mention that I'm an ex-con."

Without a good answer, Dante had accepted the obvious. He was piling up the bricks, but the wall still wasn't high enough to contain Mike Tedesco. There was more work to do.

Dante watches Sanda rise to her feet, open the drain, then turn on the shower. She allows the water to play on her breasts for a moment before closing the shower curtain. Dante grins as he empties the last vial, then follows up with the oxycodone. Sanda appears totally unself-conscious, as if the net effect of her naked body on the male libido has somehow eluded her. Meanwhile, Dante had been ready to go again before the first time ended.

Far and away the most beautiful woman Dante has ever had the good fortune to bed, Sanda Dragomir is a stunning woman, even more so unclothed. Her small breasts are crowned with pink nipples that leave her pale skin all the whiter. Her legs are long and toned, her belly resilient, her crotch shaved smooth. When he'd brought his mouth to her thigh, he was able to easily trace each of the underlying muscles. They felt, as they contracted and relaxed, like small burrowing animals.

If so, they were animals that knew their way through the jungle. Sanda hadn't just brought expertise to the game. She'd plucked his neurons like harp strings. Without him having to say a word, she'd known exactly what he wanted, then made those wants serve her own ends.

Sanda steps out of the tub and wraps herself in a towel that leaves her splendid ass half-exposed. "Come," she says, "I wish to show you my novel." Then she turns and walks past Dante, leaving him no real choice except to follow. She's issued a command, after all, not made a request. Dante trails her to her computer and seats himself before the monitor while she pulls up the files.

A moment later, he finds himself reviewing a series of black-and-white drawings, a couple of dozen in all. He only has to glance at the first few to realize that Sanda Dragomir is extremely talented. The panels are haunted by shadows, a dark alley off a sunlit plaza, a dim corner in a glitzy nightclub. In one drawing, Russian dissidents sentenced to the gulags stream across a flat plain overhung by ragged clouds. Backs bent, they march, men, women, and children, between an ice-choked river in the foreground and a line of rocky cliffs that rise almost straight up. The cliffs are pockmarked by caves.

Intrigued, Dante stays at it for a good half hour, skipping from panel to panel. "Is there any real money in this?" he finally says.

"Everyone asks this question, Dante. And sad truth is that money does not pay for work. By hour, this is minimum wage."

For some reason, Patti O'Hearn's wholesome features make an unexpected appearance, the red hair, the freckles, the teasing smile. As a cop, Dante's sure that Patti believes herself tough and cynical. And maybe she is too. But Patti's not in Sanda's league. Or his, come to think of it.

"So, how do you pay the bills?"

"Why is this your business?"

"Because I'm a cop and I don't step in shitholes without knowing how deep they are."

Sanda's eyes narrow and her mouth tightens, her overall expression seeming to Dante more disapproving, than angry. Either way, he doesn't react and Sanda turns away for a moment. When she turns back, she's smiling.

"I have cottage industry."

"Which is?"

"Which is none of your business, but I will anyway describe this shithole of yours. How deep is for you to calculate." The smile remains in place. "For living, I sell marijuana in small amounts, one-half ounces. Price is between a hundred and twenty and a hundred and thirty dollars for each. Always quality is same, very good but not best. Money-back guarantee means marijuana doesn't have to be smoked before paying. No smell, yes? To alert Mrs. Jiang? And I am making delivery too."

Dante considers the information for a moment, then laughs softly. "I scared you, right? When I grabbed Musetta?"

"He is my . . . connection is how you say? He is supplier. He is how I pay rent. I was afraid you would arrest him."

"So—and this is a blow to my ego, Sanda, a bitter blow—it seems like you're tellin' me you didn't go to Tasso's hopin' to meet the love of your life. You went there to resupply."

"This is true. As for love of life, only future will reveal."

Dante marvels at the obvious. Sanda's telling him that Mike Tedesco's not coming back and she's now on the prowl. Dante likes the idea of it, but can't make himself believe that she's telling the truth, her whole life being, as she's already described it, a lie.

Just before he leaves, as he's standing by the door, he shows Asher's photo to Sanda. "Do you recognize this man?"

"Yes, I have seen him in Tasso's."

"With Mike Tedesco?"

"Sometimes, but he mostly plays with the . . . the darts. You know, that they throw. I think he is crazy for this game."

* * *

127

Dante's inside the Three-One's squad room at six, two hours before the squad's tour is scheduled to begin. He's had a bare three hours of sleep, but he's energized nonetheless and he quickly settles into the paperwork necessary to move the case forward. That finished, he reviews the data from the security camera attached to St. Mark's Church. The video confirms Myra Cuffee's version in every detail, right down to the presence of a dog, but the shooter's wearing a mask and the quality, obscured by the rain, is too poor to be used for identification.

By the time Lieutenant Kelly Barnwell arrives, he's fully prepared. Just as well because Barnwell's a middle-aged, no-nonsense Black woman who's already passed the captain's exam. All that remains before promotion is a review of her leadership skills.

As Barnwell crosses the room on the way to her office, Starbucks bag in hand, she signals to Dante. He's shooting the breeze with a pair of veterans, Colby Harris and Jeanine Lawson, but he responds without hesitation despite it still being a quarter to eight. Dante's never been a boss hater, never been lazy, never been anything that might offend his superiors. True he cuts corners, ignoring, for example, Ralph Musetta's demand for a lawyer and the drugs he possessed. But that falls into a category familiar to every detective: Don't Get Caught. Especially having an affair with a witness who might be a co-conspirator.

"I'm not in the best of moods." Barnwell pulls a container of coffee from the bag and removes the top, unleashing a tiny cloud of steam. She lays a pastry on the table and unwraps it. "The Yankees lost again, the same damned way. They were two-for-ten with runners on base. I mean, I know the team has to be rebuilt, but this is a nightmare."

Dante's not into baseball, or any other sport. He's also in a hurry. "Well, I have good news," he announces, his tone upbeat. "I know who killed Asher Levine. A man named Mike Tedesco, the manager at Legrand Transportation. The only question is whether or not we have enough to make the collar." Dante stops as the odor of Barnwell's coffee reaches his nostrils. He looks down at the half-filled mug in his hand, its contents brewed in a low-end coffeemaker that hasn't been cleaned in months. "But not to worry, Boss. If we don't have enough right now, there's plenty more to get."

Dante makes his case, much as he'd made it in his own mind when he assured Stella Levine that he was close to arresting the man who killed her son. Mike Tedesco knew the truck's route and didn't show up for work. Asher Levine had the skill to disable a GPS unit, and he was murdered at the scene. Both men frequented a bar in Long Island City, Tasso's Bar and Grill. A third patron, Ralph Musetta, claims they spent a lot of time together.

Barnwell takes a moment to scan the paperwork laid on her desk before she arrived, the complaint and a series of DD5's. Dante watches patiently. The lieutenant's always been a quick study, and results-oriented to a fault.

"What about Theodore Legrand, the owner?" she asks.

"Best guess, he's dirty, but I got nothin' on him. They call him Skippy, by the way, Skippy Legrand. Sounds like a little kid's name, but the jerk's gotta be six-four."

"And the girlfriend?"

"Sanda Dragomir. What about her?"

"She shot a man who broke into her house." Barnwell runs her finger over Sanda's DD5. "Paul . . . Bancroft."

"Bancroft worked for Skippy Legrand, alongside Mike Tedesco.

I don't know what he was doing at Dragomir's apartment, probably looking for Tedesco. According to Dragomir, she took Bancroft for a burglar or worse."

"Do you believe her?"

"Not entirely. I think Tedesco warned her and she was expecting someone to show up. Not that it matters. The locals at the Seven-Two are writing it off as self-defense, at least for now. Sanda's free to come and go as she pleases."

"What about Tedesco? Did she know what her boyfriend was up to?"

"She claims she didn't, but Tedesco told Ralph Musetta that he had a big job coming up, so it wouldn't surprise me if he also told his lover."

Barnwell picks up her tart, takes a bite, wipes her mouth with a small napkin. "The driver, José, he's the key, right?"

"He's in the wind, like Tedesco. But we have a witness to the hijacking, an old lady named Myra Cuffee. According to her, José was yanked out of the truck and held at gunpoint while Levine tried to disable the GPS unit. Levine gave up on the GPS unit a few minutes later, whereupon the gunman shot him, but turned José loose. Then he shot Levine again, this time in the head. Finally, he jumped into the car driven by Asher, him and his dog, and took off. There's a video as well, taken by a security camera about a block away. It confirms Myra Cuffee's statement."

"But. . . ?"

"But the shooter wore a mask and it was pouring hard and the camera was a block away."

Barnwell sifts through the paperwork for a moment, then raises one of Dante's fives and quickly reviews it. "Cuffee can't make an ID, so what's the point?" She gives Dante a second to answer. When he doesn't, she continues on. "Look, if José Sepulveda didn't recognize the shooter, if the shooter was a stranger to him, he would have called us or his boss the minute he got clear. The man's hiding because he can identify the man who killed Levine. Find him, Dante. Find him and close the case."

TWENTY-FOUR

Mike Tedesco wakes up horny at six o'clock in the morning, a common occurrence. Not being a man given to postponed gratification, he rolls over, prurient intent uppermost in his mind, only to come nose-to-nose with Pug. As Pug's nose is both wet and cold, Tedesco jerks away.

"Damn."

Pug jumps to the carpeted floor, but doesn't run off, though he looks contrite as he lowers his massive head and whines softly.

"Jesus Christ, Pug," Tedesco says. "What am I gonna do with you?"

In light of the fact that Skippy's more or less ordered him to get rid of the dog, this is not an idle question. But Skippy isn't running the show anymore, a message he's yet to internalize.

Tedesco slips into the same clothes he wore yesterday, including his still-damp socks. He completes the outfit by shoving a pistol inside his belt, then walks down a corridor into the living room where he finds Daniela seated before her altar. Daniela's wearing Oshun's colors. Beaded bracelets, sun-yellow, run from her wrists to the center of her forearms. Red and yellow necklaces, three of them, drop onto a kimono-like robe. Too large to be real, ruby-colored rings grace the fingers of both hands.

Daniela doesn't glance up when Tedesco walks into the room. With her eyes closed and her expression lazy, she has the look of a stroked kitten. Tedesco's seen her in this state before and he's not tempted to interrupt. He walks into the kitchen, finds a plastic supermarket bag, puts a leash on Pug, and heads out the door. His route along Riverside Drive takes him past the charred remains of Asher's Lincoln and he pauses, but only for a moment. The sky above the river is streaked with long wispy clouds and the humidity continues to rise, second by second. The cool spell is about to end, ozone time about to begin. Tedesco looks across the Hudson at the retreating blue skies, while Pug stands before a light pole, one leg raised.

"Hi, is that a rescue dog?"

Tedesco glances up to find a young woman, a student by the look of her, walking a small terrier. Despite the terrier being a third of Pug's size, it pulls its master toward Pug, who drops his leg to the ground. Tedesco represses a smile. Pug could—and very well might—eat this mouse for breakfast. But Pug's apparently retired from the game. The two dogs stand nose-to-nose for a moment, flanks tense, then abruptly relax.

"Yeah," Tedesco says, "he is a rescue. The cops picked him up when they raided a dog fight in the South Bronx. They took him to a vet I know, Dr. Lincoln. Jim didn't think Pug would survive, but he's doing real well now. How about your pup? Did you rescue her?"

The lies come easily, as they always have, but there's no payoff. The girl smiles, shakes her head and says, "Ashley's not mine. She belongs to my boyfriend."

That's enough for Tedesco. He guides Pug up the long hill leading to New York–Presbyterian Hospital, taking his time as he focuses on an immediate goal, one of many. He has get away from Daniela and *Regla de Ocha* or Santería or whatever the fuck they call it. The whole thing's making him crazy, just like it did last time he stayed with Daniela, and he can't afford to be crazy now. He has to keep his mind straight, especially this morning.

Tedesco now wants the cops to find him, wants to confront them, see what they do when he tells them to go to hell. The outcome hinges on whether or not they've found José. José will definitely talk if the cops dig him up. Likewise for Sanda Dragomir. Tedesco hasn't been stupid enough to confide in Sanda, but he's had Asher Levine over to Sanda's apartment. Given Sanda's past, that was a mistake for which he can only blame himself.

"I was illegal immigrant," she'd told him early in their relationship. "Hiding in shadows. Then police come to me with offer. I must testify against lover, Teddy Winuk. In return, they will give me green card. I take this deal, yes? In three more years, I will be citizen."

Tedesco had assumed the revelation was meant as a warning. Watch your ass, because if Sanda has to choose between Mike Tedesco and Sanda Dragomir, little Mike's going over the cliff. Meanwhile, the woman's taken it a step further by killing Paulie Bancroft. Another warning? Tedesco knows he might have to do something about Sanda. The problem is that Sanda also knows it, as do José and Skippy, and maybe even the scumbag cop who's looking for him. Dante Cepeda? There's probably nothing in life that would give him more pleasure than watching the prick die. Slowly.

Lots of fun, right? With survival the ultimate longshot?

Tedesco drops to one knee and scratches the thick scars on Pug's head. Talk about longshots. But the dog's tongue hangs through his ripped mouth and he pants happily, his small eyes narrowed to slits. Not a care in the world, not . . .

Suddenly, in the distance, Tedesco hears the drums, so far away at first they seem little more than a suggestion, then closer and closer, growing louder and louder, until they're on top of him. Only then does he look up to find, not a descending Orisha, but a gigantic Mercedes sedan, its sound system cranked to full volume, heavy on a throbbing bass that repeats the same note, over and over again.

Boom, baboom-boom. Boom, baboom-boom. Boom, baboom-boom. Boom, baboom-boom.

Fifteen minutes later, when Tedesco walks into Daniela's apartment, he finds her exactly where she was, at her altar. She looks over her shoulder this time, her expression speculative, but Tedesco's not in the mood for a lecture. He raises his head to stare into the poster above the altar, *La Caridad del Cobre*, Our Lady of Mercy, in her golden robes, bearing her sacred child. Then his eyes drop to the fishermen in their little boat and for just a moment he feels their terror, trapped on a vast sea, the waves crashing into the boat, the boat on the verge of tipping, death seemingly assured.

With nature turned against them, they naturally looked to a god for rescue. Tedesco understands because he, himself, had prayed for rescue on the day three social workers, backed up by a pair of cops, took him out of his mother's house. Against her will? Given that his mother was at the bottom end of a bipolar mood swing, not to mention stoned on heroin, there was no way to tell.

Tedesco shakes his head. He's been fighting his way through an oncoming tide since boyhood, a tide that never ebbs, that keeps on coming, throwing punches, relentless.

"Miguelito?"

"What?"

"You need this."

Daniela's holding out a bracelet made from black and green beads in clusters of three. Tedesco knows that he's supposed to slide the bracelet over his wrist, to show proper gratitude, but he can't make himself pretend. Just the opposite. Tedesco's decided not to return to this insanity, not tonight or any night, even if he has to sleep on an office chair in the warehouse.

"Look, Daniela," he says, "I'm not buyin' what you're sellin', simple as that. Tell what's her name . . ." He points to the figure on the poster, the woman in her golden robes. "Oshun? Yeah, Oshun. Tell Oshun to mind her own business."

"Oshun doesn't want you, Miguelito. It's Ogun. Ogun wants you."

"Oshun, Ogun, the man on the fuckin' moon. Right now, with what's goin' on in my life, I don't need this bullshit."

Daniela's out of the chair and standing in front of him, the transition seeming instantaneous. She slides the bracelet over his left wrist. "Ogun is a ferocious warrior, especially where his survival or the survival of those he protects is threatened. You will serve him because he's chosen you to serve, as warrior or as sacrifice remains to be seen."

"And I have to do what? Wait around to find out which?"

Daniela smiles for the first time. "The orishas are vain, all of them, and insecure. They need to be worshipped and they hate to be rejected." She places a gentle hand on Tedesco's chest. "Now, go. Go and don't come back. Your troubles flow around you like vultures over a dying animal, Miguelito, and I have troubles of my own."

TWENTY-FIVE

Skippy Legrand's day is in full swing when Mike Tedesco, trailed by a leashed Pug, enters Legrand Transportation. Tedesco's walk is close to a strut, the smile on his face a smirk that widens slightly when Skippy's employee—four drivers and six warehouse workers—stop in their tracks. It's like a bad science-fiction movie where time stands still and everyone shares the same expression, mouths open, eyes narrowed, somehow keeping Tedesco in full view without looking at him directly. They know about the hijacking and the murder, of course, and that Mike Tedesco didn't come to work yesterday, and that a detective spent an hour in the office with the bookkeeper.

"Hey, Skip, what's happening?"

"You're late."

"Sorry, Boss. What could I do? I had to pick up my car, only it got towed. I been an hour bailin' it out."

Skippy stares down at Pug, who returns the compliment, his black eyes so empty they might have been placed there by a taxidermist. "This is a workplace, Mike. No dogs allowed, so the first thing you need to do is get your mutt the fuck out of here."

"Hey, don't worry, I'll tie Pug up in the back. It's too hot to leave him in the car."

Skippy wants to assert his authority, but has no idea how. He should have kept his big mouth shut. "Yeah, fine," he says, "but you're gonna clean up after him. And I swear on my mother, if he gets loose, I'll run him over with a forklift. He's too ugly to live, anyhow."

As Mike walks off, Pug in tow, Skippy scratches at a patch of psoriasis under his right arm before turning to his new driver, Adelberto Gomez, José's replacement. Released from their time warp, Skippy's workers also resume their tasks. Skippy knows they're drawing conclusions that link Skippy to Mike to the hijacking, as he knows that Tedesco's unexpected appearance will be the sole topic of conversation over lunch. Skippy knows these things, but doesn't care. Brazen is what he and Mike's new relationship is all about. You don't like it, find another job.

"Let's get the trucks out of here. We're already twenty minutes late."

Skippy means to shout, but he's too tired. He was awake half the night playing poker at an offshore website, his luck strong from beginning to end. By the time he passed out in front of his computer, he was ahead more than fifteen large, which brought his total winnings on the day to thirty thousand dollars.

Skippy should be a happy man, what with his luck now turned and his debt to Alebev canceled. And he would be—in fact he'd be overjoyed—if not for Mike Tedesco, who can put him behind bars for decades. And there's nobody else, not a single thread, tying him to the hijacking. Tedesco had kept Asher Levine and Skippy far apart because Asher was Mike's leverage. The job couldn't be pulled off without Levine.

The obvious being the obvious, Skippy's mind keeps returning to an obvious solution. Eliminate Tedesco. But that's easier said than done, what with Paulie gone and him, Skippy, not having the balls do it himself. Not yet, at least. But soon, because something's happened to Mike Tedesco. The man's always been relatively cautious, measuring risk and reward, a natural crook who's been to prison and doesn't want to return. Maybe the law means nothing to him, maybe he has the conscience of a cockroach, but those bars were as real as real gets.

All of that's gone, all the caution, vanished, like a silver dollar in the hand of a close-up magician. That's the way Skippy reads it. Mike Tedesco knows he's toast and doesn't give a shit. He's drawing to an inside straight-flush with a full house showing on the table. Yeah, he's got a chance, assuming the card he needs hasn't already been played.

"Yo, Skippy," Tedesco calls from the other side of the warehouse. "We're short on Newports. Whatta ya wanna do?"

For the next hour, it's all about loading the trucks and getting them on the road. One truck, the early truck, was loaded on the prior afternoon and kept in the warehouse overnight. The rest, the trucks in the yard, protected only by a chain-link fence, were left empty. So, the rush is on, with Skippy micromanaging, as usual. Tedesco's basically doing the same thing with an added duty thrown in. Once the trucks are fully loaded, Tedesco will take the manifest into the truck and compare it to the actual cargo. Theft is a constant problem, one that includes insiders as well as outsiders. In New York, there are three items that can be sold almost instantly on the street: cigarettes, alcohol, and disposable diapers.

By the time they finish at eight thirty, everyone's sweating, Skippy, Tedesco, the workers. The temperature's already in the low eighties and the humidity's all-enveloping, an extra layer that can't be washed away. Skippy's anxious to get into the air-conditioned office despite the near-certainty that Martha Proctor will demand answers to questions Skippy's not prepared to answer. Martha's a yenta's yenta, a real pain in the ass, and she always has been. Skippy would have fired her ten years ago if she didn't do the work of three people. As it is, her skills allow him to spend his mornings huddled over the racing form, a job he's eager to begin. That's because a trainer named Byron Candell, a bottom-feeder known to juice his animals, has a fifteen-to-one shot entered at Monmouth Park. Skippy wants to examine the horse's past-performance charts as soon as possible.

The new hire, Adelberto Gomez, is last to go out, in part because the man barely speaks English. That's fine because Adelberto's route is through the southernmost part of the South Bronx where Spanish is everyone's first language. It's fine, as well, that Adelberto's almost certainly an illegal. When Skippy asked Gomez for a green card, the man had offered a dog-eared social security card, which was not the same thing, but more than enough for Skippy.

"All right, Gomez, off ya go. And don't get lost. If ya don't know where you are, call in."

"*Si, si*, yes."

Tedesco comes up as Adelberto's truck departs. "Everything cool?" he asks.

"Cool?"

"Between us." Tedesco lays a hand on Skippy's shoulder and look up into his eyes. "Are we still on the same page?"

Skippy looks down for a moment, only then noticing the bracelet on Tedesco's left wrist, black and green beads strung on a coarse thread. "What the fuck is that, Mike? You turnin' gay on me?"

"It's for luck," Tedesco says after a brief hesitation. "Which me and you are definitely in need of."

Skippy's about to add something about Tedesco being the one in need—the cops aren't after Skippy Legrand—but the words flee his mind when Detective Dante Cepeda walks through the door, a smile hard enough to crack a bank safe pulling at the corners of his mouth.

"Hail, hail," he says. "The gang's all here. How ya doin', Mike? Haven't seen you in a long time. In fact, until I heard you worked for Skippy, I thought you were still in prison."

Tedesco stares at the cop for a moment—Skippy thinking the two are going to go at it for sure—but then he steps back. "Well, if it ain't the punching bag." He looks over at Skippy. "This spic, he spent his teenage years in a boxing gym. Getting punched in the face. Me, I preferred weed and pussy."

"That's true, Mike, I went into the gym and you went to . . ." Dante's voice trails off as Pug ambles across the warehouse floor, nails clicking on the concrete, leash dragging behind him, tongue dangling from the side of his mouth.

"That your dog, Skippy?" Dante asks.

Skippy folds his arms across his chest. "I got nothin' to say to you, Detective. You wanna ask questions, talk to my lawyer. And by the way, unless you got a warrant, get the fuck out of my warehouse."

Dante responds by kneeling in front of Pug. Early on, before he was promoted to the detective division, Dante and his partner had responded to stray pit bull complaints many times. Most were in decent condition, but there were others very much like the dog who now sniffs at his fingers. Dante harbors a particular hatred for humans who abuse animals, and especially for men who set dogs against each other, who extract the last bit of their courage, only to throw their fighters out on the street when they're too old for the pits.

"Hey, Skippy." Dante dusts off his knees as he rises. "You wanna hear something funny?"

"I want you to leave my place of business."

Dante shakes his head. "You need to wise your buddy up, Mike," he tells Mike Tedesco. "He's comin' off a bit naive."

Tedesco reaches into the pocket of his shirt and extracts a damp business card. "My lawyer's name is on the card. He's waitin' for you to get in touch."

Dante accepts the card, but he's already turning to Skippy. "So, what I was sayin' before, about something funny? We have a witness to the murder. Saw the whole thing. Of course, it was rainin' pretty hard, so the witness didn't have the greatest view, but this witness was sure about one thing. Before your truck arrived, the witness saw a man sittin' in a doorway, maybe tryin' to stay dry. And guess what? There was a dog sittin' beside him. You believe that? A dog? I mean, who brings a dog to a hijacking? Who brings a dog to a murder?"

Skippy swallows his initial impulse, to attack Mike Tedesco, and his second impulse as well, to name Mike Tedesco as the dog's owner.

"Wise up, Skippy," Dante continues. "This asshole?" He jerks his thumb at Tedesco. "He's gonna take a fall, which is what happens when you kill people for no good reason. But you? You weren't there, Skippy. You were at work and you have a dozen witnesses to back you up. So, why do you wanna go down with the ship? Which, let me add, was never seaworthy in the first place?"

Dante pauses for a second, as if expecting an answer, then slams his fist into Mike Tedesco's chest. Tedesco drops onto his ass and slowly falls over backward, his diaphragm temporarily paralyzed. He's nearly unconscious, but he understands Dante well enough when Dante says, "You call me a spic again, I'll beat you until you cry."

"Hey, enough." Skippy positions himself between the two men, both his gaze and tone defiant. "You made your fuckin' point."

"Actually, I think the dice are still in the air, Skippy, but I'm gonna leave anyway." Dante walks through the door, then turns back to stare at Pug for a moment. The dog's expression is nearly serene, but when Dante calls, he responds instantly.

"C'mon, boy. Let's get outta here."

As if he'd only been waiting for a better deal, Pug lifts himself from a sitting position and follows Dante Cepeda down the street. He doesn't so much as glance at his fallen benefactor.

TWENTY-SIX

Mike Tedesco doesn't resent the shot he took from Dante Cepeda, not after the years in prison when being manhandled, slapped around or beaten unconscious by the COs was simply how the prison cards were dealt. One thing sure, unless you were a complete asshole, you didn't fight back. The few who did, who wouldn't give up the battle, spent their days, weeks, months, and years in an isolation unit, talking to the walls.

No, what you did was suck the rage deep inside where it could do you some good. Then you found the right COs, the ones who'd smuggle in just about anything short of a gun, and open for business. At one point, two years into his bit, Mike Tedesco had paid a CO nine hundred dollars for thirty minutes of passionless sex in a small pantry off the kitchen. That would be Sergeant Harriet Krueger, who needed the money to pay her daughter's college tuition.

Perspective is everything in the end. It certainly was for Corrections Officer Harriet Krueger, who decided that a half hour with Mike Tedesco was preferable to the 10 percent interest charged each week by a loan shark. Same with Cepeda's punch, which actually plays to Mike's advantage. Dante was fast and there's no getting around the fact, fast and powerful. If they went to war, one on one, just their hands, little Mikey would probably come out second best. Knowing that in advance doesn't hurt.

Tedesco's on his way to Sunnyside, José Sepulveda's stomping grounds, a journey of perhaps thirty minutes on a good day. But it's not a good day. Harlem River Drive is at a dead stop and it's still a mile to the Triborough Bridge off-ramp. Tedesco sticks his head out the window in an attempt to see past the SUV in front of him. He's hoping for the flashing lights of a police cruiser, but whatever's blocking the traffic is still out of sight. For all he knows, it might be on the other end of the bridge.

With nothing to do but stare out over the Harlem River at the equally-slow traffic on the Major Deegan Expressway, Tedesco's thoughts settle on the one development that's truly gotten under his skin. That would be Pug walking off with Cepeda. Mike had fed the mutt, cleaned up his crap, bought him a leash and a bowl, even named him. Forget about Pug actually making the right long-term choice, the one he'd make in Pug's position. Loyalty had to count for something.

A man without permanent friends or permanent enemies, Tedesco laughs at himself as he flips on the radio, pre-set to a Sirius R&B channel. Loyalty? He's already thinking about Skippy Legrand, about having to do to his existing partner what he's already done to his dead partner. But Skippy has a definite problem. He can't tie Mike to the hijacking without implicating himself. That makes José Sepulveda the most immediate threat. Tedesco was crazy to let the man go. Talk about a moment of weakness, talk about asshole sentimentality. If Mike had pulled the trigger when he had the chance, as every instinct demanded he do, he wouldn't be dealing with the obvious. José will identify Mike Tedesco if the cops (meaning Dante

Cepeda) catch up with him. And Dante hasn't, not yet. If he had, Tedesco would already be in cuffs. Or dead.

At the scene, when José told Mike that he had a brother in California, Mike had advised him to pay the man a visit. That was good advice, no doubt, but Tedesco needs to know whether or not José took it.

The traffic ahead inches forward, the average speed gradually increasing, until Tedesco's moving along at a steady eight miles an hour. He travels a good half-mile before the traffic comes to a stop once again. Tedesco can now see the off-ramp leading to the bridge, and that no one's moving up that ramp, not at all, not a fucking inch. In the car next to him, an apple-green taxi, the turbaned driver pounds on the steering wheel.

Five minutes later, having advanced less than ten yards, Tedesco's on the phone with Sanda Dragomir. He's using a burner, one of several picked up on the prior afternoon. Given his goal this morning, it clearly wouldn't pay to leave a record of his movements, an electronic trail embedded forever in some Verizon databank.

"So, what's new?" he asks.

"What's new is that a man breaks into my apartment yesterday and I have to kill him."

"Yeah, I heard about that."

"You are knowing this man, yes?"

"Paulie Bancroft. He works for Skippy." Tedesco looks down at the black-and-green bracelet on his wrist. Sanda's tone is cool and deliberate, a mirror of her general disposition. Daniela, by contrast, is all passion, willing to abandon herself whenever the orisha comes calling. Personally, he prefers Daniela, or he would if he wasn't afraid of her world. "Congratulations, by the way. Paulie was no match."

"This is all you have to say?"

"Hey, I warned you. I told you somebody might show up."

"And you are the cause of this showing up."

Tedesco slows himself down. He can feel the anger rising. "What'd you think, Sanda? When you invited me to live with you? Did you think I was an accountant, maybe a stockbroker? How 'bout a computer fucking engineer?"

Sanda abruptly changes the subject, another annoying habit. "Last night I was at Tasso's. There was cop there. Detective . . ."

"Dante Cepeda."

"Yes, Cepeda. He asks questions about Asher and you, Michael. He asks if you are buddies."

"Asks exactly who?"

"Everybody in the bar."

Tedesco curses softly. "And did he question you, Sanda?"

"I am telling him that we have separate lives. That we are keeping our business to ourselves. I didn't know where you are being yesterday, which is truth."

"Anything else?"

"Don't worry, Michael, I have not mentioned Asher's name. But you must not return to here. I want quiet life, not men with guns coming to hurt me."

"Just like that? You're throwing me out? I'm askin' because I been payin' half the rent and I got nowhere to go at the moment."

"Hotels, yes? Give them money and they will give you place to live."

"Is that supposed to be funny? Because I'm not gettin' the joke. And don't confuse me with Paulie Bancroft. Bancroft had the IQ of a dead tree."

147

"Michael, you don't understand. I am becoming citizen of America. Nothing gets before this thing, especially not lover who is criminal and who sends men to kill me."

Sanda hangs up without saying goodbye and Tedesco feels the loss, not of love, but of attachment itself. First Pug, now Sanda, like his fate is so obvious that even dogs know enough to get free of him. And why not? Because it's always been like this, from his first day in foster care when four older boys had come for him. He'd gotten to one of them later on, sliced through the boy's throat, barely missing the jugular, driven purely by hate. Now, as he stares at the phone in his hand, the hate again explodes inside him, a skyrocket blazing in every cell, nose to toes. He wants to get out of the car, open the trunk, take up the shotgun, and start killing. Simple as that. Just keep pulling the trigger until blood flows along the roadway, until blood spills into the Harlem River, until the river runs red.

Tedesco closes his eyes, letting the images flash through his brain. He imagines himself walking from car to car, imagines the panicked faces of the drivers and the passengers, imagines human faces exploding, imagines gore splattering against the windows, imagines pulling the trigger again and again and again.

By the time Mike Tedesco turns onto Barnett Avenue, forty minutes later, he's recovered his generally positive attitude. He's telling himself that he's already been lucky twice this morning. First, he left the Colt under the seat in his car when he got to the warehouse. If he'd been carrying it when Dante showed up, he would have used it before allowing himself to be searched. Second, as he'd driven from the impound yard to the warehouse, the host on an all-news radio station reported the discovery of two bodies in the trunk of a car. As both victims were Russian gangsters and the car was parked in the Russian-dominated neighborhood of Brighton Beach, the police were focusing their efforts on the usual mob suspects.

To Tedesco's left, a long line of attached, cinder-block garages perch at the edge of the Long Island Railroad's elevated tracks. On the other side, brick townhouses, two stories high and plain as vanilla pudding, face away from Barnett Avenue. There's no one about, not even a dog walker. The heat, probably, which rises from the blacktop in waves, shimmering and seductive.

Tedesco parks toward the end of the row of garages, where Barnett Avenue gives way to 38th Avenue, across from the home of Chiapas Electronic Repair, a narrow, whitewashed building. He remains behind the wheel for a moment, listening to a faint drumming that he finally recognizes as the beating of his own heart. Then he steps out of the car, the heat seizing him, the sweat instantly flowing, the glare from a swollen summer sun forcing him to squint. The air horn of a passing train, a howl that seems to him almost painful, breaks the silence. Tedesco watches the train rush by, then whispers to himself, "Showtime."

Mariano Herrera, seated in an ancient swivel chair behind an equally old, equally battered desk, is José Herrera's cousin. He and Tedesco have met several times, usually when Mariano gave José a ride to work because the subway wasn't running. They'd recognized each other instantly, convict-to-convict, the wary calculating look giving it away. But they only talked business weeks later when Mariano delivered his pitch. A locksmith before he went up for the first time, he was now a burglar and a small-time fence. Thus, if it should happen that a few boxes of cigarettes fell off the back of one of Skippy's trucks, he, Mariano Herrera, was prepared to offer cash payment on the spot.

Always quick to seize an opportunity, Tedesco was able to occasionally liberate a few dozen cartons and Herrera proved as good as his word. And while they never became friends, they'd shared a beer or two in the back of Chiapas Electronic Repairs, a store without customers. Mariano and José, as Mariano explained, were very close as young children in Mexico. Neighbors called them *los gemelos*, the twins. And even though Mariano had come north five years before José, they'd renewed their friendship without hesitation, their very different values and lifestyles notwithstanding.

When Tedesco comes through the door, Mariano attempts a smile, but doesn't quite make it. He knows why Tedesco's here, which means he's probably been in touch with his cousin. Or so Tedesco decides.

"You like choices, Mariano?" he asks. "You good at making quick decisions?"

"Wha'chu got in mind?"

Tedesco pulls a small wad of money from his shirt pocket, fifteen C-notes. He fans them out on Mariano's desk, then pulls the .45 cal from his waistband and points it at Mariano's face. "Option *numero uno*." Tedesco gestures to the bills before giving the Colt a little shake. "Option *numero dos*."

"Amigo, please . . ."

Tedesco waves him off. "Don't even go there. It's yes or no. Yes means you take the money and tell me where José's hiding. No means I kill you. Probably within the next fifteen seconds."

Mariano's small brown eyes fade for a moment, then turn prison-hard. Maybe he loves José, but he can't bring himself to challenge Mike Tedesco's resolve and he's not ready to die for his cousin. Head down, eyes riveted to the C-notes, he reveals José's location, a nephew's apartment on McClellan Street off the Grand Concourse in the Bronx. Tedesco shoots him anyway, putting a single round through the top of Mariano's head. He watches the man drop face down to the desktop, watches his fingers twitch for a few seconds before they go still. Then he quickly scoops up the money before a spreading pool of blood contaminates the pile and heads for the door.

TWENTY-SEVEN

Dante Cepeda's still pondering Tedesco's presence at Legrand Transportation when he walks into offices of Schuster & Schuster, an architectural firm with offices on Beekman Street near city hall in Manhattan. The Schusters, Irv and Joseph, are Asher Levine's cousins, the twins who Cepeda first approached at Tasso's. Dante had received a call from Joe Schuster early in the morning, urging him to pay a visit. The twins wanted to help.

The receptionist in the waiting area is a knockout, a light-skinned Black woman with a smile so bright and warm that Dante can't help but return it. The smile's automatic, of course, a gift to anyone coming through the door, but it widens considerably at the sight of Pug on his leash.

"Oh," she asks, "is he a rescue?"

"More like evidence of a crime."

"Ah, you must be the detective. Irv and Joe are waiting for you. My name's Cynthia."

Cynthia lifts herself from her chair in waves, like a dolphin cutting the surf. She leads Dante and Pug through the waiting room, past a line of cubicles staffed by men and women focused on their monitors, past the only architectural table in the office, to a well-appointed conference room. Dante, as he comes through the door, is impressed by the entire setup, the ultra-sleek couches and tables in the reception area, the diligent workers in their cubicles, but especially by the long table and matching chairs in the conference room. The gleaming surface of the table, made from a single piece of what he imagines to be tropical wood, is figured with a dark, twisting grain that flows from one end to the other.

The Schusters, Irv and Joe, are equally impressive. Tall, blond, and seriously fit, the bald patches at the backs of their heads only make them look more serious, more like the solid professionals Dante imagines them to be. They wear pressed jeans, polished loafers, and white-on-white shirts open at the neck. Their blazers, one black, one camel hair, hang from a free-standing coatrack next to the room's only window.

The Schuster to Dante's left offers his hand. "Joe Schuster," he says. The Schuster to his right nods, then extends his own hand. "Irv Schuster. And if you get our names wrong, don't worry about it."

"Yeah, we're hard to offend. You want coffee?"

Irv jumps in before Dante replies. "Great idea," he says. "Cynthia, would you bring coffee, please? And some of those cupcakes."

"See, that's Irv," Joe explains. "He's using you as an excuse to break his diet. So, what's up with the mutt?"

"The dog's part of the investigation."

Dante's patience is already wearing thin—he's got plenty to do—but it's apparent that if he wants to hear what the twins have to say, which he does, he won't be going anywhere soon. He settles into a chair as Pug drops onto a carpet thick enough to pass for a mattress.

"First thing, let me thank you in advance for your cooperation," he says. "I know we all want the same thing. We want your cousin's murderer to pay the price for what he did."

"Yeah, we do," Irv says. "But about Asher, which is why you're here." He waits for Dante to nod, then begins a rapid-fire exchange with his twin. "The first thing you should know about Asher is that he was a loser."

"All his life, Detective."

"We loved him, right?"

"Right, Irv. As kids, the three of us, me, Irv and Asher, we always hung out together."

"And Asher, he was always . . . What's the word, Joe?"

"Unpopular? Unaccepted? Low man on the totem pole?"

"Bullied, Joe. That's the word. Asher was bullied at school, starting in kindergarten. He wanted to be a tough guy, but the only person he convinced was himself."

Bearing a large tray, Cynthia chooses that moment to return. There's a carafe on the tray, along with three Schuster & Schuster mugs and a half-dozen mini-doughnuts topped with sea-green frosting.

Dante nibbles dutifully at one of the doughnuts and nods, though he finds the frosting overly sweet. "Excellent, now . . ."

"Excuse me." Cynthia pops back into the room, the tray now tucked beneath her arm. "It's Clarence Lorrianko. For Irv."

Irv Schuster's face darkens momentarily. "You'll excuse me, Detective, but I have to take this."

Dante's not unhappy to see Irv go. He and his brother obviously enjoy playing off each other, bouncing the conversation back and forth with the apparent ease of vaudevillians, but there's work to be done.

"Mr. Schuster . . ."

"Joe, please. I'm on your side."

"Joe, then." Dante leans forward to lay his arms on the table. "Let me be frank, Joe. Asher's unhappy childhood? That's for the family, not the police. I'm here in the hope that you have information directly related to the hijacking."

"You want to know if Asher shot off his big mouth. That it?"

"Yeah, that's exactly it. See, I think I know who killed Asher, but I don't have enough to arrest him and it's drivin' me crazy."

Joe sits back in his chair, smile gone, his blue eyes suddenly focused. "Speaking of the family, we're worried about you putting Asher at the center of a crime. The boy's dead, Detective, and his mother doesn't want to think of him that way. If it should become public knowledge . . ."

Dante traces the grain on the table's surface with a fingertip as he considers his response, what to reveal, what to conceal. Finally, he says, "What might or might not be introduced at trial is up to the prosecutor. My job is to gather as much evidence as possible, then pass it along. That said, we currently plea bargain more than ninety percent of all indictments, in which case there's no trial and no public record."

"OK, but that doesn't tell me why you think Asher committed a crime. Is there hard evidence? Or are you guessing?"

"What we have is a video of the entire incident, from beginning to end. This video shows the Legrand Truck climbing the hill at 141st Street. It's maybe two thirds of the way up when a car, a Lincoln, pulls into the intersection at Convent Avenue, blocking the truck. The Lincoln's driver—that would be Asher—then approaches the truck, raises the hood, and begins to work inside. A second man appears at the same time. He pulls the driver out of the truck and holds him at gunpoint. A few minutes later, the man with the gun and the man working under the hood get into an argument. A few seconds after that, Asher's shot for the first time."

"And you think the second man, the man with the gun, is Mike Tedesco?"

"That's exactly right."

"And you have a video?"

"Yeah, but the shooter wore a mask and it was raining hard, so the video can't be used to make an identification. Otherwise, Tedesco would already be in jail."

Joe Schuster pulls an electronic cigarette from his pants pocket. "You mind?"

"Knock yourself out."

Joe puffs away for a moment, then begins to speak, his tone steady. "Asher wanted to be a tough guy. It doesn't exactly make sense, but that's how it was going all the way back. And Mike Tedesco? I only had a few real conversations with Tedesco, but every time I felt like I was being probed. Like he was examining a business plan, lookin' to make a profit. Irv felt the same way. Tedesco's a natural predator. So, with Asher . . ."

"Moth to a flame?"

"You got it. And we tried to warn him, me and Irv, only Asher wouldn't listen. He kept talking about a big break and how he was gonna make changes in his life. No more overalls. No more grease so thick under his fingernails that he can't scrub it out. No more paychecks so small that he can't afford his own apartment. Asher's gonna take his fate into his own hands. He's gonna make his own luck."

"Did he mention Tedesco?"

"No, but Irv did. First thing, Irv said, 'Don't tell me you're hooked up with Mike Tedesco. Because, this asshole's been to prison once and he's gonna go back. That's his only fate. You don't need to make it yours.'"

Dante reaches for another piece of doughnut, then changes his mind. "Did Asher respond?"

"Yeah, he shrugged and said, 'A man's gotta do what a man's gotta do.' That was two days before the jerk got himself killed. Two days before he broke his mother's heart." Joe raises his head, finally meeting Dante's gaze. "That it, Detective?"

"One more question, Joe, and if there was any way to avoid asking it, I would. Was Asher gay?"

"How is that relevant?"

"C'mon, man. Yes or no?"

Joe nods once. "Yeah, he was, only his mother didn't know. You understand? This is not something she needs to deal with after he's dead."

TWENTY-EIGHT

Joe Schuster's tale isn't definitive, not at all, but it does qualify as evidence in a circumstantial case. And that, Dante's coming to believe, will probably be vital, the cumulative weight of all those coincidences finally pulling Tedesco beneath the waves, finally drowning the son-of-a-bitch. Even without José, even without turning Skippy Legrand.

As he drives over the Pulaski Bridge, from Queens into Brooklyn, Dante reviews his schedule. The dog first. Myra Cuffee mentioned the presence of a dog at the crime scene, a dog that left with the shooter, and the St. Mark's video confirms her version. That makes the battered pit bull another piece of evidence, another rock in the bag already dragging Tedesco down. Evidence, of course, has to be preserved, but the dog can't be put on a storage shelf in the property clerk's warehouse, and Dante isn't prepared to trust his welfare to the pound. Pug's on his way to Sanda Dragomir's Sunset Park apartment.

The dog also factors into another stop Dante plans to make. At some point during the day, he'll visit Legrand Transportation and ask Skippy a simple question. Who brought the dog to work? Then he'll brace Skippy's workers, see if they confirm his version.

He can work on Skippy at the same time. Dante's making it 80–20 that Skippy breaks at some point. It's only a matter of applying the right pressure.

At the moment, Dante's priority is José Sepulveda, or Herrera, or whatever he's calling himself today. But the dog has to go first because it's way too hot to leave him in the car and he's too ugly to inflict on cooperative witnesses. Dante smiles, imagining the dog being led into a courtroom, the jury gasping at his condition and blaming Tedesco for every scar.

Dante finds Sanda's door at the top of the stairs unlocked, as she'd promised when he called ahead. Sanda's at her computer, seated on a battered office chair. She looks from the dog to Dante and back again, a thin, speculative smile playing at the corners of her mouth.

"You have bought a pet?"

"Not exactly . . ."

Pug ends the exchange when he abruptly crosses the living room and sits at Sanda's feet, his eyes rising to meet hers, his tongue hanging through the gap on the right side of his mouth. Sanda stares back for a moment, then her rock-hard eyes soften and she drops to her knees, her fingertips curling around the dog's ears.

"What is dog's name?"

"No idea."

Pug moans softly as Sanda's scratches the hollow spaces behind his ears. His eyes close for a moment, then open into narrow slits. To Dante, he seems about as content as a living creature can be, the past forgotten, as if it never happened.

"I think he is very brave," Sanda says. "He does not give up, even after this." She gestures to Pug's scars. "He does not turn away from own life."

"Like he didn't turn away from a fight?"

"Yes, this. Always he wants to go forward. I will call him Marius after brother I once have. Very brave man, my brother, and always seeing sun through the clouds. They kill him, yes? Gangsters? For what reason I do not know. One night, he didn't come home. Two weeks later, he is found floating in Dambovita Canal."

Dante's touched, truly, but he recognizes the bad news. "So, this dog, Marius, he doesn't belong to Mike Tedesco?"

"Mike does not have pet, not even goldfish. He is too selfish for this."

"Do you know where he might have picked up a dog?"

"Please, Dante, no more talk of Mike. See Marius? He is smart dog to put the past in the past."

Dante's eyes harden. Whatever he's got going with Sanda, it's not love and not likely to become love. "I'm gonna ask you a question, Sanda, but I don't want you to answer right away. I want you to think about it. Mike and Asher? I know they had plans together and I think you know it too. I also think you can help me put Mike Tedesco where he belongs, which is in some hellhole of a maximum-security prison. So, I'm asking you to tell me what you know about Asher's and Mike's plan to hijack a Legrand Transportation truck. How often did you see them together? Where and when did you see them together? And if there was pillow talk between you and Mike, I want to hear every word."

"You would throw me away for this, Dante?"

"I'm a predator, Sanda, like every other detective. I'm a predator on the hunt and Tedesco's my food. If you feed him to me, I'll be ever so grateful. I'll even let you scratch my ears. But if you don't help me? If I stay hungry? Well, how do you know that I won't eat you instead?"

Dante looks back as he goes through the door, at Marius, who still hasn't taken his eyes off Sanda Dragomir.

Dante's walking back to his car, still pissed off by Sanda's reaction, which was not to react at all, when he decides that what he really needs is leverage. Sanda's not the giving type. That much he knew going in.

So, it's time for a change of tactics. Dante places a call to Lieutenant Barnwell, finding her in a decent mood with the Yankees coming off an 8–0 win. Dante wants Barnwell to place a call to the chief of detective's office at One Police Plaza. By Sanda's own admission, she earned her right to become an American citizen by informing on a former boyfriend. If she isn't lying outright, she has to be a confidential informant with her name and history registered in the data files kept at 1PP. So, what did she do and when did she do it? And to what individual or agency is she currently beholden? And is there anything, any little bit he can use against her?

Dante knows Barnwell to be a gung-ho type and scrupulous about keeping her promises. She makes a commitment now, to call over, request a favor. It's this last part that assures Dante. The lieutenant's not going to put in a formal request, not going to fill out the paperwork and wait for the boys to come through. She's going to access her personal network, a strategy much more likely to produce results in real time. Instead of cop-bureaucracy time.

Twenty minutes later, Dante completes the run from Sunset Park in Brooklyn to Sunnyside in Queens without encountering a breakdown, an accident, or a road repair crew. He finds parking as well, only a block from Sofia Herrera's apartment. He's already considered his options, sadly limited by his threat to return with enforcement officers from ICE. If Sofia's still living in the apartment, she'll know he's full of shit. On the other hand, if she believed him, she's probably gone.

The old man answers Dante's knock. He looks Dante up and down, but doesn't move out of the way or attempt to close the door.

"*¿Como te llamas?*" Dante asks, his tone sharp. What's your name?

"Francisco Herrera," the man replies. "Do you want to see my driver's license?"

Dante smiles. Francisco has only a trace of a Spanish accent. Without doubt, he's been in the country for many years, probably from boyhood, and he's also a citizen, whether because he immigrated legally or took advantage of the Reagan amnesty in 1987. The situation—a mix of legal and illegal immigrants, usually related, living in the same apartment—is one Dante's encountered many times, the advantages obvious enough.

"That's all right, Francisco. Keep your driver's license in your pocket, but get out of my way. I'm looking for Sofia."

Francisco doesn't argue the point. Although his harsh expression remains firmly in place, he steps aside.

Dante traverses the hallway to again find Sofia on the couch, only this time, she's sewing what appears to be a First Communion dress. A Latino soap opera, a *telenovela*, is plays on a large flat screen, but she pauses the show when Dante appears.

"You have come back," she says, her own English heavily accented. "Please, sit."

Dante obeys, lowering himself into a chair and crossing his legs. Francisco joins him, choosing a chair as far away from Dante as possible. Another example of Latino macho, or so Dante thinks. The man has to show his disdain.

"There is coffee, if you wish," Sofia says.

"I can definitely use a cup, Mrs. Herrera. I've been running all morning."

"Cisco, *por favor*."

Francisco rises from his chair, a sure indicator of who's paying the rent, and heads for the kitchen. Sofia continues to sew, her needle diving into the many pleats and folds of the white dress, then rising up before plunging again. She only stops for a moment when her two children peek around an arched opening that leads to the bedrooms.

"*En su habitación*," Sofia says, her tone even. Go back to your room.

The children seem confused to Dante, confused and frightened. Where is Papi? Why hasn't Papi come home? This is good for Dante, the bottom line of his argument. He relaxes into the chair as he awaits Francisco's return, and even then, he sips at a mug of incredibly strong coffee several times before speaking.

"Your children don't seem all that happy, Sofia," he says.

Sofia finally looks at Dante. In her thirties, she's a pretty woman, with dark eyes that reflect her exhaustion. Almost surely, she and her children live their lives at the economic margins. Now they face utter chaos.

"They miss their *papi*," Francisco says.

Dante turns to stare for a moment into Francisco's eyes, then says, "They want him back, I understand that. And by the way, I've checked José out and I know he was a good man." This part is true. Even beyond the witness and the video, Skippy's bookkeeper described José as a "mouse." Dante leans forward, drawing Francisco into his space, and raises a finger. "But I think it's pretty clear by now. José can't come home as long as Mike Tedesco's on the street."

"And whose fault is that?"

Dante hesitates for a second before delivering the same message he delivered the day before. "It's Mike Tedesco's fault. His and his alone. But there's a way out, a simple way out. If Mike Tedesco's arrested, he'll be charged with murder and he won't get bail. *¿Comprende?* No chance, no how. He'll be held without bail and get a sentence, at minimum, of fifteen-to-life. That's problem solved, Francisco. That's José coming home to his family."

"Not if you arrest José."

"I have an eyewitness and a video of the hijacking. The man who yanked José out of the truck put a gun to his head. José's not a suspect."

"So you say."

Dante's not insulted. In fact, he's been thinking about taking José into custody, as a material witness. Call it a guaranteed outcome. No judge, given José's illegal status, would cut him loose until the case is resolved.

"Look," he says, "here's the bottom line. José's in hiding and I'm willing to leave him there until I arrest Tedesco. I'll meet him anywhere he chooses. All I want is a written, signed statement identifying Tedesco as the shooter. At that point, trust me on this, your problems will disappear."

TWENTY-NINE

Dante's pleased with his smooth delivery, which he instantly deems convincing, but his satisfaction proves to be short-lived. First, even as the sound of his voice lingers in the room, he hears a sharp knock on the door. Then, less than minute later, Francisco Herrera leads two uniformed police officers, a sergeant and a patrolman, into the living room. The sergeant steps forward, drawing a sharp breath quite familiar to Dante. She's come to deliver the bad news.

"Are you Sofia Sepulveda?" she asks.

"*Sí.*"

"Is José Sepulveda your husband?"

Sofia's voice drops to a whisper and she begins to tremble. "*Sí.*"

"I'm very sorry to tell you this, but your husband was pronounced dead earlier this morning. A homicide, ma'am. He was the victim."

"How . . ."

"I don't know, ma'am, but you'll definitely hear from the detectives investigating the case. They'll want to talk to you."

Although Dante closes his eyes and locks his jaw, the sound that erupts from Sofia—not a moan or a cry, but something far more elemental—grips him all the harder for his being taken by surprise. What Dante feels at that moment is something like fear, something like the emotions that swept through him all those years before when he finally realized that he'd been abandoned. He compensates by telling himself that he'll find some excuse to kill Mike Tedesco, that it's eye-for-an-eye time. Does he mean it? Dante's not sure, but he feels better anyway.

The sergeant's name tag reads Federer, and she appears relieved when Dante flashes his gold shield. Neither of them, Dante knows, has any comfort to offer, not to Sofia, not to Francisco, who stands in the middle of the room, tears flowing along the deep seams in his cheeks, and especially not to the children. Resigned, he takes Federer into the hallway.

"This guy, José, he witnessed a homicide," Dante explains. "I've been trying to locate him for two days."

"Well, you won't have any problem now. Sepulveda bought it in Joyce Kilmer Park, in the Bronx."

"Where in the Bronx?"

"On the Grand Concourse, a couple of blocks from Yankee Stadium."

Dante considers his options for a moment, then says, "Are you gonna put a uniform on the door, make sure nobody disappears?"

"Absolutely, I got someone on the way. What about you? Is this your beef?"

"Me and José's killer, we both started lookin' for José at the same time. He got there first. So, yeah, it's definitely my beef. I failed José and I take full responsibility."

Just like, he tells himself, *I failed Paco Altoona, who disappeared without a trace.* Dante, along with several other kids, had pestered the counselors with questions about the search for Paco. Those questions had stopped when one of those counselors, Mrs.

Bingham, had turned on them. The cops, she'd explained, her hand on her hips, think he went into the river.

A detective named Ike Samuelson guides Dante through the crime scene. Samuelson's grateful for the intel on Mike Tedesco and the Legrand hijacking. No mystery here, praise the Lord and pass the chicken. A suspect has been dropped into his lap. Dante's grateful as well. In this case for the sheet that conceals José's body.

"All we know is that Sepulveda was sittin' on the bench when someone shoved a knife into his back. The perp didn't bother to pull it out, which limited bleeding, but still . . ."

Samuelson gestures to a pool of coagulating blood on the grass beneath the bench. The blood is the color of the chocolate in a lava cake.

"He must've stayed upright for some time before he fell off the bench and a bystander called nine-one-one. I'm gonna leave exactly how long up to the lab rats, but I'm guessin' anywhere from thirty seconds to a couple of minutes."

Dante looks around. The closest security cameras are on the other side of Grand Concourse Boulevard, ten lanes away and screened by trees planted in the median. There are no cameras in the park.

"Any wits?" he asks.

"No witnesses, not yet, but we're still canvassing." Samuelson waves his arm at the surrounding neighborhood. "This is the South Bronx. The good citizens mostly aren't stupid enough to testify against the bad citizens. Especially, if the crime looks like a professional hit, which this crime definitely does. Plus, you gotta figure, if the vic didn't fall off the bench right away, if he just sat there and died, it could be that no one noticed."

More good news. "What about the knife?" Dante asks.

"A hunting knife, big blade. Won't get the maker's name until it's pulled out of his back." Samuelson glances over his shoulder, at a cluster of pines separating the pathway and the bench from the sidewalk. "Way I figure, the perp came from between the trees and slammed the knife into the vic's back, one stroke, and then fled the scene. José what's-his-name didn't see it coming and he probably died before he figured it out. Here, you wanna see?"

With no ready alternative, Dante follows Samuelson around the bench. They stare down for a moment at the sheet covering José. Taken from the trunk of a cop's car, it's dirty, threadbare, and stained with blood. But it does shield José from the assembled gawkers standing fifty feet away behind a double row of crime-scene tape. That, and whatever dignity it confers, is about to end. Dante can almost feel the gawkers draw a collective breath. Time for the show.

Samuelson pulls the sheet down, revealing José Herrera to Dante for the first time. A small man, José's head is arched and his unseeing eyes stare out, blank and empty. His lips are drawn back, exposing prominent front teeth, the teeth, Dante decides, of a mouse. As Dante kneels to examine the knife still in José's back, he wonders if Tedesco took even a fraction of a second to consider the consequences before he drove the knife into José with such force that it's now buried to the hilt.

Dante reviews his options as he rises. The Crime Scene Unit and a death examiner from the ME's office are expected momentarily. The forensic equivalent of a paralegal, the death examiner will conduct a preliminary examination before José's body is shipped to the morgue, the knife still in his back. There it will remain until the pathologist conducting the autopsy first removes, then examines it, weighing and measuring, swabbing the handle and blade for DNA testing. Knife and swabs will then go upstairs, to the ME's testing lab, one of the finest in the country, where a technician will check it for prints. Dante's not holding out hope when it come to the prints. He's not thinking that Tedesco's a fool. Nevertheless, there's a distinct possibility that Tedesco's DNA will turn up. Of course, he might have purchased the knife recently and never touched it with his bare hands, or even breathed on it. Or he might have scrubbed the handle and blade with bleach and a toothbrush, then worn gloves when he slammed it into José's back. But the ME's forensic lab can detect microscopic amounts of DNA, as little as five cells, then amplify it until they have enough to match against a known sample like Mike Tedesco's. The process, unfortunately, will take months, way too long to leave him on the street.

Dante uses his cell phone to take a quick photo before Samuelson again covers the body. Dante's thinking that Tedesco knows the system, inside and out, which means he also knows that once he's charged with a murder committed in the course of a robbery, he'll be denied bail. And even if he eventually secures an acquittal or the charges are dismissed, he'll spend many months on Rikers Island.

That's why he's taking care of business while he can. He's cutting his losses, correcting his mistakes, limiting, as the pols say, his exposure, and there's only one important question left to answer. Who's next?

"So, whatta ya say?"

"About what?"

"About takin' the case?" Samuelson's eyes blaze with hope. "You wanna fold it into your investigation?"

"Are you askin' me if I wanna hang out in Joyce Kilmer Park for the next five hours? Are you askin' me if I wanna spend three hours after that doin' paperwork?"

"Well . . ."

"Don't answer, Detective, the thing speaks for itself."

THIRTY

t's not a sure thing, Skippy Legrand tells himself, *because there's no such thing as a sure thing.* Meanwhile, his heart's pounding like the hooves of a ten-horse field in mid-stretch. With three minutes to post, the horses entered in the first race at Monmouth Park, a six-furlong sprint, are approaching the gate. Including Byron Candell's five-year-old gelding, Call Me Later.

Skippy's done his homework, looking deep into Call Me Later's past, including races that don't appear in the current *Daily Racing Form.* A year ago, the horse was competing in allowance races, winning twice and consistently finishing in the money. Now, after a series of new owners, he's been entered in a fifteen-thousand-dollar claiming race, running against the lowest of the low. Skippy's checked out every other horse in the eight-horse field and these pigs don't look as if they'll make it from the starting gate to the turn at the end of the backstretch. Of course, that can also be said of Call Me Later, and Skippy would have zero interest in the animal if he wasn't trained by Candell. Skippy's cleaned up on Byron Candell several times in the past, relying exclusively on the trainer's bad reputation. Candell never wins when the odds are short, never. Instead, he dopes his horses, loading them up with ketamine, until they're too sluggish to compete. He gets away with this tactic because only the first four horses across the finish line are drug-tested.

Call Me Later is a perfect example. Last year, when he was still competitive, the gelding went to the front every time out. Meanwhile, for the past six months, he's been running at the back of the pack, the only clue to his relative fitness a pair of workouts where he ran five furlongs in a few ticks over a minute.

Was this brief display a little test on Candell's part, maybe to be certain that his horse still had that good speed? More important, how likely is it that Candell, given the cost of shipping the animal from Aqueduct to Monmouth Park, came to lose?

There's no such thing as a sure thing, Skippy again tells himself, the proof becoming apparent a few seconds later when Detective Dante Cepeda, his shirt soaked with sweat, walks into the office. Skippy watches in disbelief as Cepeda closes the door behind him. Martha Proctor having gone outside for a cigarette, that leaves the two of them alone.

"Whatta ya say, Skip?"

Skippy glances at the monitor. He's got fifteen thousand dollars tied up in this race, nine to win and the rest in exactas with Call Me Later on the top and bottom. If the horse finishes first with the right horse second, Skippy could pocket as much as three hundred grand.

"I thought I told you already," Skippy complains, "that I'm exercising my right to remain silent."

"Grow up, Skippy, this is the real world. You don't have to answer, but I still get to ask my questions." Dante hesitates for just a moment, then says, "First, who owns the dog, you or Mike?"

Skippy smells the trap, though he can't quite see it. He's angry, as well. Only yesterday, he told Mike to get rid of the dog, but the asshole didn't listen, as fucking usual.

"It ain't my dog," he tells Dante, "and that's all I got to say on the subject."

"OK, then try this one. Tedesco was here this morning when I showed up, but now he's gone. Tell me when he left."

"I don't know exactly?"

"An hour ago? Two? Three? Five minutes after I took off?"

"I don't know exactly."

"Did he sign out? Did he punch a clock?"

"No and fucking no."

"You're tellin' me he sets his own hours? He comes and goes whenever he wants?"

Again Skippy glances at the monitor. The last horse is being led into the gate. "Look, I don't have time for this bullshit. Why don't you go back to wherever the fuck you came from and get a warrant?"

"Because we're not finished. In fact, I'm just gettin' started."

Skippy curses, under his breath to be sure. He's got a big problem. Martha Proctor's outside because Skippy gets crazy when he watches a race, especially when he loses, and she wants no part of his tantrums. But there's no room for tantrums here, not with the cop watching, and Skippy resolves to play his cards close to the vest. That resolution vanishes when the starting gate slams open and the track announcer, Frank Mirahmadi, shouts, "And they're off!"

It's almost as if Call Me Later is the only horse to heed Mirahmadi's words. The gelding charges out of the gate from the five hole, accelerating so fast that Skippy's reminded of a time when jockeys concealed small batteries, called buzzers, in the palms of their hands. The gelding's four lengths ahead after an eighth of a mile and ten lengths in front at the quarter pole. Better yet, he appears to be running smoothly, hugging the rail, saving ground.

"Please, Lord, please, please, please." Skippy's jaw is so tight he can barely get the words out. His hands have tightened into fists and his knees literally shake. "Just this once," he says, giving voice to a sentiment he's expressed many times in the past. "Just this once and I'll never ask you again."

Call Me Later maintains his lead almost to the head of the stretch before he begins to fade. Skippy watches the jock's whip rise and fall, rise and fall, but the gelding fails to respond and his stride shortens. The only good news is that Skippy was right about Call Me Later's competition. These pigs can't run a foot and nobody emerges from the pack to challenge. Instead, they come up on Call Me Later in a wave, like a pack of wolves in pursuit of a lumbering buffalo. Skippy can almost hear them howl.

His hands on his desk, his breathing shallow, Skippy leans forward. *Not now*, he thinks, *not now when I'm so goddamned close.*

"Run, you fucking pig," he screams. "Run, run, run."

In fact, the race actually seems to slow, the gap between Call Me Later and his competitors narrowing with every stride, until Skippy feels it will go on forever, a preview of the hell that surely awaits him. But the last eighth of a mile does eventually become a sixteenth, and the sixteenth does narrow into a hundred yards, then fifty, then ten, until the entire field, including Call Me Later, sweeps across the finish line.

The camera moves to the tote board and Skippy's eyes widen as he waits for the order of finish to be posted. The PHOTO FINISH light comes on instead, its crimson letters seeming to actually mock him. So close, so close, so close. It's the story of your miserable fucking life.

"I think the four horse got it," Dante says.

"Yeah? You think?" Call Me Later is horse number five.

"Sure, it's a lock. But, hey, Skippy, I didn't come here to harass you. Really, I'm a results-oriented guy. I don't believe in wasting time. But there's something I want to show you, something you have a right to see. I mean, it was your cigarettes on that truck, right?"

Dante doesn't wait for a reply. He takes out his phone, pulls up a photo of José that reveals both his face and the knife in his back. "Check this out," he says before dropping the phone onto Skippy's desk.

Skippy doesn't want to look, absolutely, 100 percent does not, but the image is impossible to ignore. It's that dead thing, nobody home, that gets to him, even more than the knife. Skippy's father had cautioned him: Don't make friends with your employees because they're only a means to an end. But José? Talk about harmless? Talk about hardworking? Talking about making the most of a shitty deal? The little jerk never stopped smiling.

"You with me?" Dante asks.

Skippy looks up. "I don't know nothin' about this." He gestures to the photo. "I was here all that morning and I got ten people can swear to it."

"Stop with the bullshit. I'm not makin' an accusation and we both know it." Again, Dante hesitates. "Look, Skippy, Tedesco's comin' for you, sooner or later, and we both know that too. Not here with all the cameras and witnesses. Mike'll try to catch you unaware, like he caught José, who was sitting on a park bench in the Bronx, one minute alive and the next dead. And you? You have a choice. If you give Tedesco up, I'll put him in a cage for the next twenty-five years. If you don't? Best go about your business armed. Best have eyes in the back of your head. Best be sure you have a will and it's up-to-date."

A bell sounds from the monitor's small speakers and Skippy eyes leap to the screen. The Photo Finish light is off and the order of finish has been posted with the four horse, Black Light, on top, and Call Me Later second. Skippy has five hundred dollars on the 4-5 combination.

The various payoffs have also been posted. Black Light, fifth choice in the race, is paying $18.90 for every $2.00 bet on the horse to win. The exacta payoff, $256.80 is even better, what with Call Me Later a twenty-to-one shot.

Skippy tries the math in his head, but he's off his game and he finally resorts to Martha Proctor's calculator. Five hundred divided by two, multiplied by $256.80. The number that pops us, $64,200, while not the gigantic payoff he'd envisioned, is nevertheless satisfying. He's eighty fat ones to the good over the last two days and he's got a legal, 9 mm Sig-Sauer in the middle drawer of his desk. Mike Tedesco's not gonna stop him, and neither is this cop.

"I'm only gonna say this once, Detective," he announces. "If you don't fuck off, I'm gonna call my lawyer and ask him to get a restraining order. Maybe I'll sue your dumb ass, too, for harassment."

Skippy watches the cop leave, thinking good riddance, but a minute later his phone gives off a little ping. It's a text message from the cop, no words, just José with the knife in his back and that gone-goodbye expression on his face.

"Shit," Skippy mutters as Martha Proctor walks into the office. "Shit, shit, shit."

Her response is prompt. "Skippy, you promised. No more cursing when you lose."

THIRTY-ONE

Mike Tedesco wracks his brain in search of an explanation that doesn't mean what he knows it means. He's sitting behind the wheel of his Dodge Charger, watching Sanda Dragomir walk toward him. She holds a small blue purse, leather probably, in her left hand. In her right, she holds a leash that runs to the collar spanning Pug's thick neck.

How could this happen?

The question answers itself because there's only one possibility. It tears into the center of his mind and implants itself like a remora on the belly of a shark. Sanda's fucking Dante Cepeda.

In the blink of an eye, right? Out with the old, in with the new, the "in" part to be taken literally.

Tedesco sucks in a breath as he shuts off the engine and opens the door. He's thinking he should just kill the bitch and be done with it. And he would, too, except for the witnesses sitting on their stoops and in their tiny front yards. And then there's the distinct possibility—no, the likelihood—that she's armed.

Sanda stops in her tracks when Tedesco steps onto the sidewalk, but her features remain without a trace of fear. Pug stops beside her.

He also remains composed, though he does glance up at his new master, perhaps for direction.

"The mutt's got a short memory," Tedesco says. "Only this morning, he was eatin' out of my hand."

"What are you wanting, Mike?"

"Gotta give it to ya, baby. You always get right to the point." He kneels to scratch Pug's head. "But I was just wonderin'. What did it feel like, watchin' Paulie Bancroft die after you put a bullet in him? You feel bad? Good? Tell me what?"

Sanda draws a long breath. She's exasperated, that much is obvious, though exactly why eludes Tedesco. The question, to him, seems perfectly reasonable, and he only asks because he's curious. He's killed two men this morning and he's so jacked up that he can barely keep his feet on the ground.

"When I was a child in Romania, men are using me for a toy. They take my heart and my soul, and now I am left to live life without these things. So, when man you call Paulie comes to hurt me, I prevent him from succeeding. How long do you remember cockroach after you step on him?"

Tedesco manages a tight grin as he gets to his feet. He wants to smash her, to punch her in the face, to keep on going until she's dead. And not even because she's a threat, though she is. It's because she's telling the goddamned truth, because she'd grind Mike Tedesco into the dirt if it became necessary, because she'd put a bullet in his head, then go out to lunch, maybe have a glass of wine by way of a celebration.

"You took my money," he says. "I paid the rent, the cable, the electric, but now you're tellin' me to get out. That ain't right, Sanda. And it ain't right that you're fuckin' the cop, either. It's like you're goin' out of your way to shit on me."

"You are doomed man. You are man who dooms himself. You are ship I am not to go down with."

Tedesco wipes the sweat from his brow. They're standing beneath an oak that towers over the surrounding houses, but the dense shade offers little relief. It's been like that all day, even inside the car with the air-conditioning on full blast. He can't shake the feeling that he's being driven.

"Doomed? Maybe so, but I'm not a punk you can dismiss with a wave of your hand. You don't wanna go down with the ship, don't chain yourself to the mast. Just about everything I own is in your apartment and I want my property. I'm tired of wearin' the same clothes every day."

Once again, Tedesco struggles with the urge to kill her on the spot. If he's doomed—and he doesn't really dispute Sanda's judgment—what difference does it make? Kill her and the dog, both of 'em, then take off for parts unknown. He's got his weapons and his money in the trunk, and even if he doesn't get far, he can make the world pay a price to bring him down.

Tedesco's train of thought is interrupted by a rumble that reminds him of a subway train approaching a station. But the rumble's emerging from Pug's barrel chest and not from a tunnel in the ground. Tedesco reaches beneath his jacket as Sanda reaches into her purse. Both come to a halt when a baby-blue cop car turns onto the block. He watches it slowly approach, watches it pull to the curb, watches the window roll down, and a female officer wearing a sergeant's stripes lean out.

"Is that a rescue?" she says, pointing at Pug, who, no fool, abruptly stops growling.

An hour later, Tedesco's in a ratty hotel room near La Guardia Airport, unpacking his three suitcases. He's wondering what to do next as he watches a cockroach wander across the far wall. One part of him wants to sleep, to lie down and not wake up until the nightmare ends. Another part knows that sleep is out of the question and if he wants the nightmare to end, he'll have to write the final act himself.

Once his clothes are sorted, he jumps into the shower, his first in a couple of hot summer days. The water is tepid and the bar of soap, unwrapped, is the size of a credit card. He'll have to buy a few things if he means to stay beyond tomorrow morning.

The shower refreshes him, despite the greasy tiles on the bathroom floor, and he dresses quickly, reaching last for the bracelet given him by Daniela. He's tempted to throw it away, but that would be admitting that he's out of control, something he'd vowed to never let happen. Finally, after a brief hesitation, he slides the bracelet over his wrist. Daniela's god, Ogun, is a god of war, afraid of none, feared by all. That's good, right?

Tedesco laughs softly. He knows one man who doesn't fear him, a man who punched him in the chest, then turned his back and sauntered off. That would be Dante Cepeda.

So, it's back to the real world, back to his real problems. Tedesco heads out to the Buccaneer Diner on Astoria Boulevard, only a short distance from the motel. The Buccaneer is legendary, a finalist every year for best diner in New York. Its menu is eight pages long, broken into a dozen categories. From The Grill, From The Sea, from a fajitas omelet to prune hamantaschen. Tedesco enjoys a full meal, onion soup, tossed salad, fried shrimp, and sautéed broccoli. He lets his mind wander as he eats, admitting almost from the beginning that the situation's become personal. He wants to hurt Dante Cepeda, his hatred for the man running back to their days at the Youth Hope Center. They couldn't avoid each other—the home was too small for that—and Tedesco had endured the contempt in Dante's eyes rather than risk losing the fight sure to follow a challenge. Tedesco had put the issue behind him on the morning Dante left Youth Hope, but the man had turned up again. Wearing a badge. Carrying a gun. Determined to put Mike Tedesco in prison for the rest of his unnatural life.

THIRTY-TWO

When Tedesco walks into his office at seven o'clock, Skippy Legrand's sitting behind his desk. He's got a 9 mm Colt taped to the bottom of the desk, right between his legs. Trust is not an issue here. No, the issue, for Skippy, is the Yankees-Orioles game. Scheduled to begin immediately, the players are already on the field. Skippy's got a three-bet parley going here, a parley that began earlier in the afternoon, when he put five grand on the Boston Red Sox. The Sox were playing a day game in Fenway Park, and they won going away. His winnings, plus the five he'd bet, are now riding on the division-leading Yankees. If they win, the total will carry forward to a Dodgers-Astros game being played later on the West Coast. If the Astros win that game, what with the varying odds, he'll be up approximately thirty-six grand.

As with his bet on Call Me Later, Skippy's divided his parley between several offshore casinos. To him, even the biggest casinos have one thing in common with every neighborhood bookie. If they owe you too much, you'll never get paid.

"You look like shit," Skippy observes, "like you're ready to jump out of your skin."

Tedesco drops into a chair on the other side of the desk. "That's what comes of doin' somebody else's dirty work."

"Asher wasn't my idea. Alebev and his bodyguard, either. And now José. You told me nobody would get hurt." Skippy walks over to a small refrigerator next to the window. He removes a bottle of vodka from the unit's tiny freezer, pours two stiff ones into a pair of coffee mugs, and carries them back to the desk, carefully examining Tedesco on the way.

Covered by an oversized, short-sleeve shirt, there's a slight bulge at the waistband of Tedesco's pale slacks, the sort of bulge any cop would spot. But Skippy's not a cop and he's thinking, *If I kill the prick now, just reach beneath the desk and pull the trigger, nobody could prove it wasn't self-defense.* Tedesco is, after all, the prime suspect in two murders and a hijacking. But Skippy can't bring himself to make the move. He's a businessman with a gambling problem, not a killer.

"The cop, Cepeda, was here a couple of hours ago," he says.

"That I already figured. What'd he want?"

"He showed me a photograph. José with a knife in his back. Then he appealed to my conscience."

"And what'd you say?"

"Talk to my lawyer."

They drop into an uneasy silence as the Yankees' pitcher, James Taillon, throws his first pitch to Cedric Mullins, a sinking fastball that darts below the batter's knees. Undaunted, the free-swinging Jones drops the barrel of the bat on the ball and lifts it into the right-field seats.

"Who'd you bet on?" Tedesco asks.

Skippy doesn't reply, but the answer becomes pretty obvious after a few minutes as the Oriole lineup, one of the weakest in baseball, pounces on Taillon. Watching, Tedesco almost feels sorry for the Yankee pitcher. Taillon's desperation shows in his eyes and the set of his shoulders and the way he circles the mound after every pitch. If his performance doesn't pick up, he'll be riding a bus for some minor league team. And he knows it.

Five runners later, with the Orioles up 6–0, Taillon records the last out on a leaping grab by the Yankees' center fielder, Brett Gardner, and Skippy settles back in his chair. He's on the run of his life. He can't lose. He could pick winners out of a hat.

Invincible, he thinks, *that's the word*. Then he opens his eyes to find Tedesco with a knowing little smile on his face.

"You got a problem?" he asks.

"I got lots of problems, Skip, which you already know."

"How about José? Was he a problem? How'd it feel to whack a man you worked alongside for almost a year."

"It felt lucky, Skip."

"Lucky?"

"Yeah, lucky. See, I had an apartment number and an address when I drove up to the Bronx. But I had no fuckin' idea how I was gonna get into that apartment, or how many cameras I'd have to pass along the way. So, what I did was dump the car in a space near this little park on the Grand Concourse and take a look around. Man, I could not believe what I was seein'. There he is, sittin' on a park bench, half-asleep, with nobody near him and no cameras in the park. As for what I did next? Well, some guys have all the luck and some guys never catch a break from the minute they first draw breath to the minute their hearts stop. José fits into the last category like he was made for it. And by the way, I gave the little jerk a choice. José told me he had a brother on the West Coast, and I told him to pay the man a visit or pay the price. He decided to stay in New York where the cops could lay their hands him. You gettin' this Skippy? It was José's own fault. You wanna blame someone, blame him."

Skippy's mouth is hanging open. He understands the threat behind Tedesco's explanation, understands it fully. Asher, Alebev, Alebev's muscle, José Sepulveda. Adding Skippy's name to the list wouldn't cost Tedesco a minute's sleep.

"One more problem to handle, Skippy," Tedesco says, his tone even. "We do this and we're done. I'm gonna get out of town, let the cops find me. And that's *if* they can get an arrest warrant."

"You gonna name a name, or keep me guessin'."

"Sanda Dragomir."

"Your girlfriend?"

"Me and Asher, we met in her apartment a few times, including the night before . . . Listen, Skippy, I know this cop, Dante Cepeda, because we once lived in the same group home. He'll squeeze Sanda until she gives me up, simple as that. And Sanda? Trust me on this, loyalty is not her strong point. No, I gotta get to her first. I gotta take her testimony off the table."

Skippy stares into Tedesco's dark eyes. Something's coming, something Skippy won't like, but there's no way to prevent it. He glances at the monitor as Giancarlo Stanton strikes out, ending the Yankees' half of the first inning. No runs, no hits, no walks, nobody left on base. The story of the team's entire season.

"Why are you tellin me this?" he asks.

"Because this is the woman who killed Paulie, the woman who won't hesitate to kill Mike Tedesco and the woman who will definitely see me comin'. But you, Skippy? She doesn't know what you look like. She has no reason to fear you. You can get close."

Skippy's hand inches toward the gun taped to the bottom of

the desk, only stopping when Tedesco crosses his legs, obviously unafraid.

"OK, Mike," he says, "pretend I'm an actor and you're my director. Explain my motivation here. Why would I want to kill a woman I never met?"

"Self-preservation. That what I'd tell you if I was your director. Think about it? José? Asher? No matter what story I tell, you can always claim you weren't there. But Alebev? He bought it right here, inside the building with our security cameras runnin', and no matter who did the killin', you, my boss, are the only one with a motive."

THIRTY-THREE

Detective Cepeda makes his case, using every argument at his command, including the presence of a dog at the crime scene and the statements given by Asher's cousins, but Assistant District Attorney Harold Biondo never stops shaking his head. One of a number of prosecutors who work the various precincts, he's generally tasked with deciding whether the detention of a suspect warrants a formal arrest. Always keeping in mind that cops work for the mayor while prosecutors work for the district attorney, that cop careers are based on arrests, while the careers of prosecutors are based on convictions.

This conference is a bit different because Dante wants Mike Tedesco off the street before he kills someone else, someone as innocent as José Herrera. An arrest warrant would do the job nicely and still leave plenty of time to find more evidence. But Biondo's far from convinced.

"Do me a favor, Detective, and consider for a moment, in light of the simple fact that the dog population of New York reaches into the millions, what a defense lawyer would make of your dog evidence. And these conversations your suspect had with Asher Levine? By your own admission, Tassso's Bar and Grill is a place where everyone knows everyone else. Thus, you could have displayed a photo of any regular and come up with the same result. What I need is a shred of physical evidence or some direct statement on your suspect's part. Keep in mind, just because Tedesco hasn't supplied you with an alibi, doesn't mean he hasn't got one."

"I need time to gather that evidence. Look, there's a detective at the Four-Four in the Bronx, Ike Samuelson. He's gonna pull the footage from every security camera surrounding the park where José Sepulveda was killed. If Tedesco entered that park—and I know he did—we'll catch him in the act."

"And when you do, you'll get your warrant."

"Jesus Christ." Dante pauses long enough to calm down, at least a bit, before he makes a final plea. "Tedesco's already killed twice, and I can guarantee that he'd got at least two more victims on his must-kill list. If one of them turns up dead tonight, what're you gonna tell yourself?"

"I'll tell myself the truth, Detective. The criminal justice system isn't perfect. Sometimes innocent people are convicted, and sometimes the worst of the worst get away with the most heinous of crimes. And what's the alternative? Do away with trials altogether? Go directly from arrest to prison?"

If this was a TV show, Dante tells himself as Biondo turns away, *I'd grab this asshole by his lapels and slam him into the wall.* Instead, Dante returns to his desk and makes a series of phone calls to Barnwell's connections at the Puzzle Palace, the aim to establish Sanda Dragomir's informant status. Placed on hold for extended periods, he's unable to avoid a conversation with his neighbor, Detective Leon Taylor. Taylor's a big-time whiner and today's no different.

"So," he begins without invitation, "you got crazy Black men shootin' cops, including Black cops, of which I'm one. And you also got these terrorists goin' around killin' everybody in sight. And then you got the rest of the population—which you're tryin' to serve and protect—givin' you whatever grief they can get away with. OK?"

"OK."

"I mean, you go out on the street and the looks you get, it's like everyone thinks you're a murderer. And you don't know who's carryin' what." Leon wipes his brow. The thin stream of cold air discharged by an air conditioner stuck in the window barely reaches the desks at this end of the room. "Point I'm makin' here, Dante, is there's times when you just need to get the fuck away. Times when you gotta put some space between you and these mean old streets."

Leon's desk phone rings and he turns back to his desk, leaving Dante to his own thoughts. The pattern they follow is predictable and becoming more common, which frightens him a bit. They begin at about age thirteen when his pals in the group home began to hang out on the street. Dante knew, even at this early age, that the streets of the Bronx led only to one destination and that was prison. But rejecting your peers carried unpleasant consequences, like being ostracized, like having to fight every day.

Always good at school, Dante's first preference was for afterschool classes, but that strategy never had a chance. If he chose school over his peers, he'd have to fight *twice* a day. Dante could almost hear the words they'd lob in his direction: punk, pussy, bitch, suck-up, and the worst of the worst, acting white. Words you couldn't accept, words that demanded a response.

Dante chose another path, one that offered relative safety if not personal satisfaction. He went into a boxing gym and began to train. More tolerated than encouraged, the gym provided him with a reason to be out running in the early morning hours, to spend his afternoons skipping rope, to work out on the weekends. The gym kept him off the street and the skills he acquired inside the gym, meager relative to the other boxers, kept boys like Mike Tedesco off his back.

Bottom line, his strategy worked. He first passed through high school without catching the attention of a single cop. This was a relative triumph because three of the boys in the home were already in juvenile detention, while another had been sentenced as an adult. Still, Dante hadn't rested on his laurels. Two days after graduating, he climbed onto an US Army bus that transported him from the Port Authority bus terminal on Ninth Avenue to a combat training center in Columbia, Georgia. Four years and a tour in Iraq later, again without getting into trouble, he traded his military career for a cop career with the New York Police Department. His advance since then, from patrolman to narcotics to the detective division, had been steady, if unspectacular. At no time had he looked back.

"Hey, you with me, Dante? 'Cause you look like your brain's been domiciled on the moon."

"Yeah, I'm with you, Leon. Keep goin'."

"Right. So, I talk it over with Kashina, about needin' to get away, and she's in complete agreement, which, trust me, is a first. What we'd like to do is spend a week in the Adirondacks, but I already took my vacation, so that can't happen. No, we have to settle for what we can get, which is a day at Jones Beach. Just us, the kids and the ocean. So, first thing, we deal with the food. Sandwiches, fruit, drinks, and plenty of ice for the cooler. Then the towels and the umbrellas and the beach chairs. Then I pack everything into the Explorer, including the kids and off we go. An hour and half, OK? And two stops for the little one—that would be my two-year-old, George—who keeps needin' a bathroom but doesn't do anything when he gets to it."

Dante glances at the telephone, a hint that doesn't escape Leon Taylor, who taps his desk and nods. "All right, lemme wrap this shit up. Jones Beach? Let's just say it's a long haul from the parking lot to the water and I ended up makin' three trips. Musta taken a half-hour, but we finally put it together. The chairs and the coolers were under the umbrellas and the kids were stripping out of their shorts and T-shirts. We even caught a break on the ocean. The surf can be rough at Jones Beach, too rough for kids, but it was real quiet that afternoon. If I remember right, I was grinnin' like a fool when I took my little one by the hand and led him toward an ocean he was seein' for the first time in his life."

Leon reared up in his chair and glowered. The punch line was on the way. "You are not gonna believe this, Dante, but a split-second after we put our toes in the water, this lifeguard blows his whistle and puts a no swimming sign on the tower. Then these other lifeguards come out of nowhere and stick red flags up and down the beach. Me? I'm going, What the fuck, what the fuck, only under my breath because of the kids. Finally, a lifeguard walks over and plants one of the flags in front of me.

"'Sorry, sir,' he says, 'but a shark's been spotted offshore. No swimming until further notice. You'll have to go back to your blanket.' A shark, Dante? A mother-fuckin' shark? Man, I gotta tell ya, bein' as I was the one made the original suggestion, the rest of the day was pure hell."

The thing about it, Dante tells himself as he turns back to his work, I always knew what I was running from, but I can't recall spending ten seconds defining what I was running toward. I only prepared myself for escape. Or even worse, Sanda Dragomir.

Dante's again reminded of Sanda when he runs into Patti O'Hearn as he heads out the door. Patti's wide engaging smile, her ultimately mischievous smile, is so obviously genuine that Dante pulls up short. This is the smile of someone who enjoys her life, the smile of an optimist.

"Hey," she says, "I been lookin' for you. We did that canvas of the apartments on Riverside Drive."

"Anything turn up?"

"Lotta witnesses after the firefighters showed, but no one saw the Lincoln get torched. Like we figured." Patti shifts her weight without taking her blue eyes off Dante. "Haven't seen you around the last couple of days."

"What could I say, Patti? This case, it's eatin' me for dinner. The driver's dead, by the way. The one Myra Cuffee saw runnin' down the street in the rain. He bought it in a Bronx park, stabbed through the heart, and I can't even get a fuckin' arrest warrant."

Suddenly, an image pops into Dante's mind. Detective Leon Taylor, his big belly hanging over his swim shorts, reaching out for his son's hand. For Taylor, the gesture must have been as natural as breathing.

"I'll see you around, Patti. I gotta go."

As he passes through the lobby, Dante's commander, Lieutenant Barnwell, comes through the door. She's aware of José's demise, but hardly sympathetic.

"I'm just comin' back from a Compstat meeting," she tells him, "and they were all over me. It appears that somebody's whisperin' in somebody's else's ear and the bosses have linked up the homicides. You know what they say, my friend? When you take the man's pay, you do the man's job."

"They want an arrest?"

"Like, pronto."

"Then review the material I left on your desk and have a talk with Assistant District Attorney Harold Biondo. I've spent the last half-hour beggin' him for an arrest warrant."

Dante starts to leave, but his boss restrains him. "Fuck Biondo," she says. "I'm gonna go over his head."

THIRTY-FOUR

It's near to closing by the time Dante reaches the Legrand Transportation warehouse. He's hoping Mike Tedesco showed up for work this afternoon. If not, Dante will settle for another chance to convince Skippy that his life's at risk. But Tedesco and two other men are busy unloading an eighteen-wheeler backed into the yard when Dante pulls up. All three are slick with sweat and Tedesco's hair, usually curled alongside his ears, hangs to his shoulders like the pelt of a dead animal.

Dante measures Tedesco as he approaches. The man can't be sure that he's not about to be put in cuffs, but his glittery eyes radiate defiance. Still, with his shirt off, he's obviously unarmed.

"What the fuck do you want?" Tedesco opens up before Dante gets within ten feet.

"What's the matter, Mike? All of a sudden you don't like me?"

"I never liked you in the first place."

"True, enough." Dante smiles. "Wanna tell me why? Because I don't recall ever gettin' in your business."

"You and me, Dante, we lived in different worlds. You were a suck-up. I fought back."

"I can't argue with that, either. I stayed out of trouble, but you never stopped lookin' for a way to beat the rules. Slick is how I'd put it. But what exactly did it get you? Besides the prison sentence you already served and the one you can look forward to servin' for the rest of your life?"

"Look, if you're gonna cuff me, do it. Otherwise, talk to my lawyer."

"No, I'm here to talk to you. I'd rather do it in private, but . . ."

Tedesco glances at his coworkers. One stands behind him, the other stands inside the truck, looking out over the tailgate. They know, of course, about José. He's all they've been talking about this morning, that and the fact that Mike Tedesco probably killed him.

Resigned, Tedesco leads Dante to a patch of shade at the edge of the building. He turns to his coworkers as he goes, ordering them back to work.

"Before you get started," he tells Dante, "I got somethin' I wanna get off my chest."

"Go right ahead. Voluntary statements given after repeated Miranda warnings definitely work for me."

Tedesco kicks at the loose gravel for a moment, then says, "You were such a good boy, Dante. No risks, not ever. So, tell me what it got you, huh? You have yourself a little house out on Long Island, maybe a little wifey and a couple of snot-nosed brats? You countin' the days until your pension kicks in? Until you get to stay home and mow the grass?"

Dante laughs, thinking, *Not even that.* "Whatever I have, it's gotta be a lot better than what you're facin'."

"Fuck you, Dante. Fuck you twice."

Dante lets the sentiment hang for a moment, absorbing Tedesco's hatred. He notes the lower jaw thrust forward, the tight, barely controlled grimace. Dante wants Tedesco off the street and assaulting a police officer will serve that end nicely. That's why he's here, to provoke that assault. Overlapping security cameras protect every inch of the yard alongside the warehouse. What Dante and Tedesco say to each other will always be a matter of dispute, but not what they do to each other. If Tedesco throws the first punch, he'll go directly to jail.

"I didn't come here to reminisce," Dante finally says. "In fact, I don't have any good reason for talkin' to you, nothing beyond curiosity. You'll notice that I haven't rattled off a list of your rights, plus I fully admit that you've asked me for a lawyer, not once but several times. I'll even let you pat me down for a wire if you want."

Tedesco swipes at his face with the back of a hand as sweat-slick as his forehead. "Two minutes, Dante. Then I'm gonna go inside and lock the door behind me."

"OK, so yesterday I had this conversation in the office with Martha Proctor. And maybe you should think about whacking her, too, because she loves to talk. I asked her about José, of course, and she told me that José was a mouse. That's the exact word she used, Mike. She said he was a mouse and I was just wonderin' how it feels to step on a mouse. Another notch on the belt? A cost of doin' business? Or once you wiped off your shoe, was it like the whole thing never happened?"

"Sorry, Dante, but I'm not bitin'. I don't know shit about what happened to José."

Dante shakes his head. "Like I said, you've always been slick. You set up the hijackin' away from security cameras. Likewise for when you burned the car and stuck that knife in José. But here's the thing. The detectives up in the Bronx? They're gonna pull the footage from every security camera surrounding the park. So, if you entered Joyce Kilmer Park this morning, and we both know you did, those cameras will provide the kind of proof I can show to a jury."

Tedesco's hands curl into fists and Dante responds with a delighted smirk, the kind that resulted in thrown punches when they were kids. "But about that mouse thing?" he continues. "If I remember right, back in the day it was all about mice. Swear to God, you had all the younger kids workin' for you, the ones you could step on. But the funny thing is that I don't remember you ever fightin' someone your own size. That's why I kept away from you, Mike, because for all your talk about takin' risks, I made you for a punk."

Tedesco rocks from side to side, barely able to contain himself, and Dante's thoughts drift back to a class he took at John Jay College of Criminal Justice. That's where he first heard the word *decompensation*. At the time, the professor applied the concept to serial killers who break down toward the end. They kill more and more often, taking fewer and fewer precautions, as if the demons inside had finally taken over. Tedesco's not a serial killer and Dante knows it, but the man appears to be falling apart, the pressures too much for him.

"You think I don't know what you're doin'?" Tedesco's words are spoken through a clenched jaw. "So, let's just say we'll settle up at some later date."

"Still slick, but somehow I'm not threatened. I mean, by the time you get out of prison, you'll have to come after me in a wheelchair. But we'll let that go because I really came here to ask you about Asher. And don't tell me you never heard of him because I rounded up ten people say you were as thick as . . . as thieves, Mike. Thick as thieves."

"So, I knew Asher. So what? I know everybody at Tasso's."

Dante waves him off. "Knowing Asher's not what this is all about. What I want you to tell me, because I've really been wonderin', is whether or not you were fuckin' him. What with Asher bein' gay and you bein' so slick. And I don't want you to think I'm prejudiced. My first partner was gay and we got along great. No, I'm just curious."

Behind them, the rear doors of the trailer slam shut and the eighteen-wheeler, in low gear, begins its journey home. The bellow of the revving diesel engine blots out any hope of continuing the conversation, a pause for which Dante finds himself grateful. He waits until the truck clears the corner before resuming, his tone almost gentle.

"All your life you've been quick to spot weakness, and to exploit it whenever possible. So, Asher's sexual orientation—confirmed by his cousins and the gay porno I found in his room—would naturally catch your attention. Kind of like a shark spotting an injured seal. So let me guess what happened next. At some point, Asher casually mentioned that he installed and repaired tracking units. Right away, your buzzer went off. This was a talent you could definitely exploit. The only problem? Asher was a little wimp. Armed robbery was not his game, not even close. You had to convince him."

A tremor runs through Mike Tedesco's body, his mouth opening and closing as he tries to come up with a response. Finally, he mutters, "Asher was a friend of mine."

"C'mon, Mike, don't bullshit a bullshitter. We both came up in foster care, plus you spent time in prison. Man-on-man sex is not something unfamiliar to us. So, what'd you do? You cozy up to Asher for a while, move in slow, wait until he was hungry then lean in for a quick kiss?" Dante stops suddenly, a grin lighting his face as he taps the side of his head. "I just thought of something. Do you remember a kid named Paco Altoona?"

"Who?"

"Paco Altoona? Small, skinny kid? He disappeared one day? Took off for school and never came back?"

"OK, what about him?"

"Well, you were fuckin' him, right? That's why I thought you were probably gettin' it on with Asher. Because you were fuckin' Paco."

"What are you talkin' about? I never . . ."

Dante waves him off. "Forget the bullshit, Mike. I know you were screwin' Paco because I saw you."

Tedesco eyes dart across the yard. That he's on the verge of losing control doesn't escape Dante. Mike's not used to being disrespected, not to this extent, not even by prison guards. He wants to act, but what with Dante being armed with a badge and a gun, there's no action to be taken.

"You finished, Dante?"

Dante takes a step back, then another. He's failed, obviously, but he has one last message to deliver. "Do yourself a favor. Give yourself up. Make a full and complete confession. Because I'm tellin' you from the bottom of what little heart I still possess, if you give me an excuse, any excuse at any point, I'm gonna kill you."

THIRTY-FIVE

Dante walks past Sanda and into her apartment. He's come directly from the Legrand warehouse and while the sweat covering his body has dried, he's having trouble tolerating his own stink. Even the dog, after a brief greeting, heads for a corner.

"You are needing a shower," Sanda remarks, her tone not unkind.

Dante holds up a paper bag. "Brought a change of clothes. Give me fifteen minutes."

True to his word, Dante emerges a quarter of an hour later, freshly shaved and scrubbed. He's barefoot, wearing faded jeans and a WE RULE THE NIGHT T-shirt cadged off a Street Crimes veteran. Smiling now, he reaches for the beer Sanda's already poured and drains the glass.

"Yummy, yummy, good for the tummy." He pulls Sanda into an embrace, just long enough to check for resistance. But she only laughs, and he heads for the kitchen, returning almost immediately with a handful of takeout menus.

"You hungry?" he asks.

"Why you are doing this?"

"Doing what?"

"Coming here and taking over my house? You are not owner here."

"Hey, slow down. Next thing you'll shoot me."

Sanda's standing quietly by the door, her expression serious. She's not about to take any crap from a man, which Dante already knows. Unfortunately, crap is all he has to offer tonight, crap in heaping doses.

"Tell you what," he says, "why don't we go out for dinner? My treat."

Without speaking, Sanda opens the door. She knows exactly what he wants. Information he can use to convict Mike Tedesco. But she owes Dante Cepeda exactly nothing. Kneeling, she puts a leash on Marius, who licks her ankle, a show of gratitude for being included. Then she leads dog and lover to a Thai restaurant with an outdoor café, a restaurant that tolerates dogs, including a shaggy Pekingese at one table and a Jack Russell terrier at another. Both, along with their owners, cringe at the sight of Marius, but Sanda ignores the reaction. She guides Marius to a table at the edge of the café, and he quickly settles down by her chair.

They talk about Sanda's book, *Mirrors*, for the most part, of what might happen after it's published. There's the hope, however remote, of a runaway bestseller, maybe even a movie deal. But that's not her most important motive, not according to Sanda.

"All my life I want to be artist, but I am no good at drawing," she tells Dante. "I practice, yes, because this is how you get to Carnegie Hall, only I am not becoming proficient. That is the right word? Proficient?"

"Yeah, that's good enough."

"Basically, I am giving up until one day I am in store and see drawing software on shelf. I buy this, yes, and discover that software makes up for not having skills. With this, and much practice, I can be artist."

They discuss the plot of Sanda's novel for the rest of the meal, their talk casual and frequently interrupted as the food is served and consumed. Sanda harbors a deeply seated hatred of Eastern European governments, especially Russia's, and she reveals herself to be a true American patriot. It's the lack of appreciation that irks her. American ignorance is only matched by American ingratitude. Americans are super-coddled. Americans know nothing of how the other 90 percent live.

Dante doesn't dispute any of her positions. Truly hungry, he concentrates on his dinner, rushing it because of the heat. It's only a bit cooler now that the sun has set, and what little breeze sweeps over the café feels as wet as Marius's drooping tongue. By the time they get back to Sanda's air-conditioned apartment, Dante's tempted to put his policing duties to one side, to retire to the bedroom and see if the second night holds enticements equal to the first. Not happening, though, not immediately, and it's more than likely he'll have to be up early tomorrow morning. Resigned, he heads for the bathroom.

Sanda's sitting on the floor when he returns, scratching the dog's flanks. Satisfied, he settles into a chair and watches her closely while he recalls Lieutenant Barnwell's admonition: Take the man's pay, do the man's job. Even if it costs you a relationship you really want to pursue.

"I spent half the afternoon on the phone, Sanda," he begins. "Running down your history as a confidential informant." Dante pauses, but Sanda continues to stroke Marius. "I first spoke to a detective in Brooklyn named—if you can believe this—Irwin Littlewood. He told me about Teddy Winuk, the guy you ratted out. Winuk's now a confidential informant, too, so I guess the affair had a happy ending. Oh, by the way, according to Littlewood, you worked as a prostitute and Winuk was your pimp."

This isn't exactly what Littlewood told Dante. Littlewood's version had Winuk playing the role of agent, and the two severing that relationship before Sanda turned on him. Dante's offering it in an attempt to stir the pot, but Sanda's pot refuses to stir. In fact, she breaks out laughing.

"This is why you play games for two hours?"

"No, there's more. From Littlewood, I jumped to a lieutenant at One Police Plaza, Detective Bernstein. Bernstein knows you well, Sanda. He told me that your file's been dormant for a long time, but as far as the NYPD's concerned, once a confidential informant, always a confidential informant. You're expected to cooperate."

Sanda's laughter fades to an amused smile as she gets to her feet, approaches Dante's chair, and leans over him. "Does this arouse you, Dante? That I am prostitute once? Do you believe there are things I could be teaching you?"

"Yes to both questions, but we're not goin' there, Sanda, not yet." Dante tugs Sanda onto his lap, the spicy fragrance of her shampoo drifting into his nostrils. "Bernstein was only a stopover. From him, I went to a woman named Bernice Colfax. Ms. Colfax works for Immigration and Naturalization. In fact, she's handling your application for citizenship. But I have to say that she's not your champion. No, Bernice thinks former prostitutes who entered the country illegally should never become citizens, or even allowed to reside here, but . . ."

"But she is not having a choice?"

"It's not about a choice. It's about an excuse. Which is what she's looking for to drop your citizenship application in the toilet."

Sanda lays her head on Dante's shoulder and settles her weight against him. Though his radar is up and running, he detects no resentment in the gesture, not even the urge to manipulate. Betrayal, he knows, has been a factor in Sanda's life for all long as she can remember. Dante's, apparently, comes as no great shock and she appears to be accepting. At least his cards are on the table.

"Tell me why," she says. "Why you are making these phone calls, these threats?"

"Because I was the one who told Asher's mother that her son was dead, shot down like a dog in the street. And I was there when a woman named Sofia Sepulveda learned that she was now a widow with two young children because Mike Tedesco stuck a knife in her husband's back. We're not talkin' about an athletic contest, me against Mike with a gold medal at the end. This is real murder with real people really dead. I know because I've seen the bodies. I want Tedesco off the street before I have to see another one."

"And you wish . . ."

"Hang on, I'm not finished. I got a call just now as I drove over, from Francisco Herrera, José Sepulveda's uncle. Francisco lives in the apartment with José's family, which is how I met him. He told me that a cousin of José's named Mariano was killed this morning in a little machine shop he owned, shot through the head. He also told me that José and Mariano had been close since childhood and that Mariano knew where José was hiding out."

Dante finally shuts down, leaving Sanda to ask her question. "And you wish exactly what from me?"

"I want you to connect Asher to Mike and the hijacking."

Sanda bites, very gently, into Dante's earlobe. "What about truth, Dante? Do you want me to say the truth?"

"I want you to say anything you're willing to repeat in front of a jury. And I want you to say it now."

Sanda shakes her head as she rises to her feet and walks toward the bedroom. "We will save this talk for the pillow. Come."

And what can Dante say to that? Sanda's beyond stunning, a woman's who's thoroughly integrated her past and her present. He follows her into the bedroom and slowly undresses her, his lips gliding over her skin. He finds himself wanting to stay right here, his mouth on the satin of her inner thigh, at the peak of expectation, listening to her soft moans, her own expectations equal to his. When he finally slips into her and she lifts her legs, the sensation is so exquisite his mind finally goes to sleep. Now there's just the two of them, twisting and rolling, moving now slow, now fast, sensations rising and falling, neither wanting an end to the pleasure, not even the final rush of orgasm. But they do finish eventually, and they do fall back on the sheets, their breathing finally going quiet. Neither speaks, though, not for a good ten minutes. For Dante's part, he's simply exercising a strategy common to cops. Let the tension build, don't be first to speak. Sanda's motives are more obscure, at least to him, but she finally rolls over to face him.

"The day before this hijacking, they are here in apartment, Asher and Mike. I am not listening to conversation because I know they are talking about committing crimes. But when Asher is leaving, I hear Mike say, 'Don't fuck it up, Asher. I am expecting to see you tomorrow morning. If you are not showing up, I will come to look for you.'"

Dante rolls onto his side and pulls Sanda toward him, sliding his hand across her belly and onto her breasts. He's growing hard again. Already.

"This is my reward?" Sanda asks.

"No, Sanda, it's mine." Dante smiles to himself. Do the man's job, take the man's pay? If his time with Sanda, however brief it may turn out to be, isn't the pay part, he doesn't know what it is.

THIRTY-SIX

Mike Tedesco, as he approaches Daniela's front door, stops in his tracks for a moment, halted by the pounding of the bembe drums and the chanting, so fucking loud the stereo might be on his side of the door. The same rhythm, the same words, over and over again, come down, come down, come down, take my body, take my brain, take my soul. As though Daniela's been expecting him. And maybe she has, the witch. Maybe she's been playing him all along.

Tedesco tells himself that he's mad and finds no dissenting voice within his own mind. Mad as in angry. Mad as in crazy.

Impatient now, he unlocks the door—no surprise that the locks haven't been changed—and steps inside. He doesn't know what he'll do if he discovers twenty people in the room, if it's tambor night at the Castillo *hacienda*, but he finds Daniela by herself, seated before the altar, eyes rolled back in her head, unaware of his presence. She comes around pretty quick, though, when he shuts off her stereo. Her irises slide down, and she lifts her chin as she draws a breath.

"What do you want, Miguelito?"

"How 'bout you not callin' me by that name? How'd that be for fuckin' starters?"

Daniela merely shakes her head. "I told you not to come back here."

"Yeah, you did, you and that other bitch in my life, and my mother, too, come to think of it. You're rats deserting the ship. Funny how you were so friendly before the ship started to sink."

This is true, at least in Tedesco's mind. His ship is definitely sinking. And the funny thing is that he'd been totally unaware of his fuckup until Dante spelled it out. Yeah, he'd checked for cameras once he spotted José, his search thorough enough to guarantee there were no cameras in the park. But he hadn't expected to find José on that bench and he'd walked from where he left his car to the park without taking any precautions. If the Bronx detectives follow through—which Dante will pretty much guarantee—Mike Tedesco's goose is not only cooked, it's burnt to a crisp. You'd think he would've realized that without Dante having to tell him.

Bottom line, he's going down, into the ground or into a prison cell, the only consolation being the simple fact that he's not going alone.

"What do you want?" Daniela asks, her tone now more concerned than condescending.

"I want you to remove the spell."

"I put no spell . . ."

"I'm talkin' about this god, Ogun, or whatever the fuck he's called. I can't think straight anymore and right now I really need to think straight. You gotta take him off my back."

"I don't have that power, Miguelito. This is something only you can accomplish, and maybe not even you. When the orisha has . . ."

"Stop right there." Dante walks across the room and opens the closet door to reveal a pantry loaded with herbs and small bottles of sludgy liquids. "*Palo Malambo, Abre Camino, Quita Maldición,*

Paraiso . . . Shit, Daniela, I've seen women coming here with my own eyes, and more than once. *'Por favor, retire esta maldición.'* Please, take this curse away. So don't tell me you can't do it."

Tedesco flops down on the couch. He needs to get his head straight, to think. There's an answer out there. He can sense it, and maybe it's reachable, but he just can't focus. His mind drifts when he tries to concentrate, drifts to a single point, a black hole in his personal universe named Dante Cepeda. There are times when Tedesco thinks he was born hating Dante.

Daniela rises, walks to the closet, and begins to pulls herbs from the shelf. Watching, Tedesco smiles to himself. "Whatever you're makin'," he tells her, "you're gonna drink it first."

Daniela shakes her head as she begins her work, mixing the herbs in a bowl, laying the bowl on her altar. She fills small dishes with black, white, and brown beans, spiced yam and finely chopped vegetables mixed with cilantro, vinegar, and jalapeño. These, too, go on the altar, laid before a dozen figurines. Above the altar, on the wall, *La Caridad del Cobre* looks down, her gaze sorrowful, compassionate, but only at the fishermen in the boat.

Daniela's preparations almost complete, she turns to Mike Tedesco. "Ogun needs a blood sacrifice, Miguelito. If you want, I can go out and get a chicken, but your own blood will do."

Tedesco's smile borders on a snarl. Nevertheless, he's genuinely amused. Daniela was always good at setting him up, just the way she set up the old ladies who knew their diabetes was the result of a curse and not the five liters of soda they drank every day. Tedesco's not about to let her out of the apartment until their business is completed. And the blood part? That's good too. Daniela whacks a chicken at every tambor, cuts its throat. Sometimes she cooks it and feeds it to the congregation, sometimes she buries it in a graveyard at midnight. The one thing constant is the blood.

"Get the knife," he says. "No, I'll get it."

Tedesco pushes himself to his feet and walks into the kitchen. He comes back with a ceramic paring knife and a plate. The knife, he knows, is incredibly sharp. "Hope you're not looking for a long hot drink because you're only gettin' a few drops."

Without flinching, he pricks his finger with the point of the knife, just deep enough to produce the required drops of bright red blood. For a moment, he's afraid that she'll lick it up, like a kitten at a saucer of milk. But Daniela merely places this offering in front of the others on the altar before carefully choosing a CD from her large collection.

The drums seize him within a few seconds. They lay hold of him, their grip relentless, the talons of a hawk in the flesh of a careless rabbit. Then the chant begins, with Daniela joining the chorus, and Tedesco feels his world dissolve. Lost and gone forever. The words are Yoruban, straight out of Africa, the only one he recognizes, Ogun, present in every call and response. But the message seems utterly clear to him and he feels the walls dissolve as he slips under. No more tiny apartment, one of millions, no more Harlem or New York or America or even Earth. No more here, no more now. He falls into a universe that's much too big for him, a current that's too powerful to resist.

Even if he wanted to, which he doesn't.

Tedesco has no way to measure the time until he returns, until he opens his eyes and lifts himself to a sitting position. The silence reaches him first, then the realization that he's perfectly calm. An image pops into his mind, a memory. In the small anteroom of the group home that he and Dante once shared, a poster of Martin Luther King Jr., chin raised, staring off into the distance. The legend beneath was written in bold black letters: FREE AT LAST/FREE AT LAST.

When he finally looks around, he's not surprised by anything he sees. Not by the destroyed altar, not by the smashed stereo, not by the figurines and offerings scattered across the living room, not by the poster torn to shreds, not by Daniela lying motionless on the carpet. Except for her twisted neck, she might be asleep. As it is, what with her lying on her belly while she looks up at the ceiling, she's obviously dead.

Tedesco stares down at his hands for a moment. No blood. Excellent. He rises to his feet, fetches a plastic trash bag and begins to clean the room. Just in case someone arrives unexpectedly, like the cops. Tedesco hasn't the faintest memory of what happened, or how much noise he made.

Daniela's saved for last. Tedesco slides his hands beneath her armpits, drags her into the bathroom, and dumps her in the tub. He feels absolutely nothing. Ogun needed a sacrifice? Well, he got one, didn't he?

Tedesco heads for the kitchen, finds the remains of a chicken stew in the refrigerator, heats the food in the microwave. He adds a beer to his meal and consumes it standing up. The funny thing, he realizes, is that his situation has changed. Or, not his situation, exactly, but his understanding. Yes, Dante or the Bronx cops will examine footage from the security cameras surrounding the park. But some won't produce an image clear enough to show to a jury and some won't be working at all. He still has a shot here.

He eats slowly, and just as slowly works through the events that brought him to this point, to the events and the only remedy available. That much hasn't changed. Sanda can drive a nail into his coffin, maybe the final nail, and she'll rat him out in a hot second if Dante threatens her. No, make that *when* Dante threatens her.

Tedesco packs the remains of his meal into a plastic bag he'll dump somewhere along the way, then calls Skippy Legrand at home. It's baseball time and his boss most likely has a bet down. Tough shit.

"How ya doin', Skippy?"

"Better before you called."

"Why, Skippy? Because nothing's changed. *¿Comprende?* Not a fucking thing. And there's something else you might wanna think about. You're way too fat and way too old for survival of the fittest. I been in prison, Skippy, and I don't see you makin' a go of it."

Tedesco opens the refrigerator door and looks around. He spots a half-gallon of mocha-fudge ice cream in the freezer and pulls it out. "You got nothin' to say?"

"I'm still waitin' to hear why you called me?"

"Yeah, well I got it worked out. What we're gonna do tomorrow morning. You just be sure to meet me at five thirty."

"Just like that? Tell me who died and made you my lord and master?"

But Tedesco's not buying. He dips a spoon into the ice cream and brings it to his mouth. "You got nothin' to worry about, Skip, and I'll explain everything in the morning. I'm just tired right now. I been goin' hard all day."

"Then how 'bout a hint, like what you're gonna ask me to do."

"Hold it right there, man. There's no askin' here. You don't show up tomorrow morning, I'm gonna come to your house lookin' for your miserable ass. I don't care who's home and who's not. This ain't a fuckin' negotiation."

THIRTY-SEVEN

Skippy Legrand digs his nails into a patch of psoriasis newly erupted on the inside of his right thigh. He's sitting inside a stolen Honda minivan with a handgun, a Browning semi-auto, tucked beneath the seat. He's expected to use the gun to kill a woman named Sanda Dragomir, a woman he's never laid eyes on. That's not a problem because she'll be coming out of a townhouse three quarters of a block away and he'll recognize the dog she's walking, good old Pug.

So, that's why they're here, him in the van, Tedesco parked around the corner in his own car. To kill Sanda Dragomir, the entire project as crazy to Skippy Legrand as his partner, who's now replaced his agitation with a calm more appropriate to a zombie.

"Dogs gotta be walked," he'd told Skippy. "Rain, sleet, snow? Don't matter. Dogs gotta be walked. Plus, Sanda's an early riser, so there's a good chance we'll catch her alone."

Alone or not, his job, Skippy Legrand's, is to drive down the street, jump out of the minivan and shoot Ms. Dragomir through the head. Twice. Then he's expected to jump back in the car and drive to a rendezvous point near the South Brooklyn Marine Terminal where Mike Tedesco will undoubtedly kill him. What with Skippy Legrand being the last piece on the chess board.

Tedesco's armed, of course. Worse yet, he's a ruthless killer who obviously enjoyed his work the night he killed Alebev, wrapping layer upon layer of tape around Alebev's head, watching as Alebev's face initially flamed, then slowly whitened. With no choice, Skippy had watched, too, and he'd taken the lesson to heart. Tedesco was willing to go places that Skippy Legrand wasn't. Hell, Mike Tedesco was already there.

What now? Skippy's been asking himself that question ever since they arrived thirty minutes ago. What now? It's the definition of insanity, asking the same question over and over, each time expecting a different answer, especially when there's only kill-or-be-killed on the table.

Meanwhile, on a separate track, as if he had one foot on Earth and the other on Mars, Skippy had enjoyed another good night, betting two baseball games, winning both. He's up over a hundred grand now, money he's unlikely ever to spend. And the part that hurts the most? He'd never have agreed to the hijacking, or been in debt to Alebev, if the streak had started a week earlier.

It's like the gods are rubbing it in, his whole stupid life. Take a good look, asshole, put your face in it and draw a deep breath. If you don't smell shit, your nose ain't working.

The pity party evaporates a moment later when the door to Sanda Dragomir's townhouse opens and the mutt appears, the one Tedesco dragged into the warehouse. Only it's not Sanda holding the leash. It's the cop.

Skippy gets on the burner supplied by Tedesco. "Hey, guess what, Mike?"

"Don't fuckin' play with me."

"It's not me playin' with you. It's the cop who's playin' with your girlfriend. He just came out of the house. Him and the mutt."

"What's he doin'?"

"He's watchin' the dog piss on the neighbor's trash bags."

"Is that supposed to be funny?"

Skippy doesn't answer right away. He watches the cop lead the dog to a car, a Chevy, parked at the curb. A few seconds later, with the dog pacing back and forth on the back seat, the Chevy pulls out of the parking space.

"He put the dog in a car and they're coming our way," Skippy tells Mike Tedesco. "Looks like you're gonna have to come up with a Plan B."

Skippy scrunches down until his eyes are below the arc of the steering wheel. He's not surprised when the cop sails past, slowing but not stopping at the red stop sign. But Mike Tedesco's immediate pursuit catches Skippy off-guard and he realizes, after a moment, that he was right in thinking his partner insane. And also that he's finally caught a break. He gets out of the van, leaving the gun behind, and draws down a lungful of steamy summer air, not resenting the faint smell of ozone, or the stench of the garbage piled at the curb. Then he marches down the block, climbs the few steps to Sanda's door and rings the bell. A few seconds later, as if she'd only been waiting, the door opens to reveal Sanda Dragomir, gun in hand, finger curled through the trigger guard, already bringing pressure to bear.

"Please," he says, pushing the words past the constriction in his throat. "Please," he repeats.

Sanda advances a step, forcing Skippy to give ground. She looks to her right and left, then drops the barrel of the gun.

"You are not armed."

It's not a question, the way she says it, and Skippy merely nods. He's taken with her beauty, especially the slanting eyes and the direct gaze, which hints at some knowledge he, himself, will never possess. Even the way she holds herself, firm and confident, as if she knows exactly who she is, and who Skippy Legrand isn't.

"Why are you here?" she demands.

"To warn you."

"About Mike? I am already warned from him."

"Yeah, but he's crazy. Right now, he's following the cop. I don't know which one's comin' out alive, but probably not both of 'em."

Across the street, a door opens and a woman exits. Dressed in a lightweight business suit, she's on her way to work. Sanda glances at her, then steps to the side. "Come up," she says. "I will hear this confession."

Skippy's impressed with the apartment, with the loaded bookshelves and the computer on the desk and especially the air-conditioning. According to Mike, Sanda was halfway to becoming a street whore when he met her. That's obviously not true, but then Mike's always been a liar.

Sanda directs Skippy to the living room couch, then fetches a glass of iced tea that tastes of peaches, honey, and lemon. He drinks, lays the glass down, and leans back, closing his eyes for a moment.

"What with Paulie and all, I already figured you knew about Mike," he finally begins. "But you're thinkin' of the old Mike. I mean, I've known the guy for a long time and if he never had exactly what you'd call a conscience, he at least gave a damn about his own survival. That's gone now, completely. Like he'd shoot you in a supermarket with a hundred people watching. Like he's expecting someone to take him off the count. Like he's decided to go out in a blaze of glory."

"Glory?"

"OK, blood, then. But what I'm gettin' to is that it's hard to go up against a guy who don't care how it comes out. Understand my point. Nobody's safe, not me or you or the cop, while Mike's walkin' around. The prick even threatened my family. That's how bad he wanted me to kill you. Right here on the street, while you were walkin' the dog. Only it turned out to be the cop . . ."

Skippy grinds to a halt. Sanda's expression hasn't changed and the gun's in her lap where she can get to it quickly. But when she reaches down, it's to retrieve her cell and punch in a number. A few seconds later, she declares, without preamble, "Mike is following you."

Skippy can't hear Dante's reply, but Sanda, after twice saying yes, makes his response clear. "He says that he already knows."

"That's all?"

"No, he is telling me that he leads Mike to the graveyard."

The words cheer Skippy, a light at the end of that black, black tunnel. Mike Tedesco dead, with no tales to tell? That would leave Skippy Legrand in the clear. It could just as easily come out the other way, of course, with the cop dead and Mike's rampage ongoing, and without a reason to end.

"I'm a degenerate gambler, in case you didn't know." Skippy's hand rises toward his neck—his psoriasis is itching madly—but he controls himself at the last minute. He's pitiful enough already. "I'm the kind of asshole, when I get on a winning streak, like I am now, I only bet more."

"Until finally you are losing everything?"

"Yeah, but not this time. I'm gonna use my winnings to pay down the mortgage on the house, which is in my wife's name. I love Fay . . ." Skippy shakes his head. "Lemme just make this one point. With me gone, Fay's gonna need a head start."

"This is why you have come to my home?"

"Uh-uh. No, what I want you to do is tell the cop, if he comes back alive, that I'm sittin' at home with my lawyer. Ready to cut a deal."

THIRTY-EIGHT

Dante comes out of Sanda's bathroom at six o'clock in the morning, freshly scrubbed and shaved. He glances through her bedroom window, the one closest to the street, the look purely reflexive. All those hours in a cruiser, eyes constantly moving, searching for anything or anyone out of place? This was Policing 101, the first thing you learned, and Dante's eyes naturally wander along 47th Street to the corner.

The appraisal stops suddenly when Dante comes upon Skippy Legrand, but not because he recognizes him, not initially. What Dante notices, first, is an adult male inside a minivan parked against the curb. The man is slumped down and his hands are in his lap, not on the wheel, the classic pose of a rank amateur running a surveillance. Dante's conducted numerous stakeouts and surveillances, and he understands the difference between the two. You sat behind the wheel, fully exposed, when you conducted a stakeout because you didn't give damn if you caught the attention of passersby. On a surveillance, you took pains to conceal yourself.

Dante stares out for a moment. It's a long way to the corner and he's not sure, not at first, but when he finally decides that he's looking at Skippy Legrand, he smiles. Knowing, as he does, that Mike Tedesco cannot be far behind.

The choices roll through Dante's brain as he dresses, as he slips into his shoulder rig, as he tucks his service weapon, a 9 mm Glock, into the holster. He's obtained a signed statement from Sanda that not only places Tedesco and Asher Levine together on the night before the hijacking, but has them planning to reunite on the following morning. More than enough.

What he should do now—what he's *supposed* to do—is call the Seven-Two, where he spent his rookie year, and request backup on the takedown. That tactic, though it flows through Dante's mind, enjoys a very brief life. Legrand and Tedesco can only be here for one reason, to put another notch on the gun. They mean to kill Sanda. Him, too, if he shows his face.

Dante slides into his jacket, then walks into the living room. He finds Sanda in the apartment's small kitchen, making coffee. The dog's with her, as usual, but he responds immediately when Dante pulls down his leash, rushing to the door, dropping onto his haunches, his whole body vibrating with excitement.

"All right, mutt, stay still for a minute," Dante mutters as he tries to attach the leash.

"He is not mutt. His name is Marius."

Dante ignores the comment. "Listen, Sanda, right now, even as we speak, Skippy Legrand is sitting in a parked van at the corner. Somehow, I don't think he's here to pay a social visit."

"And Mike?"

"I didn't see him, but I don't figure Skippy to have the balls for murder, not on his own. As for Mike, I'll try to lure him away. I don't want bullets flying, not around here. Too many civilians. But if he doesn't bite, I'll circle the block and take him from behind."

"And if he is not there?"

"I'm sure he is, Sanda, but if I'm wrong, me and Skippy are gonna have a short, pointed conversation in which I make him responsible for your welfare. Like, if you should suffer so much as a hangnail, I'll run him down some quiet night and put a bullet in his head. Now if it was Mike Tedesco in that car, I'd be wasting my breath. But Skippy? Skippy's a schmuck who stepped in one of those deep shitholes I mentioned. All I have to do is make him more afraid of me than he is of Mike."

Dante reaches for the doorknob, but stops when Sanda utters a single word: "Why?"

"Why what?" he says without turning around.

"Why you are not calling for . . . what's this word?"

"Backup?"

"Yes, tell me why."

There's an issue here, whether anything in their relationship grants Sanda the right to make demands, but Dante lets that one slide as he reaches down to pat the dog's head. The poor animal's been holding it in for twelve hours. "When I was a kid livin' in group homes, bullies like Mike usually didn't mess with me. I was too tough for that. But you couldn't get in their way, either. You had to avoid challenging them. It's like politically correct speech. If kids like Mike sense disrespect, they have to respond. That's how they survive. So, I had to look the other way." Mike shakes his head. This is territory he usually avoids. "There was this one kid, Paco Altoona, a couple of years younger than Mike. Paco was too small and too skinny to fight. Simple as that. He might as well have had a sign on his back: Exploit Me. And that's exactly what Mike did, not only sexually, which was pretty common, he also made Paco mule drugs around the Bronx. I hated what was happening, Sanda, and I seriously wanted to intervene. But only the strong survive, right? The strong and the smart. One thing I knew for sure, if I took on Mike, I'd have to fight his whole gang. So, I minded my own business and one day Paco disappeared. Gone without a trace."

"This is sounding like prison. How can you call it a home?"

"Actually, it was called the Youth Hope Center." Dante's smile expands as he's struck by a random thought. "Sanda, if I didn't know better, I'd think you actually cared. That can't be true, of course, because you already told me that you don't have a heart."

Sanda fails to return Dante's smile. "Are you wanting to die? Because you must be knowing that Mike will kill you if he can."

"No, I don't want to die." Dante finally opens the door. "I want Mike Tedesco to die."

All patience lost, Marius darts down the stairs, only to be whip-sawed when he reaches the end of the leash, his head snapping back. He looks up at Dante, who's braced himself in the doorway, and whines softly.

"Look in the mirror," Dante says. "First there was Teddy Winuk, a mid-level drug dealer who killed the son of a mafia boss. Then there was Mike Tedesco, who needs no explanation. Now there's me, the crazy cop. I'd call this behavior a pattern, Sanda."

"So are people around me coming to bad ends."

Outside, Dante watches Marius relieve himself. Across the street, two bleary-eyed men converse as they walk their dogs. A third man stands by his car, a Ford sedan. He's washing the windshield. A woman jogger approaches on Dante's side of the street. She's dressed all in red, her T-shirt, her shorts, her sneakers, even her wristbands, and Dante's instantly transported back to his time in foster care. The kids in those group homes rarely had a good day, but the worst of the worst, by far, was Christmas. There'd be a scraggly, half-decorated tree in the common room, a Santa Claus dressed in a faded costume and a little pack of volunteers, over-come, naturally, with their own virtue.

In truth, the volunteers had been well-meaning. Dante under-stands that now. But at the time, viewed through a child's eyes, he knew only that after they completed their missions, they'd go home to their families, leaving the foster kids to dwell on the simplest of simple truths. Nobody wanted them.

There were more fights in the home on Christmas Day than on any day of the year.

Dante watches the jogger for a moment, reminding himself that she's a civilian and that flying bullets commonly find their way to innocent bystanders. Dante may not have all that much of a conscience, but the need to protect civilians, especially when the dispute is personal, runs too deep to ignore. Dante makes it about one chance in ten that Tedesco will surrender peacefully unless he's taken completely by surprise, an equally unlikely outcome.

"You finished?" he asks the dog. "You wanna go for a ride, test the waters?"

Marius jumps into the back seat when Dante opens the door, seeming more resigned than eager. Dante closes him in, then glances to his left. Nothing happening. He slides behind the wheel, starts the car and pulls out of the parking space. He doesn't look to either side as he crosses Sixth Avenue, though he slides his weapon from the holster and lays it in his lap. A few seconds later, a car turns onto 47th Street behind him, a Dodge Charger. Rather than close the gap, the driver hangs back, even when Dante slows to make a right turn onto Fifth Avenue.

Dante's heart rate jumps, as it commonly did when he stepped into the ring at the gym. He draws a long breath through his nose and lets it out through his mouth. The tension drops off, but not by as much as he'd like, what with the stakes here being a lot greater than a quick flurry followed by a vicious left hook to the lower ribs.

The landscape passing on either side, a mix of apartment buildings and storefront businesses, is at once so familiar that it escapes notice, and as foreign as the suburbs of Beijing. You could spend your life in Sunset Park and never leave this community of restaurants and laundromats, of lawyers specializing in immigration law, of we-buy-your-jewelry pawn shops, of beauty parlors, nail salons and barbershops. Most of the stores are still closed when Dante glides past at six thirty, but the citizens are up and out, driving to work or taking a bus that stops in front of Dante, blocking the road.

Dante glances at the rearview mirror without moving his head. The Charger's about a hundred feet behind. With the sun pouring through the driver's side window, a hundred feet is close enough for Dante to recognize Mike Tedesco. Dante again looks around, at the stores, the pedestrians, the smoke-tinged exhaust pouring from a bus's vertical exhaust pipe. So familiar, so alien, as if he'd never become a part of the whole, not even after he aged out.

Aged out. That was the term the social workers used. The message it conveyed was simple enough. On your next birthday, two weeks hence, when you turn eighteen, foster care will no longer care for you. Nor will anyone else. True, you've been forced to attend twelve low-performance schools since we took responsibility for your welfare. Also true that the skills you developed were clustered around a single truth: the strong survive, the loser gets stomped.

Tough shit.

* * *

What you did was pretend indifference. Them mean old streets didn't scare you. But inside, where it counted, you were half-paralyzed by the near-certainty that you wouldn't make it out there, not in the legit world. No, the next stop on your train was Rikers Island.

For Dante Cepeda, the battle out of the great trap, out of the shithole of shitholes, had begun long before he aged out. Guided only by instinct, the struggle had almost been moment-to-moment. But he'd done it somehow, the proof apparent whenever he returned to his apartment, whenever he started his car, in his savings account, his pension plan and his health insurance.

Dante's not given to auditory hallucinations, but this time he feels himself at a great distance from the little voice inside his head. *You're an idiot*, that voice tells him. *All those years? What exactly did you hope to achieve? If not for what you now have?* The Seven-Two is six blocks down and one block over and you're heading right for it. Call ahead, let them know you're being tailed by a murder suspect, set up a trap, take the fucker down. The bosses will love you for closing the case and you won't have to share the glory, what with your partner being on vacation. Can a promotion to detective, second grade be far behind? Think of Sanda, too, of her sleek body and knowing ways. Think of all the nights to come.

Good advice, but the image Dante considers, at that point, isn't Sanda awaiting him in the bedroom, but José Herrera lying on the blacktop before a park bench, of the knife in his back, the amazed look on his face, the frightened look in the eyes of his children when they'd studied Dante from the safety of a bedroom door. And Tedesco hadn't denied it when Dante accused him of exploiting

Asher's homosexuality. He'd gotten angry, but he hadn't denied the accusation.

Startled by the growl of the bus's engine as it moves forward, Dante smiles to himself. In Iraq, where he spent the second year of his enlistment, the firefights, with a single exception, were always from a distance. Afterward, you counted the corpses, but who killed who was a matter of pure speculation. The exception occurred about halfway into his deployment. He and another grunt were conducting a routine search of a home in Anbar province when the homeowner, a middle-aged man whose smile never left his face, snatched an AK-47 from behind a couch. Although caught by surprise, Dante had been much faster, leveling his M16 and firing off a ten round burst that stitched the man from his waist to his forehead.

At the time, he'd felt little more than relief, even when the man's family rushed into the room and began to howl.

THIRTY-NINE

Dante continues up Fifth Avenue, taking his time, his heart rate gradually slowing as he formulates a strategy. He glides past Sunset Park, already peopled by dog walkers and joggers out for a pre-work run. Dante's headed for 36th Street on the north side of the Jackie Gleason Bus Depot, nearly a million square feet devoted to the maintenance of ten Brooklyn bus lines. A subway train-yard behind the depot, protected by razor wire, runs along the south side of 36th Street from Fifth Avenue to Fort Hamilton Parkway. There are no residences on either side of the road—no live residents, anyway—because the north side is bordered by Green-Wood Cemetery.

Dante was already on the job when the cemetery was designated a national landmark in 2006. Assigned to the security detail at the dedication, he'd listened to one speaker after another laud the cemetery's historic importance. The graveyard, he'd learned, covered more than four hundred acres, almost the size of nearby Prospect Park, and its gates and gothic chapel had been city landmarks for decades. Albert Anastasia, the gangster, was buried in Green-Wood, along with the abolitionist, Henry Ward Beecher, and Laura Keene, the actress onstage when Lincoln was assassinated. There were crooked politicians, too, like Boss Tweed, and artists like Currier and Ives.

Though he'd found the presentation interesting, only one thing now matters to Dante as he turns onto 36th Street. The cemetery's main entrance is located on Fifth Avenue, almost a mile away. This section of the graveyard, protected by a wrought-iron fence of black spikes joined to fluted posts, is usually deserted. That makes 36th Street, between the cemetery and the train yard, the perfect spot for a confrontation. But Dante's timing proves unfortunate. The night shift at the bus depot is leaving, the day shift arriving, and the street is humming with activity as the workers jockey for parking.

Dante glances into the side mirror to find the Charger temporarily stopped by a car backing into a parking space. As he again looks forward, his eye is drawn to the fence bordering the cemetery. A section of the wrought iron is missing, replaced by fifteen feet of common chain-link fence. Dante pulls up, takes a close look and nods his head. One end of the chain-link fencing has come loose. It's his lucky day. Dante yanks the Ford into a U-turn, setting off a cascade of horns as he slides into an open spot next to a fire hydrant. Acting now on pure instinct, he shuts down the engine, stuffs his Glock into its holster, and opens the door, only remembering Marius when the dog barks softly. Reluctantly, Dante unhooks the dog's leash and steps aside to let Marius jump to the sidewalk. A few seconds later, with the chain link fence kicked aside, they enter a field marked by scattered gravestones, most so weathered their inscriptions can no longer be read. Perhaps fifty yards away, a grove of tall maples offers the nearest available cover.

Dante breaks into a run, the dog loping alongside, his head turned to Dante, his expression quizzical.

"We're trying to avoid a bullet in the back," Dante explains, "a possibility I might have considered earlier. While I had the chance."

Mike Tedesco is somehow aware of an inner rage that he does not actually feel. His fury drives him without showing its intent, like the molten core of an ancient volcano. As Dante frees Marius and heads for the cemetery, Tedesco jams his car into the nearest parking space, ignoring the Toyota already backing in, then opens the door and slides out. The driver of the Toyota, carrying an aluminum baseball bat, also gets out. A big man wearing a tank top bearing the likeness of a diving eagle with its talons extended, he stops short when Tedesco opens the Charger's trunk, leans inside, finally emerges with a sawed-off shotgun. But then he recovers his bravado.

"Whatta ya gonna do with that, asshole?"

Tedesco turns and fires without uttering a sound, the full force of the pellets smashing into the man's gut, opening a wound the size of a baseball. The other workers on the sidewalks freeze for just a second, then scatter, some diving behind cars, other running for their lives. Tedesco ignores them, pausing only to take inventory as he crosses the street. Seven rounds still in the Remington, seven more in the Colt tucked beneath his belt, three spare clips for the Colt. Enough firepower to settle the issue, one way or another. Still, there's a problem. The shotgun, with its sawed-off barrel, is the perfect weapon for a small, enclosed space, but the graveyard before him is large and very open. That makes the odds against him hitting anything more than thirty yards away pretty dismal. On the other hand, each shell in the Remington's magazine holds twelve pellets and the semi-automatic shotgun will fire as fast as he can pull the trigger. Anybody on the receiving end of those pellets will surely dive for cover, a matter of pure instinct.

The point here is to settle the issue, what with him being doomed. The point is to make Dante Cepeda share that doom, to make him finally admit there was no escape from the world they once shared, that all their roads led to the same destination, to this moment in this place, neither meant to survive.

Tedesco pushes the fence aside and half-crawls into the cemetery. Dante's on the other side of an open space marked by haphazardly placed gravestones, a phantom half-concealed by the smoky-blue summer haze. Tedesco watches him vanish into a grove of trees on the far side of a small pond bordered by a thick bed of tiger lilies. The dog follows, his tongue hanging nearly to the ground. That would be Pug, Mike Tedesco's dog, brazenly stolen by Dante Cepeda with Skippy Legrand to witness the disrespect.

Gotta move, Tedesco tells himself, sure that one of the asshole workers has already called the cops. Still, he lingers, looking up at a yellow sun that remains hot enough to draw sweat from every pore despite a layer of high cloud the color of a soiled sheet. The buzzing of the cicadas surrounds him, so loud it might be mistaken for the drumming of a god. On the other side of the open graveyard, the leaves on the maple trees hang straight down.

Tedesco finally takes a step, then another, before realizing that Dante's game might be nothing more than an elaborate trap. The shotgun and the Colt are both illegal, the shotgun with its sawed-off barrel doubly so. If Dante's called for backup, if a little army of cops is already speeding toward the cemetery, Mike Tedesco's time on Earth is rapidly coming to a close. Smiling, he drops his hand to the top of a gray headstone.

"See you soon," he says.

* * *

Dante's seated behind a thick bed of orange tiger lilies, peering between their closely packed stems. He watches Tedesco's head swivel, the man's gaze running past Dante without slowing down. Tedesco's maybe a hundred yards away, too far. Dante's not a terrible marksman, but his training and experience are with targets set at half that distance. Take the shot? Get lucky? If he misses—the most likely outcome—he'll give away his position. No big deal, really, because the shotgun Tedesco's toting is about as useful as Dante's Glock. Eventually, they'll have to close the distance.

Maybe, he thinks, they can walk toward each other, ten paces and fire, an old-fashioned duel with modern weapons. An *honorable* duel.

The scenario brings a smile to Dante's lips. Honorable had played no part in Dante's childhood, Tedesco's either. As an adult, Dante's learned to respect his neighbors' rights, the basic deal cut by anyone rising into the middle class. But it's never been about honor, not for him. It's been about . . .

Dante's not sure, not about the why of his life, or why he's in this graveyard stalking a murderer, or exactly what he'll tell his superiors, assuming he survives. He knows only, as he brings up his Glock, as he sights in on Tedesco's back, as he reminds himself that given the humid conditions, any bullet he fires will drop as it crosses the field, that there's no going back.

Whether or not to pull the trigger becomes irrelevant when Marius wanders into the picture. The dog's moving quickly, nose to the grass, his path erratic. He's obviously agitated, though at what eludes Dante because the bodies in this field have been underground for a hundred years.

Marius comes to within twenty feet before Tedesco notices the dog. He stretches a hand out, the gesture seeming almost hopeful to Dante, and signals for Marius to approach. Marius takes his time, but does finally come near enough to sniff at Tedesco's fingers before moving off.

Tedesco's reaction is as harsh as it is ultimately predictable. He raises the shotgun and points it at Marius's retreating tail. With no choice, Dante fires off a shot without bothering to aim. Tedesco drops to a knee, then spins as he pulls the shotgun's trigger. The .00 pellets tear through the leaves of a tree at least thirty yards to Dante's left. As for his own shot, he has no idea where it went, certainly nowhere near Tedesco who leaps to his feet and sprints for the back of a mausoleum at the edge of the field. Tedesco moves fast, but not as fast as Marius. His super-cool persona forgotten, Marius streaks for cover, wisely choosing a direction opposite that of Mike Tedesco.

Now what? Dante has a single advantage. His position is unknown. He can take his time, hoping Tedesco will move toward him. If not, he'll at least have an idea where the man's headed. What with the cemetery being so big, if they get separated, they could wander for hours without making contact. But those are hours they won't have. Dante hears the wail of a distant siren. Surely, Tedesco hears it as well, and that means he has to move.

Mike Tedesco does hear the siren, and he does, in fact, move. But not away from the road on 36th Street. Tedesco moves closer to the broken fence, the point at which the cops will surely enter, to a tall obelisk just wide enough to hide him. He takes his time, exposing his back to Dante, half-expecting a shot that never comes.

As he settles in, Tedesco listens to the siren grow louder and louder. The first shot fired by Dante had drawn Tedesco's full attention. It had also saved the dog's miserable life. But it hadn't come close to finding its mark, almost surely because the cop was too far away.

Too far away to hit anything, but not too far away to witness the game Mike Tedesco's about to play. No, Tedesco's never been more calm, and never been more calculating. He wipes the sweat from his forehead. Cop lives are now at stake with only a cop named Dante Cepeda to warn them, to save them. Which he cannot do, of course, without exposing himself.

And if he doesn't? If Dante allows those cops to walk into a slaughter, if he simply watches them, bleeding and dying on the grass, if he proves himself a coward? That, Tedesco decides, would be revenge enough.

The scream of the siren jumps in volume as the cruiser, lights flashing, turns onto 36th Street, drawing the attention of the few workers who haven't taken cover. Tedesco seizes the moment, staying low as he moves thirty feet to his left, finally dropping to the ground behind a pair of gravestones fronted by a newly planted tree. He stretches out on his belly with the shotgun's barrel covering the only way into the cemetery.

The cruiser slams to a stop, the screech of tires nicely complementing the howl of the siren, which shuts down abruptly as two cops, both women, jump out of the car and run over to examine the fallen worker. Dead being dead, the cops turn to the graveyard. Tedesco nods to himself, thinking that Dante will now be doubly motivated. The white-knight cop will not let the little girl cops walk into a massacre.

Outside the fence, several workers point toward the obelisk, thirty feet away from where Tedesco lies in wait. He watches the two cops draw their weapons, push the workers back, then come to the fence and hesitate. They're looking in the general direction of the obelisk, and it's obvious, even from a distance, that they'd sooner bite off their tongues than enter the cemetery. At another time, Tedesco might have laughed. As it is, he simply lies there in the grass, unmoving, prepared for whatever comes next.

Dante listens to the rise and fall of a siren as a second police cruiser approaches from Fort Hamilton Parkway. Aware of Tedesco's new position, thirty yards from the fence, he watches the cruiser slam to a halt, watches two cops, both male, jump out. The older of the two wears a sergeant's stripes on his sleeve. He'll be the decider.

Careful not to expose himself, not yet, Dante unclips the gold shield attached to his belt and cups it in his left hand. He understands the risks. Shots already fired, four jumpy cops? Who's to say they won't shoot first and ask questions later? Especially if Dante's holding a gun in his hand. Of course, he could tuck his weapon into its holster and raise both hands, one holding the badge. Maybe they'll hold their fire . . . no, they'll probably hold their fire. But Tedesco won't. He'll open up with everything he's got.

Buyer's remorse. The term jumps into Dante's mind as he lays his Glock on the ground in front of him, takes out his cell phone and calls Lieutenant Barnwell. The call goes directly to voice mail. Cursing, he hangs up and tries the 911 dispatcher. There's a problem here and he knows exactly what it's going to be. After he identifies himself, including his shield number, Ms. Brock, the dispatcher, asks him to name the color of the day. The point here is to prevent civilians from passing as cops.

"I have no idea." Dante looks at the fence. The four cops on the scene are huddled near the opening. They've got to enter, like it or not. "I'm off-duty."

"Well, I'm sorry . . ."

"No, listen to me. You've got two units dispatched to 36th Street in Brooklyn on a 10-24S. The four officers in those units are seconds away from entering Green-Wood Cemetery. I mean *seconds* away. It's a trap, Ms. Brock. There's a murder suspect armed with a shotgun waiting for them. It's up to you to stop them. If you don't . . ."

Dante lets it go there, knowing it's already too late. Led by their sergeant, the cops pass slowly through the gap in the fence. Dante's hoping they'll fan out, but it's not happening. They instinctively stay together as they take a few tentative steps. Dante draws a long breath. Soldiers in the field always maintain a safe distance between them, but cops aren't soldiers. Not even close.

Again left with no choice, Dante, his badge raised above his head, jumps to his feet. He's about to yell out a warning when two of the cops open fire, pulling the triggers on their service weapons over and over again. Dante's more than hundred yards away, which doesn't really matter because they're not bothering to aim and the odds against being hit are enormous. But a low-probability event is not a no-probability event, and Dante flops to the ground as a stray bullet cuts a deep groove into his right calf.

The sergeant screams, "Hold fire," but the command goes completely unheard when Tedesco opens up, the roar of the .12 gauge obliterating all other sound. Despite their vests, two cops are hit by the spreading pellets, one in the face, the other in the abdomen just below her vest. The uninjured cops fire in Tedesco's general direction, then attempt to retreat, guiding the wounded officers toward the fence. Tedesco fires again, two more rounds, twenty-four pellets, each large enough to kill a human being. He's propped the shotgun's shortened barrel on top of a gravestone and his fire is deadly accurate. Three cops go down, one wounded in the head.

That's enough for Dante. He ignores the pain in his calf, ignores the blood flowing from the wound, rising to his knees, sighting carefully, firing once, then twice. The second round goes wild, but the first throws up dirt a few inches from Tedesco's legs.

Tedesco spins, fires blindly, then takes off at a dead run, headed up the steep hill at Green-Wood's center. Dante fires again, then again, his only reward Tedesco's retreating back as he enters a wooded grove.

Now what? Limp back to the fence, wait for the ambulance, leave the hunt for Mike Tedesco to others? He has every excuse in the world, every excuse to surrender, to give Tedesco his victory. His last victory, most likely. The howl of police and ambulance sirens now fills the air, seeming to come from all directions. Tedesco will be hunted down, by helicopter if necessary, and there isn't a cop on the job who won't fire a bullet into Mike Tedesco's skull if given the slightest excuse. And more than a few who won't need an excuse.

Dante climbs to his feet and starts up the hill, using gravestones to steady himself in the open areas, the trunks of trees in the wooded patches. Unlike many cemeteries in New York, Green-Wood hasn't been industrialized. The scattered graves are not laid out in neat rows like houses in a Long Island development. Even the mausoleums, spaced along the graveyards wandering pathways, retain their individuality. Dante passes a Greek temple, a pyramid, an Eastern Orthodox church topped with an onion dome, a solid granite block built into the hillside that reminds him of a WWII bunker.

After a time, the pain falls away, as does the scream of the cicadas and the heat of the sun. Dante feels as if he's traveling through a tunnel with a single outlet and he never doubts, not for a second, that Mike Tedesco's headed for the same destination. He continues uphill, passing beneath the trees, skirting the open graveyards, until he reaches a flat clearing. There he finally pauses, half-stunned by the view out over the harbor. Stalwart as ever, Lady Liberty stands with her upraised torch, guarding the spires of Manhattan's financial district, guarding the Freedom Tower, guarding the workers and the tourists, the high-end restaurants and the food trucks, the boutiques and the street vendors. T-shirts, tacos, or a million-dollar diamond, the Lady stands between us and them.

A rustling in the grass yanks Dante into the present. He spins, gun in hand, to find Marius, nose to the ground, weaving between the gravestones. The dog's panting so hard that his tongue hangs from his ruined mouth to the top of the grass. But he doesn't slow and his search appears purposeful, though Dante can't imagine the object of that search. He's only sure it's not for him because Marius handles Dante the way he handled Tedesco, trotting up, taking a sniff, moving away, his attitude dismissive. Dante watches the dog wander off, then turns back at a sound from lower down on the slope, the crack of a snapping branch.

"Hey, Dante, you still with us? Huh? Tell me those cops didn't kill your sorry ass? Talk about ingratitude. Talk about no good deed going unpunished. You're the poster boy for asshole of the month. The great white knight brought down by friendly fire."

"I'm still breathin'," Dante calls out. "So, if you want me dead, you're gonna have to do it yourself."

Dante moves to a large gravestone topped with the bronze statue of a seated woman, naked except for a cloth draped across her upper thighs. At another time, he might have found the statue actually salacious. As it is, he's satisfied with a slight gap between her right arm and her torso, just wide enough to offer a view of the graveyard.

It's the perfect spot for an ambush. The odds against being spotted by Tedesco are very large, while the cover, between the gravestone and the statue, is near total. Five minutes later, Tedesco appears at the edge of the field, a good distance from where he'd called out. He remains in shadow while his eyes sweep the open space. They pass by Dante without a hint of recognition.

Dante makes the distance between them about sixty yards, a bit too far, and so he waits, his breathing slow, his heart rate steady, still ignoring the pain, ignoring the blood, while Tedesco slowly advances, sixty yards becoming fifty, then forty, then thirty, until Dante can't miss. Only then does he lay the muzzle of his service weapon on top of gravestone and rivet his eye to the front sight. *This is the moment*, he tells himself as he pulls the trigger, *when I'm supposed to reflect on Tedesco's humanity, to recall my Catholic upbringing, that all souls, even the darkest, can be redeemed.* But that's the point, really. To kill Tedesco before he has a chance to beg forgiveness. To send him directly to hell.

The 9 mm, hollow-point round covers the distance between Dante and his target at supersonic speed, crashing into Mike Tedesco's chest before he hears the crack of the gunshot. For an instant, a mere fraction of a second, Tedesco looks confused as his free hand starts toward the wound. Then he drops the shotgun and pitches forward onto his face.

Dante comes out from behind the statue and runs across the graveyard to Tedesco's side. He kicks the shotgun away as Tedesco rolls onto his back. At this point, and Dante knows it, he's required to call for assistance, to pinpoint his location as best he can, to render first aid. The bullet's torn through Tedesco's lung and blood flows from his mouth with every breath. But he's definitely alive and aware. His dark eyes blaze, the hate apparent, and his hand crawls toward the semi-automatic Colt tucked beneath his belt.

"Nothing to say?" Dante asks. "All choked up? Just as well, because I have plenty to say. About Asher, about José and his cousin, about the cops you ambushed, about Paco Altoona."

Tedesco makes an attempt at speech, but the sounds coming from his mouth, accompanied by small drops of blood, are unintelligible and Dante simply continues. "I failed Paco. I should have intervened. I should have beaten you so bad you'd be crippled for the rest of your life. And I knew it at the time, knew that beating you down was only honorable move on that chessboard we called the Youth Hope Center."

Tedesco's hand has reached the butt of his Colt. Dante watches his palm slowly curl around the grip, watches his forefinger grope for the trigger guard. Maybe hope springs eternal, or maybe this is some final macho gesture. Either way, Dante's not impressed. He squats down, then tosses the Colt away, Tedesco so weak he offers no resistance.

"Say again, Mike?"

"It should have been you."

"You didn't have the balls to challenge me." Dante's tone is matter-of-fact. "Paco Altoona was more your speed. You preferred your victims weak, if not actually helpless."

Dante rises to his feet, his weapon still trained on Tedesco, a matter of habit because the man poses no threat. As he watches Mike Tedesco die, his focus narrows until hears and sees nothing around him, certainly not the two uniformed cops who crest the hill, coming from the front gate on Fifth Avenue. Later they'll claim that no one told them about a cop being among the likely combatants. They'll claim, too, that they commanded the shooter to drop his weapon, not once but several times. They'll claim that Dante Cepeda continued to stand there, that he didn't react at all, not when the first shot grazed his right thigh or when a second tore into his shoulder or when the last bullet, the bullet that killed him, crashed through the back of his skull. Even dead, his brain reduced to mere pulp, he continued to stand over Mike Tedesco for a few seconds, as if determined to make a final assessment before the darkness claimed them both.

FORTY

Forced to lean on the brakes, Skippy Legrand curses when a bus pulls away from the curb without signaling. He glances at the woman sitting in the passenger's seat to his right, but she fails to react. Skippy's been driving around Brooklyn and Queens for the past two weeks, stopping every few blocks while Sanda Dragomir staples a poster to a tree, or a traffic sign, or a mailbox, or any other goddamned thing big enough to hold a likeness of the dog she calls Marius. Sanda created the likeness herself, working from memory, and the computer-generated image, what with the scars and the torn lip, is close enough to do the job, especially when backed up by a hundred-dollar reward. Meanwhile, the mutt's nowhere to be found.

"Please to pull over," Sanda says.

Sanda's wearing a short skirt and a scooped-neck top that reveals a bit of cleavage, a concession to the August heat. Skippy's eyes fall on her legs as she slides out of his two-year-old Buick, the passing glance more or less involuntary. Not that Skippy's discerned even a glimmer of seduction in Ms. Dragomir's manner. And she could have gone there right from the get-go. She could have secured his cooperation with . . . not even a kiss, much less a romp in her bed. She could have gotten him with a smile. The woman's that beautiful.

Skippy's pretty sure that Sanda can do the seduction bit, only not when she's got other leverage. The cops believe that Skippy and Tedesco planned the hijacking together. They're right, of course, and if they had a shred of proof, which they don't, he'd already be in jail. Still, they've been all over him, questioning his workers and his customers. A detective at Borough Command, a lieutenant, even had a conversation with the claims adjustor at Skippy's insurance company, which then dispatched its own investigators. The way it's going, his claim might never be paid.

That's where Sanda came in.

"Mike has told me that you are knowing everything before it happens. About stealing cigarettes. This is true. You and Mike create this plan together, then you come to my house on the same day when Mike and Dante are killed. You confess to me. You tell me to tell Dante that you are ready to make a deal."

Sanda had a way of putting a question mark at the end of every sentence. Not that time. Her tone was flat, her final statement so final that Skippy had taken a few seconds to analyze his position. Which, he'd concluded, was up shit's creek.

"Whatta you want, Sanda? Tell me straight, please, so we both know."

Skippy had stifled a laugh when Sanda made her demands. He was to act as her chauffeur while she searched for her lost mutt, who used to be Dante Cepeda's mutt, who used to be Mike Tedesco's mutt. Skippy had been expecting her to put a dollar value on her silence.

"When," he'd asked, "do we get started?"

They'd first visited every animal shelter in Brooklyn, with Sanda leaving her name and phone number just in case. That took three days. Since then, they've ridden every morning to a neighborhood like Coney Island, where they've been for the past five hours, posting the posters Sanda prints overnight, blanketing the streets and avenues.

Originally touched by the woman's devotion, Skippy's had enough. He's trying to break in a new manager. And while the kid shows promise, Legrand Transportation definitely needs the boss's attention. Somebody has to make sure the trucks are properly loaded and the drivers briefed. The way it is now, his workers could be robbing him blind. Plus, he's been on a losing streak, his only saving grace the fifty grand he used to pay down his mortgage. He needs to concentrate on the racing form, to put in the hours, to review tonight's baseball games, the starting pitchers, the disabled lists, who's hot and who's not.

Impatient now—Sanda's engaged in conversation with several passersby—Skippy turns to the newspaper lying on the seat.

The four deaths in Green-Wood Cemetery, what with one being a cop killed by other cops, have commanded the city's attention for the past two weeks, inspiring bleed-lead headlines in every newspaper. The reporters, citing the usual unnamed sources, had initially attributed Detective Cepeda's death to bad luck, pure and simple. A failure to communicate, a forgivable error, pick one. Cops responding to a shots-fired incident had observed one man firing at a second man who lay on the ground, leading to one of those split-second decisions cops later come to regret.

There it stood for three days, until a *New York Times* reporter connected Detective Dante Cepeda, the cop, to Michael Tedesco, the alleged murderer. They'd once lived, she'd discovered, in the same group foster home.

That piece of news initiated another frenzy. Had they been pals, enemies, allies? Had they maintained contact over the years? Were they both criminals? Had the cop killed his buddy in order to shut him up? Or had they hated each other all this time, bitter enemies to the bitter end?

The leaks coming from the NYPD hadn't helped, either, specifically that Tedesco had been linked, through DNA evidence, to the murders of Mariano Herrera, José's cousin, and Daniela Castillo, a former girlfriend. Coming two days apart, the revelations were fuel on the fire and both New York tabloids pursued multiple angles, including Daniela's connection to Santería and the beaded bracelet on Tedesco's wrist. The *Daily News* headline that stared up at Cal was the latest example: GRAVEYARD SLAUGHTER! The paper had obtained Mike Tedesco's autopsy report, which included a list of the many gruesome injuries done to his face and skull by the ten bullets fired from Dante Cepeda's Glock. No photos, thank God.

Skippy doesn't hesitate when Sanda returns to the car. "I can't make it tomorrow," he tells her. "And probably not the next day, either. I got a business to run."

"I am only needing from you a short time more."

"Fine, we'll go out again on Sunday when I'm closed." Skippy checks Sanda as he pulls into traffic. "See, right now? If you run to the cops? How will you explain the time we been spending in each other's company? Because I'm tellin' ya, Sanda, if you testify against me, my lawyer's gonna tear you to pieces. And I'm not tryin' to bully you. I'm talkin' cold, hard reality. You have a past, remember, and it ain't that good."

Sanda chooses to maintain a cool silence, but Skippy's used to the attitude. He pilots the Lincoln to Avenue M where he makes a left turn. Brooklyn's a driver's nightmare. The only highways trace the borough's outer edge, while uncoordinated traffic lights on every corner turn red before you travel a block. Plus, the sun's pouring through the windshield, heating the interior despite the air-conditioning, and Skippy's psoriasis, which he's reluctant to scratch due to its location, is itching madly.

The final blow? If Sanda lived any further from Legrand Transportation in northern Manhattan, she'd have to move to Staten Island. His trip home will involve some of the most notorious roads in the city.

"I wish to know something," Sanda says out of nowhere.

"I'm listening."

"All these dead people. Murdered. How are you for dealing with this?"

It takes Skippy a moment to make sense of the last part, but when he does speak, he's careful not to make any damaging admissions. "The guy went crazy for some reason. I mean all the time I knew him, he wasn't crazy and then, all of a sudden, he was."

"Michael?"

"Yeah. It's like someone put a curse on him, like he was possessed. We're talkin' about a robbery here. Mike was hijackin' one of my trucks, but something went wrong and he killed the kid, Asher Levine. Why would he do that? Why didn't he walk away? And why did he strangle his girlfriend? That would be Daniela. Why did he kill Daniela, or José's cousin, or José? Why did he want to kill you? None of it makes any sense to me, but I still got a business to run. I got a business to run, a family to support and I'm still breathin' air instead of dirt. So . . ."

They ride the rest of the way to Sanda's apartment in silence, along 60th Street, through Midwood and Borough Park, to Eighth Avenue in Sunset Park where he takes a right. Already planning his journey to Manhattan, he's within a hundred yards of Sanda's townhouse before he spies the old man on the stoop. The man's talking to Sanda's neighbor, the fat Chinese woman who's been giving Skippy the evil eye for the past two weeks, and he's holding a long leash with a scarred pit bull on the other end.

"Holy shit," Skippy says, "it's the mutt."

But he's talking to himself because Sanda Dragomir is already out of the car, shouting, "Marius," as she approaches the dog. Amazed, Skippy watches tears pour from Sanda's eyes. This is a woman as hard as glass, a woman who blackmailed him as if extortion was a game she played every goddamned day. Now she's reaching for the dog, both arms extended, and the dog's jumping into those arms, laying its head, wet tongue and all, on her shoulder. The old man drops the leash. He's grinning a grin that seem to reach all the way to the back of his head. Skippy assumes that he came on one of Sanda's posters, that he's following up on the reward. Not that it matters because Sanda jumps to her feet. She hugs the old man first, then her chubby neighbor. Then they're all hugging one another and the dog is dancing around between their legs, wriggling like a snake on a hot griddle.

Skippy moves the shift stick from Park to Drive. He takes his foot off the brake, steps on the gas, finally locks the doors. Despite everything, he feels as good as he's felt in a very long time. That's because Skippy Legrand will be spending the night at home with his family, and not on Rikers Island with the terminally demented.

"Finally," he whispers as he takes a last glance into the rearview mirror, "a happy fuckin' ending."

ABOUT THE AUTHOR

Stephen Solomita (b. 1943) is an American author of thrillers. Born in Bayside, Queens, he worked as a cab driver before becoming a novelist in the late 1980's. His first novel, *A Twist of the Knife* (1988) won acclaim for its author's intimate knowledge of New York's rough patches, and for a hardboiled style that raised a gritty look at urban terrorism above the level of a typical thriller. Solomita wrote six more novels starring the disaffected NYPD cop Stanley Moodrow, concluding the series with *Damaged Goods* (1996).

Solomita continued writing in the same hardboiled style, producing tough, standalone novels like *Mercy Killing* (2009) and *Angel Face* (2011). Under the pseudonym David Cray, he writes gentler thrillers such as *Dead Is Forever* (2004), a traditional mystery in the mode of Ellery Queen. His most recent novel is *Dancer in the Flames* (2012). He continues to live and write in New York City.

STEPHEN SOLOMITA

FROM MYSTERIOUSPRESS.COM
AND OPEN ROAD MEDIA

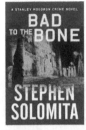
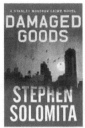

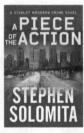

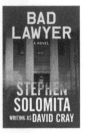

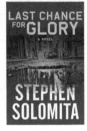

MYSTERIOUSPRESS.COM

OPEN ROAD
INTEGRATED MEDIA

MYSTERIOUSPRESS.COM

Otto Penzler, owner of the Mysterious Bookshop in Manhattan, founded the Mysterious Press in 1975. Penzler quickly became known for his outstanding selection of mystery, crime, and suspense books, both from his imprint and in his store. The imprint was devoted to printing the best books in these genres, using fine paper and top dust-jacket artists, as well as offering many limited, signed editions.

Now the Mysterious Press has gone digital, publishing ebooks through **MysteriousPress.com**.

MysteriousPress.com offers readers essential noir and suspense fiction, hard-boiled crime novels, and the latest thrillers from both debut authors and mystery masters. Discover classics and new voices, all from one legendary source.

FIND OUT MORE AT
WWW.MYSTERIOUSPRESS.COM

FOLLOW US:
@emysteries and Facebook.com/MysteriousPressCom

MysteriousPress.com is one of a select group of publishing partners of Open Road Integrated Media, Inc.

THE MYSTERIOUS BOOKSHOP, founded in 1979, is located in Manhattan's Tribeca neighborhood. It is the oldest and largest mystery-specialty bookstore in America.

The shop stocks the finest selection of new mystery hardcovers, paperbacks, and periodicals. It also features a superb collection of signed modern first editions, rare and collectable works, and Sherlock Holmes titles. The bookshop issues a free monthly newsletter highlighting its book clubs, new releases, events, and recently acquired books.

58 Warren Street
info@mysteriousbookshop.com
(212) 587-1011
Monday through Saturday
11:00 a.m. to 7:00 p.m.

FIND OUT MORE AT:

www.mysteriousbookshop.com

FOLLOW US:

@TheMysterious and Facebook.com/MysteriousBookshop

OPEN ROAD
INTEGRATED MEDIA

Find a full list of our authors and
titles at www.openroadmedia.com

FOLLOW US
@OpenRoadMedia